SHADOW SLAVE

A Trafficking Rescue Novel

Book Two of the *Never Lost Series*

D.I. Telbat

In Season Publications
USA

Printed in the United States of America

SHADOW SLAVE: A Trafficking Rescue Novel
/ D.I. Telbat -- 1st ed.
Categories: Inspirational Religious Fiction;
Christian Mystery & Suspense

D.I. Telbat / In Season Publications
https://books2read.com/DITelbat
https://ditelbat.com

ISBN 978-1-7371777-3-9

Cover Design by 100Covers

DEDICATION

To those who seem lost and need hope;
For those who seem forsaken and need forgiveness.

GLOSSARY

5TRAY – A GLOW subsidiary, **pronounced as *stray***. This fictional human smuggling network is run by Ram Garrity from its headquarters in Dallas, working closely with GLOW-connected cartels in Mexico. **5TRAY refers to: Five Tier Resource Assembly Yield**. The five tiers or divisions of 5TRAY are: Counterintelligence, Finance, Recruitment, Security, and Transportation.

ATF – Bureau of Alcohol, Tobacco, Firearms and Explosives

DHS – Department of Homeland Security

GLOW – Global Wares. This fictional human trafficking network is organized and powerful, with political influence and predators in every country.

HTV – Human Trafficking Victim

House of Leah – Based in Tampa, this safe house works exclusively with TROAS to assist recovered survivors of trafficking.

TROAS: Its fictional name stands for "**Trafficking Recovery Operative Assistance Services**." Its leader is Brody Sladrick, assisted extensively by Binsa and Greg Rotz.

CHARACTER SKETCH

Aaron Ridgewood – As a border patrol agent and young husband, this believer works under Captain Fletter on the front lines of the Texas border with MX.

Andrey Khataev – This Russian oligarch and father of Helena, baits and executes human traffickers.

Binsa: After losing her six-year-old daughter to a human trafficker, she came to Christ and joined TROAS to minister to women and children recovered from traffickers. She is a right hand to Brody Sladrick and Zayed's fiancée.

Brody Sladrick – As a veteran operative, this aged widower applies his skills for Christ as a retrieval expert to recover trafficked survivors.

Captain Fletter – This sizeable border patrol agent may prefer air conditioning over the Texas heat, but he's not afraid to stick his head out for the safety of his agents and those on the border they've been tasked to help.

Dakota Yarlin – A Canadian native, this nineteen-year-old is trafficked through the TX smuggling network.

Elliot Madison – This senator from New York has used Sladrick for years to secure himself as a trafficking crime fighter, but will he risk his reputation for TROAS when they need him most?

Felicity Torme – At twenty-one, she is a college student from Illinois who is kidnapped and trafficked through Texas into Mexico.

Greg "the Rot" Rotz – As technician & security expert for TROAS, he works closely with Sladrick and Binsa during every recovery mission. Marcy is his fiancée.

Hector Savalano & daughter Gabriella– This refugee and single father from Colombia seeks a fresh start in the U.S.

Jerome Wessel – This DHS agent has risen in his agency's ranks to hunt down Christians who place forgiveness in Jesus Christ before national security.

Kim Ward – Born and raised in a Christian home, she takes her faith for granted until she is kidnapped at age seventeen and forced into the trafficking world.

Marcy Nevins – Once a trafficked youth, now she assists TROAS operations in Tampa at Greg's side.

Nicole Pitney – At age seventy, she controls GLOW as its Executive, but this Massachusetts senator may have underestimated her enemies.

Ram Garrity – As the brains behind 5TRAY's trafficking enterprise, this 32-year-old California native now lives in Dallas, masquerading as a shipping consultant.

Sam Garrity – The father of Ram and Carmen; he takes advantage of moments to share the gospel with family and strangers alike.

Scott Carrell – Now forty-six, this dishonorably discharged Army veteran runs security for the most powerful human trafficking network in Texas, 5TRAY.

Szymon Nowicki – This eight-year-old boy is eager for adventure—if his loving mother will only loosen her protective embrace.

Yana Nowicki – As a one-armed single mother, this Polish believer hasn't allowed the scars of her past to hinder her from serving Jesus.

Zayed Aziz – From Saudi Arabia, this trafficker-turned-believer now risks his life for the needy. He is Brody Sladrick's right hand and Binsa's fiancé.

"When the world has gone crazy and is only
concerned about themselves and their causes,
the weak and vulnerable suffer the most,
and these are the ones Jesus sent us to minister to."
Patrick Klein, Founder & Director of
Vision Beyond Borders

~

*"Do not participate in the unfruitful deeds of
darkness, but instead even expose them; for it is
disgraceful even to speak of the things which are
done by them in secret."*
Ephesians 5:11-12 (NASB)

Dallas Cul-de-sac
5TRAY Headquarters

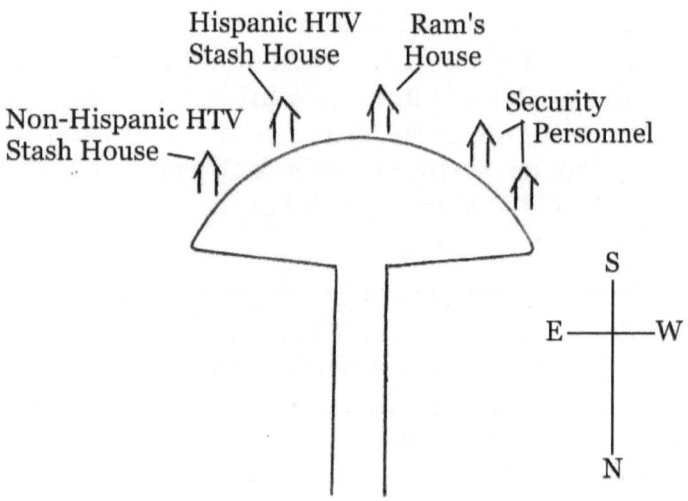

Hispanic HTV Stash House

Ram's House

Non-Hispanic HTV Stash House

Security Personnel

S

E—W

N

SHADOW SLAVE
D.I. Telbat

Szczecin, Poland, Safe House

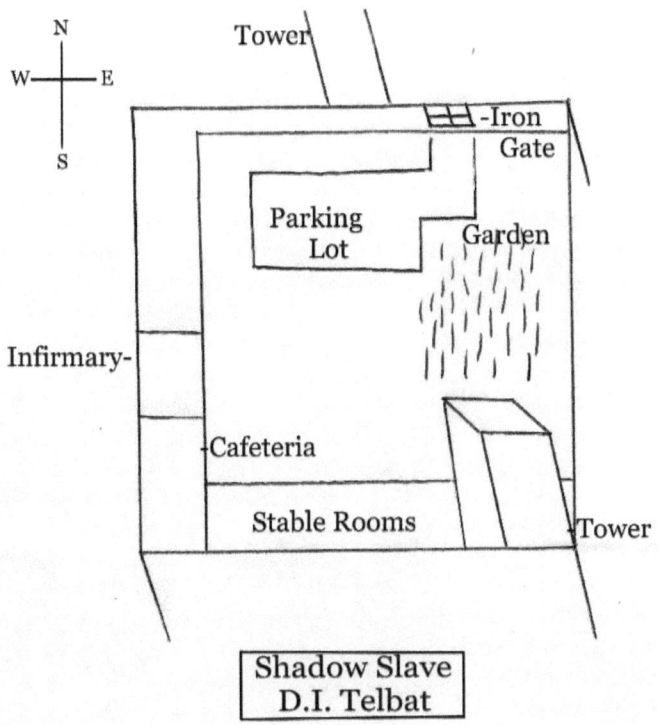

A NOTE FROM THE AUTHOR

Dear Reader,

Human trafficking is an ugly topic. Like in *Hidden Humanity*, the previous novel in this series, we have tempered the graphic nature of this horrible plague upon humanity, yet such sin must still be forced into the light. Followers of Jesus Christ should respond to human trafficking, and this book reveals not only the problem but also a believer's possible response.

In this novel, considerable attention is placed on the U.S. southern border, particularly the Mexican border with Texas. From careful research, I have mingled fiction with real events and some actual political involvement. What you're about to read in this book may seem very disconnected from your life or the America you know, but I assure you, there are dark hearts involved from places of power who are complicit in human trafficking right now.

Throughout my research, I found secular and Christian sources that sound the alarm against globalization, which makes human trafficking worse. International human rights groups have warned for years that the overwhelming influence to erase national borders only makes trafficking easier to hide and harder to prosecute. Trafficked women and children continue to increase because of globalization's war against nationalism. The more countries that lose their borders to the cause of international unity, the more victims that are lost to buyers. It is no wonder why traffickers are in support of a one-world government and globalization efforts that overlook the needs and rights of individuals.

And it is no wonder why globalists today are often politicians overlooking the trafficking problem.

Finally, as tempting as it is to ignore this terrible criminal element of trafficking in every neighborhood in every country around the world, we must remember that the forgiveness of God is not for the worthy, but for the unworthy. Survivors of trafficking need compassion and sometimes long-term aid, but the perpetrators of trafficking need the gospel of the cross no less.

We hope you will share your heart with us if this book encourages you to respond like Christ in prayer and care for all involved in the trafficking world.

God never loses those who are His!

David Telbat

CHAPTER ONE

Forty-eight dead. Ram Garrity lowered his binoculars as the police channel continued to chatter in his ear. On the bluff overlooking the El Paso highway, he stood alone observing the container truck discovered by border patrol agents earlier that morning. Something had gone wrong with the transport, and Ram wanted to know which of his men were to blame. *Forty-eight!*

He turned from the highway below and approached his dark blue SUV, which was parked next to another SUV. Scott Carrell stood in front of the bumper. The slender forty-six-year-old cradled an automatic rifle, military issue, as did his security team of five more men on the other side of the vehicles.

"I counted forty-eight," Ram stated quietly to his lieutenant. "Who was driving?"

"A couple of new boys from Arizona." Scott's face was ruddy and his crewcut was long, maybe in an effort to seem taller. "We've got them back at the house. Be assured, they'll answer for this."

Ram heard the displeasure in Scott's voice but saw the anticipation of violence in his eyes. Scott's sunken cheeks and prominent cheekbones were a consequence of his ongoing drug use, but Ram had kept the otherwise dependable man as his head of security since he'd already saved Ram's life twice. Running a Texas trafficking enterprise was dangerous.

The men gazed together at the empty desert.

"This'll make national news," Ram said. "It'll be a mess."

"Just for a few days." Scott scoffed. "Nobody cares, Ram. Not really. The politicals will pretend to be outraged and the police chieftains will guarantee swift justice, but they'll never find us. We'll be fine. Besides, you've got assurances."

Nodding, Ram wondered what was wrong with him since he felt so little for the forty-eight men, women, and children now deceased. He was responsible but he knew no one would ever catch him. Thousands of illegals weekly overwhelmed a dwindling number of dedicated border patrol agents. The agents had been told to scale back efforts. While fifty percent of the agents screened a small number of vehicles crossing the narrow entry points, the other half were swamped with humanitarian needs and mandatory social reeducation classes. And Ram just got richer.

"We've never lost a whole truckload before." Ram ran his fingers through his short cropped dark hair. "Not in all my ten years. Word'll get out. It could slow crossings, hurt payments."

"Maybe for a month, but no more." Scott signaled his security team. "We need to get back to Dallas. Some high profiles rolled in. You'll need to make a call."

"Yeah." Ram sighed loudly. High profiles usually referred to kidnapped American girls whose status was too publicized to sell them in the country. "This cursed desert. It wouldn't break my heart if we never came back to El Paso."

The doors slammed shut on the SUV as the security team settled in for the drive back to El Paso International, but Ram continued to study the desert. There could be some illegals out there that very minute, mostly Mexicans crossing in that part of Texas. Some would be smuggling fentanyl and other drugs for the cartel. Maybe they'd reach civilization, but some would die of thirst and exposure. Those with money paid Ram's Five Tier Resource Assembly Yield—known as 5TRAY—

organization for safe transport, but that hadn't worked out well for forty-eight of them that week.

"Look, Ram, I realize you're upset," Scott said, "but there are thirty agents back on that highway. You may be wearing that border patrol uniform, but that doesn't mean we should stick around."

Ram patted Scott on the shoulder, turned, and climbed into his own SUV. He always drove himself, alone. It was one of his security rules, and Scott approved, usually tailing his boss with the heavily-armed team when on the road.

They reached the airport northeast of El Paso and Ram offered airport security clearance to access the private hangars north of the main runway. Ram had learned many years earlier that he could go just about anywhere in Texas while impersonating a private border security firm. Scott had been dishonorably discharged from the Army twenty years earlier, but he'd still obtained legal clearance for his weaponized unit in the state.

After boarding his private jet, Ram changed out of the stolen uniform. Scott's men stowed their rifles for the flight to Dallas, but they kept their sidearms on their hips. They sat toward the rear of the plane while Ram sat alone toward the front. On his phone, he half-heartedly reviewed reports of African migrants from cartel associates south of the border, but he couldn't see past a number stuck in his mind. *Forty-eight*. It was now the number of death to him. It clung to his soul like the stench he'd imagined reaching his nostrils when he'd peered down at the bodies on the roadside.

Occasionally, due to careless transportation, Ram's soldiers lost an illegal or two from neglect—lack of water or air supply. But never forty-eight at once! Even brief attention from US authorities could cause a decrease in cartel revenue, but no one would confront him, not even now. He was Ram Garrity—Ruthless Ram Garrity, the gringo smuggler of Texas. Humans were his specialty, but he also had contacts for arms, fentanyl, and many pharmaceuticals.

Prearranged vehicles were waiting when they reached Dallas, and Ram drove to the quiet neighborhood of a middle-class suburb. On the south end of the suburb lay one cul-de-sac with five residences—beautiful houses built by his own contractors only a few years earlier. Ram had placed each residence under a different assumed name within the 5TRAY organization. 5TRAY had been buying up real estate wherever they frequented so they never had to worry about what neighbors saw them doing. They now owned several neighborhoods, blocks, and apartment buildings.

The middle residence of the five in the cul-de-sac was Ram's own. He parked in the garage. Before the door lowered shut, he acknowledged a pair of yard workers on an adjacent lawn. Ram owned them, too. They wore hidden military-grade comm devices and kept a machine gun and grenade launcher in the back of the truck that pulled the lawn mower trailer. As part of Scott's secondary security infrastructure, they were hired to protect Ram and 5TRAY interests and could blend into any community in the US.

The two residences on the right housed security personnel and 5TRAY's counterintelligence "division." The five divisions that made up 5TRAY, were: Counterintelligence, Finance, Recruitment, Security, and Transportation.

The two residences on the left or east side of the cul-de-sac housed HTVs—Human Trafficking Victims—and the personnel required to force them into compliance. Stash houses. One house held non-Hispanic migrants. The other held Hispanics.

Leaving his 5TRAY phone on the kitchen counter, Ram sat in his favorite soft chair in the living room and checked his messages on his civilian phone. There were three. He'd been gone two days, and both his father and sister had tried to call him. As far as they knew, he was a Dallas-based shipping consultant who traveled often to secure lucrative deals for US retailers. Not bad for a thirty-two-year-old who'd had a short rap sheet before the age of eighteen. But by eighteen, rather than reforming his behavior, he'd learned from professionals how to hide his activities—and get filthy rich.

His sister, Carmen, still lived in California near their father, Sam, where they still attended the same Sacramento church that Ram had grown up in. But neither his father nor sister were calling about their Christian nonsense—for once. The Garrity family reunion was approaching and they wanted Ram to be there. He was sure they wanted to show him off, along with his success, to the extended family sprinkled across the Midwest and West Coast.

Ram didn't respond to the messages. Not yet. It would seem suspicious if he didn't attend a family reunion. Normal people—successful civilians with nothing to hide—attended casual family get-togethers. He wanted to decline since it meant returning to California without his security team, but he would have to go. The 5TRAY counterintelligence team would need to confirm that he still had no warrants, federal or otherwise, but he guessed he could play the part of a good son and big brother for a few days.

Standing, he stretched and slowly wandered through the house for a few minutes. The height of his success had cost him much. Vigilance every minute meant he could have no distractions in life. Rival cartel bosses were a greater physical threat to him than the legal threat of the local police. His cover was extensive, the façade of a local businessman carefully built over the years. Never had he brought anyone into his home, but it was furnished like any other warm household—complete with fake family photos and bogus vacation excursions to Yosemite and Hawaii. Yet, in reality, Ram knew his life was as empty as the rooms of his house. He'd never even had a steady girlfriend.

"I'm going next door," he finally said on his 5TRAY phone, which incorporated modern encryption.

He left by the front door and walked around the edge of the cul-de-sac toward the second stash house of HTVs, which housed the non-Hispanics. Across the cul-de-sac, Scott emerged from his residence to join him, but the other five security personnel remained lounging on the deck under a canopy, with drinks and sandwiches before them. Their girlfriends came and went, all of them spoiled from and complicit with the 5TRAY operations. It may have seemed like a casual setting, but Ram knew that every man and most of the women were armed—and they were paid to kill anyone who seemed out of place venturing up their street.

Ever vigilant about satellite imaging or laser-equipped listening devices, Ram and Scott never spoke of business outside the five residences. But once they entered an HTV stash house, they trusted the "white noise" safeguards to jam any number of electronic surveillance systems.

Entering the house, Scott led the way down a hallway of reinforced doors and knocked on one. It was opened by a Venezuelan woman in her fifties, Rosa, who was paid well to feed and care for the HTVs temporarily housed in the stash house. Rosa was the only permanent resident in that house, and she was never to move or interact with the detainees beyond feeding them. After HTV departures, she was responsible for the laundry and cleaning of the cells for subsequent housing.

Ram entered the room where a custom Plexiglas cell had been constructed to contain six bunk beds for twelve occupants and a single stainless-steel toilet/sink combo, prison issue. The Plexiglas had holes for ventilation. Two cameras on either side of the room monitored the cell with feed transmitted to both Rosa's monitor in the living room and Scott's laptop in his own house. A food tray slot afforded Rosa the ability to interact with the captives without opening the heavy door.

The four other bedrooms contained the same bunk bed assembly, securing a maximum of forty-eight persons in one house. The adjacent residence of Hispanic HTVs had the same capacity, though not every bunk was always filled.

That day, Ram looked in at the frightened faces of six young white women, the cell at half capacity. He recognized two immediately from recent Amber Alerts and other nation-wide news coverage. One young woman at the back of the cell caught his eye since she wore a bandage around her head. Blood had soaked through from her forehead.

"What happened to her?" Ram asked Rosa, who spoke fluent English unless she was drunk or angry.

"It happened before we bought her," Rosa said. "They said she tried to escape. She was trouble, that's why we got her."

Ram swore and waved at the young woman to approach the glass, but she hesitated.

One facet of 5TRAY specialized in smuggling HTVs into Mexico, those who were too high profile to market in the US. Kidnappers kept giving him problems instead of simple products to sell.

"Come to the glass!" Rosa ordered the young lady.

The women in the cell shrunk away. Rosa had obviously established her authority in a profound way. Ram didn't care if it was under threat of physical harm or threat of turning off the cell's air or water, as long as the HTVs did what they were told while under his roof.

The young woman with the head wound held her midsection as she cautiously approached the glass. She, like the others, wore the clothes she'd had on when taken. Or they'd been given other civilian clothes to give them a casual appearance while being transported. Many had been drugged during transport in a family-style vehicle.

"What's your name?" Ram asked.

"Kim. Kim Ward."

She wore athletic shorts and a Seattle Mariners jersey three sizes too large.

"Take off your bandage. Let me see your head."

She slid it off over short blond hair. The cleft in her chin trembled as Ram inspected her, but her eyes met his.

"That'll leave a scar." Scott grimaced at her forehead gash. "They wrapped it without cleaning it?"

"Nobody's buying her for her looks," Rosa said, scoffing.

"Damaged goods don't sell as well," Ram said. "And I'm thinking of visible marks that could be used to identify her easier. Get her out, Rosa. Stitch her up properly. Make this problem go away."

"I'm not a nurse, Ram."

Ram cast her a glare that made the woman flinch and look away, then she moved to unlock the door. Scott drew his sidearm and trained it on the cell occupants. Rosa took Kim Ward by the arm and drew her out, then closed the door.

"You try anything," Rosa growled, "and I will end you!"

"She's not kidding." Scott chuckled. "She'll mutilate you after she beats compliance into you."

Kim may have been trying to show bravery, but tears ran from her eyes. The gash on her forehead glistened with fresh blood.

In the hallway, Ram conferred with Scott for a moment about what to do with the six high profiles. Rosa took Kim into the kitchen where she continued to threaten the young woman and ordered her to sit still at the counter.

"Get all six of them down to our friends in Coahuila by next week," Ram instructed Scott. "They all look pretty healthy. We should make a nice sum and wash our hands free."

"I'll let our guy know at Eagle Pass." Scott nodded. "But six girls at once might draw a little attention."

"Yeah. Maybe put them in a van with lots of windows. Write on the side of the van that they're with some church choir. Nobody'll stop them from going south. Then burn the van down there."

"Huh," Scott grunted. "I guess that's why you're the boss, Ram."

Scott palmed his phone to make arrangements for the six, and Ram went to the kitchen to check on Rosa's progress.

"Hold still!" Rosa snapped at Kim whose eyes were squeezed shut under her care. The house mother pinched Kim's wound, making it gush even more, while her other hand fingered a needle and thread.

"Are you waiting until she bleeds out?" Ram asked.

"What?" Rosa sniffed. "I've never done this before!"

"Could've fooled me. Get out of the way. Give me that."

Rosa surrendered the needle as Ram sat down in her place. He used peroxide to clean the gash, then gently drew Kim's skin together. It was rare that he handled any HTV personally since it was dangerous to be seen and possibly identified later. But south-bound HTVs were never heard from again. They were eventually trafficked by barge into Europe or Asia, especially to China where brides were forced to bear children in a country short on child-bearing women. Death usually followed in a variety of ways.

Still, in one day, Ram had felt the pangs of the forty-eight deceased and now he was nursing a wounded HTV. He tried to tell himself it was strictly business—to make Kim a better product before sale somewhere—but he already knew her name. Her jersey, now bloodied, indicated that she was from the Seattle area.

"Where'd they pick you up?" Ram asked as he completed a third stitch.

"At the stadium." Kim seemed much calmer in his care than she'd been under Rosa's. Her eyes were wide, watching his face.

Sports stadiums were common locations for abductions. Thousands of fans offered plenty of camouflage.

"You were alone?"

"No, I was with my dad. His name is Jack." She licked her lips. "Do you know what's going to happen to me?"

Ram nearly answered by saying, "Nothing good," but instead, he frowned for a few seconds as he considered a response.

"Just follow instructions and it'll go easier for you."

It was a lie. He wasn't used to speaking to HTVs, let alone lying to one. He'd broken into the trafficking trade by transporting drugs north and money south. His creativity in the shadows and ruthlessness toward competitors had earned him a leadership role that rivaled other smugglers in Texas. Eventually, he'd built a network highly valued by the cartels.

The truth was, Kim would probably be dead within a year. If she survived beyond a year, she'd wish she were dead.

"Why are you doing this?" Kim whispered. "You don't have to do this. Please help me. God will bless you if you help me."

Ram sat back. He even let go of the needle so it dangled on the thread from her forehead. Her eyes pleaded with him, but it was her words about God that pierced him.

He glanced at Rosa and Scott, both in the living room—a normal family room with a flat screen, lamps, and sofas. They were talking in low tones, too far away for them to hear his quiet conversation with Kim.

"I left God a long time ago," he said softly, continuing with the needle. "And God wants nothing to do with me, I promise you that."

"But He does!"

"What? By helping you? You're one naïve life. I've seen thousands just like you. Five thousand cross the border a day, a lot of them your age. If you knew what I do to them, you'd know better than to talk to me about God."

"That many?" Kim's mouth trembled. "Thousands? Where do they all go?"

"You can't be that dumb." He used the scissors to cut the thread. "There. Finished."

"Please!" She placed a small hand on his forearm. "You have to help me. My dad—he'll pay you. I know he will. Get me back home and you'll get enough money to pay off whoever you need to, even your bosses or whoever."

"I am the boss." But still, his eyes lingered on her face. So innocent. She had no clue what the future held. "You need to accept the way things are now. The life you once knew is over."

"I can't." Her eyes teared up. "I'm praying for—"

"For what?"

"For something. For someone. For you. Maybe God will help you see that I need your help."

Ram stood abruptly, but still didn't take his eyes off her face.

"Please!" Kim pleaded. "You said you're the boss!"

"Rosa." Ram snapped his fingers. "Get her back to the room."

The house mother escorted Kim away and Scott provided security. Ram watched the young woman walk down the hall. Kim Ward. She looked back and nodded, like she thought he'd really do something, as if her begging was actually penetrating something inside him. How could she know that it was? How could she be so confident that today of all days he was bothered by the loss of life more than the loss of marketable products?

❧

Brody Sladrick knew he was being followed as he drove through the dark streets of Damascus, Syria. His Land Rover was new, but he'd intentionally dented the body and scratched a large portion of the paint off to make it appear more war-torn.

His satellite phone rang. He touched the screen, his earbud already in place in his left ear.

"I could use some good news, Rottweiler." He used the handle of his trusted techie back in Tampa. Their retrieval and recovery organization—the Trafficking Recovery Operative Assistance Services, or TROAS for short—was small, but it had a long reach through the Body of Christ. "Any word from our Israeli friends?"

"Nothing yet." Greg Rotz was only twenty-three, but he'd seen action and suffered boldly for Jesus without complaining. "But as far as good news goes, you'll enjoy the evening traffic report outside Damascus."

"Let me guess: Russians?"

"Oh, yes, along with a few Syrian forces sprinkled in with Kurdish militants, ISIS outcasts, and independent armed groups that few agencies can even distinguish."

"Sounds exciting." Brody swerved off Ath-Thawra Avenue toward Abbasid Square and watched the headlights behind him keep pace. "I'm leaving Damascus now."

"Extra fuel?"

"And tires."

"Look, Brody, maybe you should wait until you have an escort to make this pickup. It'd be safer."

"Maybe safer for me, but this is their window of opportunity."

"Oh, I should've made better arrangements." Greg groaned.

"I'm not sure why we'd allow a little danger to make us hesitate now. Besides, the women are in place. Can you confirm?"

"Brody, there's so much traffic out in that desert, if the women are outside Tadmur already, they're one party of a dozen in those ruins. I can't tell who's who!"

"Is this the only encouragement you have for me?" Brody careened back onto Ath-Thawra Avenue and zoomed north. "I'm a little preoccupied right now, Rottweiler."

"Binsa said to tell you she's going to the new safe house in Poland. It's in a bad part of town, but she'll be trying to staff it with local believers."

"Keep an eye on her."

"I will. She also said it's time that TROAS made a serious impact on the US southern border. Things have been out of control there for a couple years. Forty-eight illegals were just found dead in Texas."

"What does she expect that I should do?"

"Hmm, I don't know. Maybe interrupt their networks somehow in a permanent way? You were on the border last year. Do you still know some believers who're border patrol agents?"

"Okay, well, while I'm out here playing tag with militants in Syria, why don't you find me an entrance point along the US-Mexican border? Maybe something covert. For now, let's leave our border patrol friends out of it."

"Anything specific in mind that I should target?"

"My Spanish is questionable. Try looking for a cartel target in the States for a meet-and-greet."

"I'll start hunting. And I'll be praying."

"Thanks, Rot. Gotta go."

Brody noticed the checkpoint ahead, but he didn't slow his speed. According to his GPS, he was on the edge of the city. His tail wasn't backing off and the checkpoint appeared to have one crow's nest and an armored chase vehicle. Now after midnight, he'd hoped to leave the city without any attention, but the checkpoint looked to be manned by at least a dozen people!

As his speeding Land Rover approached the checkpoint, soldiers alerted one another to the threat. Brody's only advantage seemed to be that the barricades faced a potential external threat rather than an internal one. He doubted his tail knew who he really was. They'd probably picked him up at the airport out of curiosity since he was obviously a foreigner.

He ducked his head below the dash as the first rifle shots peppered his windshield. The front bumper clipped a pile of sandbags and shifted his vehicle sideways, checking his speed by half.

Gunfire cut through the side of the Rover, then he was beyond the checkpoint. He sat up and turned off his lights. The highway continued north, but he bounced over the littered gutter and navigated around the skeletons of armored war machines to reach the rocky desert beyond.

He slowed over the rough terrain and searched for his rearview mirror to check behind him but the mirror was nowhere to be found. Once over a bluff, the few vehicle or generator lights in the ancient city of Damascus were left behind. Slowing to a stop, he listened to the night—only silence in the arid land. The neighborhoods outside the city kept their lights off for fear of air strikes from a half-dozen forces fighting for control over the chaotic region. Since the windshield was a total loss, he used the heel of his right boot to kick it completely free. It slid away over the hood of the Rover.

Brody held a flashlight in his mouth to examine his thigh. For the first time, he acknowledged the searing pain through his thick Army surplus trousers. Blood oozed from the wound and pooled in the seat under him. After examining the door, he guessed the door had considerably slowed the bullet upon entry. It was still in the muscle of his outer thigh. He cut an X in his trousers with a sharp blade and felt with his fingers for the bullet less than an inch deep.

Every second counted—not for his own safety, but for those he'd been sent to retrieve. He didn't have the luxury of performing precision surgery in a well-lit sterile operating room.

From a small first aid tote bag, he trickled betadine over his thigh and the blade, then he cut an incision above the bullet. He used the knife tip like a pry bar and torqued the bullet into his fingertips. For an instant, he studied the mangled bullet—which wasn't a bullet after all, but shrapnel from the door or a ricochet of some sort.

The blood flowed more profusely now, so he worked quickly to stitch the wound in jagged stitches. He didn't care about scarring, only functionality. His body was riddled with such scars.

The desert around him was illuminated. Turning around, he saw two pairs of headlights pursuing him into the desert. There was no more time to play doctor.

"Lord," he prayed, "I'm trusting You to be my Great Physician tonight."

Hastily, he taped gauze over the wound, then wound tape around his thigh and pants to protect the site from debris and disease. The pain threatened his focus, but he had no time to hunt for the morphine in the kit. Besides, one of the women might need the narcotic more than he did.

After pocketing his flashlight, he sped northeast toward Tadmur, a war-torn city in central Syria. It was just a rendezvous point. The women were to meet him there, and he prayed their escape had been less bloody than his own.

He watched his speed ahead of his pursuers while navigating around dry creek beds and rock formations. Every mission that he risked, he knew it could be his last. Death didn't frighten him since he'd trusted God with his soul as a teen. What frightened him was that he would fail those who were depending on him. Now at age fifty-three, the Lord had given him a partner to work with—Zayed Aziz—but that didn't ease his desire to do his part without burdening others.

But long before God had given him Zayed Aziz, Brody had been working with Binsa, a Nepalese nurse now in her late forties. In the wake of losing her young daughter to human traffickers, Brody had led her to faith in Jesus Christ. She'd been at his proverbial side ever since, running recovery work for TROAS as Brody pushed limits to retrieve the lost and forgotten.

The vehicles behind him were following his tire tracks, he guessed, since he'd kept his lights off, but Russia, Iran, and China had begun equipping more Syrian-based forces with night vision. As more of the advanced invaders moved into Syria, their equipment was stolen or sold into the hands of bad actors who made Brody's job even more difficult.

On the east side of a hill, he used fuel jugs to top off the Land Rover. He guessed his pursuers hadn't prepared for a prolonged chase into an area where little fuel would be found—unless they knew of fuel depots that he didn't.

Sure enough, two rolling hills later, the headlights behind him disappeared. He was alone. His leg ached with every dull heartbeat, but he focused on the objective. The safety of others came before his own comfort.

He reached the outskirts of Tadmur without warning except his GPS had indicated he was nearing the coordinates. There was no power in the city due to the Israeli Air Force attempting to slow Iran's advance toward the Golan Heights.

Brody stopped the Land Rover, knowing he was close to the battlefield. The only light ahead was the flickering of a burning building in the city. He couldn't continue and risk someone hearing the sound of his vehicle.

Swinging the first aid kit over his left shoulder, he walked toward the shadow of buildings. In his right hand, he held the GPS. His thigh pain made him limp, but without the shrapnel inside, he knew a little walking wouldn't cause much more tissue damage.

Two vehicles with no lights drove toward him. He winced as he crouched behind building rubble and gazed into the darkness. The starry sky offered little illumination. The vehicles parked. The second vehicle appeared to carry a camper on its bed. Suddenly, the camper tilted toward the sky. It was a portable missile battery! Men's voices shouted in Persian with a few words in Arabic that Brody wished he wasn't close enough to hear.

Fire split the night sky as rockets flew from the missile battery. In rapid succession, Brody counted nine missiles soar skyward at a sharp angle at some target he could only imagine—probably a Syrian-based foe since they were so far from Israel's northern border.

The men shouted warnings and stumbled over one another to climb into the first vehicle. The truck bounced over debris and turned back toward the city. Thirty seconds after Brody lost sight of the military unit, an unnatural glow of light arced across the sky in his direction.

Brody fell backwards as an explosion turned the spent missile battery and the rest of the second vehicle into flaming wreckage. The militants may have been firing at local enemies, but apparently Israel wasn't taking any risks. Only Israel could respond so rapidly and precisely to such a mobile threat.

Using the light from the dwindling fire, Brody crouched and ran toward the city. He reached the determined coordinates in short order where he knelt on his good leg amongst a fuel depot of barrels that he presumed were empty. Dawn was an hour away, but no one was there.

A single headlight appeared from around a building, then Brody heard the high pitch of a strained small truck engine. Brody shrunk lower behind the barrels. He didn't need to tangle with any militants, not here. This was terrible timing. Worse yet, the Toyota-sized truck with a small bed stopped on the two-lane highway only twenty yards away, the pavement pockmarked by small craters.

Carefully, he peered over the barrels as two robed figures emerged from the truck cab. These couldn't be his contacts. He was expecting ten women, not two! Maybe they'd been captured and forced to talk. That meant his rendezvous was now with killers who were there specifically for him.

As a follower of Jesus Christ, he didn't carry anything but non-lethal weaponry, such as the tranquilizer pen in his trouser pocket. Like other missions, he'd need to escape and evade on foot, which wouldn't be easy or painless with his leg wound.

Then he heard hushed voices. *Women!* They had to be his contacts, even if there were only two. He would've risked his life for only one, but he preferred to complete the objectives he'd planned against dark forces.

He dialed his phone. His partner, Zayed Aziz, picked up midway through the first ring.

"I'm in place with the cargo," Brody said quietly. "It's a hot zone."

"We're on our way," responded Zayed's scratchy voice.

The Saudi national, who was a physician, hadn't been a believer for more than six months, but he had joined TROAS with a lifetime of diverse experience, some of it military.

Before Brody turned off his phone, he stood and waved the illuminated device at the two women near the truck. When they noticed him, he pocketed the phone and approached them.

"I am Sladrick," he greeted with caution in Arabic. They wore the heavy black coverings as wives of extremist Muslims. "The friend of our suffering Servant sent me."

The nearest woman, the driver, lowered her burqa and moved closer, holding the hand of the second woman who tried to linger behind.

"I am also a friend of the suffering Servant," she stated quietly but firmly. "Where is your vehicle?"

"It's coming." Brody stopped in front of the women. At six feet tall, he looked down into the woman's face. Since he wasn't a family member, he didn't extend his hand to touch her, but he hoped she could sense his joy at seeing her safely into his charge. "I was sent ahead to guarantee a safe retrieval."

"Ah, it is a miracle we were not discovered." Her voice was steady, not frightened as Brody had expected. "We came from Dayr az Zawr. Most of the women are Yezidi girls taken from Iraq. Some have been tortured. It's the military's way to oppress different people groups."

"There are others?" Brody asked. "Not just you two?"

"We promised ten." She returned to the truck and threw a tarp off the back. "Here are nine more."

"So, eleven total." Brody raised his arms to the women who cowered in the back of the truck. "Our Lord God Almighty deserves the glory. We will find safe passage for all of you."

"No, just these ten," the driver corrected. "I need to return to the river. Sisters, climb down and stand ready. This is our rescuer sent from God."

"You're not coming with us?" Brody tried to hide his concern. "I was told to take everyone to safety."

"Yes, everyone that I brought to you." She ordered the women to stay with Brody and hushed their quiet sobs. "There is more work for me to do in the river valley."

"No one will notice you were missing?"

The woman looked up at Brody.

"My husband is a powerful man. He may beat me, but he knows I am a good wife to him. I pray he finds my faithfulness as a means to trust in Isa someday as well."

She'd used the Arabic word for Jesus.

"You're not Syrian," Brody said. "I've spoken Arabic since a boy. I recognize your accent. Who are you?"

"I am just a servant, like these women."

"You were taken as well? And forced to be someone's wife?"

"It doesn't matter." She touched his arm, maybe in an effort to calm his concerns. "I have borne my husband children now. I am no longer a frightened young girl. Our God has opened my eyes to my calling, even if it is not in my own land."

Brody squeezed her hand in his own, ignoring the cultural conventions for a moment. This was a sister in the Lord. She knew the communion of His suffering and looked above.

"Then you should leave before my friends arrive," Brody said. "In glory, dear saint, we will rejoice over all that we cannot yet talk about."

She briefly said her farewells to the ten, many who begged her to join them. But in the end, she climbed into the little truck, turned around, and drove away. The truck bounced and creaked over the ruts of the highway until it couldn't be seen or heard any longer.

"You are wounded?" one of the women asked in the darkness.

Brody guessed she had smelled the odor of fresh blood. Indeed, the walking and running had caused the wound to begin trickling down his leg.

"It will need to wait. Come with me, all of you."

He led them back amongst the fuel barrels where they stood in silence except for Brody's assurances that his friends were on their way.

Minutes later, the heavy thrump-thrump of two IAF gunships shook the desert air. Their shadowy presence caused the women to cry out, but silence was no longer necessary. One gunship circled threateningly for cover as the other settled onto the ground exactly where the truck had parked moments earlier.

Red and green light emerged from the chopper cabin when the back door slid open. A broad-shouldered figure hopped out. It was Zayed Aziz!

"Let's go!" Brody shouted over the rotor sound. "Quickly!"

They hustled to Zayed and Brody brought up the rear. Zayed helped each woman into the cabin where a gunner crouched over a forty-millimeter mounted machine gun. Finally, Zayed firmly shook Brody's hand and guided him into the chopper where he squeezed in beside the women on the floor.

The gunship lifted, tilted steeply, then leveled off and flew west. The gunner retracted his weapon on a rail and closed the door. The noise was muffled, but it was still too loud to converse.

Brody bowed his head and relaxed against the shoulder of someone—one of the women next to him. Fatigue overtook him. From the blood loss and hours of tension, his mind and body gave way. He slumped unconsciously before they reached Israeli airspace.

❧

Kim Ward didn't forget her promise to pray for the boss in Texas, but she was growing increasingly concerned for herself the farther south they were taken into Mexico.

They'd crossed into Mexico at a place called Eagle Pass and Piedras Negras. As a seventeen-year-old high-schooler, she'd never paid much attention to things outside her world of friends and interests. Although her father had warned her about the dangers of social media and human trafficking, she wished she'd taken what he'd said more seriously. The unknown now terrified her, and her careless faith in God—which she'd taken for granted as a child in a Christian home—today was ignited. Everything she knew about God now mattered exponentially.

The only thing that kept her fear in check was her faith. Two years earlier, when her mother had died in a car accident, she'd cried out to God for a few months, but then she'd returned to her focus on school, boys, and church events. However, during times when the tears of terror whelmed up, she found herself praying in a way that she knew would change her forever. The five other white girls in the "church choir" van seemed to be even less prepared for their circumstances than she was. She sat on the second seat between two other girls, Dakota and Felicity, and they clung to her in desperation. Their fingers left marks on her arm, but she didn't shake them off. Perhaps they sensed strength from her, but Kim knew it wasn't her own strength.

Once across the border and a few miles into Mexico, the van pulled off the highway to cover the windows of the van. Their two male captors, driver and passenger, didn't want them seeing out or maybe someone else seeing in. But Kim could still see out the front windshield. They were on Highway 57. Signs announced towns and cities ahead by kilometers, but the towns meant nothing to her. Mexico's vacant geography between towns was completely foreign to her.

Her prayers for God's help lacked direction, but not desperation. Every Sunday since her mother had died, her father had taken her to the Seattle suburban church with a small youth group of only one other girl her age and a boy a year younger. The leaders had been a husband-and-wife team. They'd been caring but Kim hadn't paid much attention to the actual lessons. Nevertheless, she'd learned the Bible stories and a few verses. Somehow, a little had sunk into her memory regardless of her distractions with social media. Now, everything she could recall about God truly mattered.

She was fairly certain that God had heard her recent prayers, even though she hadn't ever prayed in any meaningful way before, at least not like this! There was nowhere else to turn. Her father was hundreds of miles away. The police probably had no clue she'd been drugged and driven to Texas. The people with guns in Texas had been so organized and professional—even treating her head wound. Though she'd expected to be assaulted by now, she realized they kept calling her and one other girl "pure," which she now understood meant that they were saving them to sell for a higher price to a client somewhere.

The man who'd stitched her forehead had had a loneliness to his deep-set, serious eyes that had inclined Kim to appeal to him before she'd known he was the boss of that operation. While being cared for by his steady hands, she'd thought he might actually help her, though she wasn't sure what that help might entail. So much seemed impossible now. Her father, who was probably losing his mind from worry, was too far away to help her. And Kim couldn't imagine a US-based police force winning a gun battle against her vigilant, well-armed captors.

A few times, Kim had tried to calculate the length of time since she'd been abducted at the stadium in Seattle. She'd been forced into the back of a tractor trailer in the stadium parking lot. There'd been other sleeping girls and women on soiled mattresses in there. Pinned down, she'd been injected with something that made her drowsy but not unconscious. Nevertheless, trying to count the days and meals and additional drugging—she'd lost track.

At one such stop before arriving in Texas, she'd felt capable of escape at a highway rest stop. The waste buckets in the trailer had been thrown out, and while the back had been open, she'd lunged out. Now, she had the impression that they'd been in Arizona. Desert had surrounded the rest stop. Though she'd had no shoes, she'd run for it—straight across the hot pavement then onto the hot sand beyond.

She'd been tackled from behind and smacked her head on a rock. Kicking and screaming hadn't mattered except that she broke a couple of nails clawing at them. There in the desert, they'd drugged her again.

When she'd woken, she was in the plastic cell in Texas where she was held for two nights. Maybe she'd been missing for only a week, but it seemed like a month.

Three hours south of the border, they entered a town called Frontera, then they took a right turn to reach an airstrip outside town. They stopped in a hangar and the passenger in the front got out to speak in Spanish to other men, but the driver remained in the van.

The girls around Kim began to hyperventilate and sob with fresh gusto. Again, the unknown terrified them. They hadn't been molested by their handlers so far, but Kim knew that could change rapidly, especially if they changed handlers.

Kim held little hope that her father could find her now. He was just an accountant, even though he was committed to her well-being more in the wake of her mother's passing. But she wasn't yet out of the reach of the boss in Texas. If he was really a boss of something to do with the cartel, she guessed he could still reach out. If he remembered her—the girl he'd stitched up who'd promised to pray for him. Oh, that he would do the right thing!

The van's side door opened. With an animal-like shriek, a girl from the back seat dove at the two men who stood there. One was a slender Hispanic man with a thin mustache. He took the brunt of the girl's force and nails to his face. She kicked free and stumbled on unsteady legs across the hangar floor.

The slender Hispanic man shouted in Spanish at the others in the hangar. The order was clear—to stay back from her. The girl fled too slowly. He caught her by the hair and threw her onto the floor behind a tool box. Kim flinched as several blows landed. When the cries of the girl ceased, the attack didn't.

The two van escorts stood idly by with five other Hispanic young men who chuckled at the plight of the girl. They laughed even harder when the attacker stood, buttoned up his trousers, and dragged the girl by her hair back to the van.

"Anyone else want to misbehave?" the rapist asked with a heavy accent. He tossed the assaulted girl at Kim's feet. "Anyone else?"

Kim's hands were balled into fists. The girl was bleeding and exposed. The men sneered. Kim couldn't move. *That could've been her.* Maybe nobody cared after all that some of the girls for sale were to remain "pure." This was the fate of them all, but the panicked girl had gotten hers first.

"Good." The Hispanic boss pointed at a small jet behind the van. "Get on board. If you misbehave, I will punish you worse than what she got. Understand? *Understand?*"

Nodding or answering their agreement, the girls hustled around the van toward the jet. Kim hung back with the assaulted girl, who was now conscious and sitting upright, though dazed.

"May I help her?" Kim asked the Hispanic boss.

"Hurry up!" He scoffed at her and turned away.

Kim knelt and did her best to cover up the girl and tie her torn clothing together. As she worked, she looked up at the two van escorts from Texas. They were her last connection to anything familiar, anything related to the Texas boss.

"Tell your boss I still need his help," Kim stated softly, meant just for them. "He stitched up my forehead. He'll remember me. My name's Kim Ward. I'm praying for him. And I'm praying for you both as well."

The Texas men glanced at one another, but Kim didn't want to risk further engagement.

"Come on." She lifted the injured girl to her weak legs. "Let's get on the plane."

She held her at her side and rounded the van. Their new handlers had made an impression. In the plane cabin, the four others sat perfectly still in their seats. No one was even there to corral them. They were too scared to do anything but obey.

Kim led the raped girl to a seat and buckled her seatbelt for her. She gently touched her bleeding face.

"Hang on, okay? I'll help you clean up as soon as they let us."

She could offer no more to the girl, certainly no promises of better times to come or a light at the end of this tunnel of darkness.

Three Hispanics, including the young boss, boarded the plane and sat behind the girls. The plane taxied down the runway and took off. Kim didn't know which way they were flying, but she had a window seat, so she watched out the window. Three hours south of Texas, they were being flown to a new place. Her trail back to the Texas boss, let alone to Seattle, was practically untraceable anymore. Who could possibly track her down now?

She had to keep praying. God had to care. He could track her.

Mountains then plains of green passed below the jet. And farmland.

Kim turned from the window and gripped the hand of the injured girl. She was wiping her bloody face on the remnants of her shirt.

"Can I take her to get cleaned up?" Kim asked the Hispanic boss.

"She can go to the bathroom herself, if she wants to." He didn't look up from his phone. "Only one at a time up from their seat."

Nodding, Kim met the concerned eyes of the other girls, then whispered to the girl.

"You've got to go and wash up. Get yourself together. The bathroom's back there. Go."

"No, I'm . . ." She checked the aisle behind their seats. "I'm afraid!"

"Listen, I don't know what's going to happen next, but I think it's better for you to stay clean. The better you look, maybe the better they'll treat you."

"I'm a mess! Look, I'm still bleeding."

"Just go to the bathroom. Then come back here. I'll go after you."

"No talking!" One of the other men kicked the back of Kim's seat.

Kim faced forward and sat rigidly. These men didn't seem human. They had no conscience. No one could stop them from doing anything, and the six girls could do nothing but accept the abuse.

The girl beside her finally timidly left for the bathroom. On the way back to her seat, two of the men acted as if they were going to grab her. The girl screamed and hurried back to her seat. The men howled in cruel, disgusting laughter.

Kim stood abruptly in protest at their morbid sense of humor. She glared at the boss as he sat idly playing on his phone.

"What?" he challenged her. "You want it next?"

Lowering her eyes, she glanced sympathetically at the girl, who was trembling and whimpering again in her seat. Kim sat back down and stared through hot tears out the window at clouds and land far below, but nothing could shut out what had happened and what was probably ahead for all six.

None of the girls got up for the rest of the flight. The mistreatment of one girl was keeping the rest in line, and Kim guessed that was exactly their intention.

Near sundown, Kim spotted a coastline below. The sun was behind them, so they were on the east coast of Mexico. Gathering each detail and tracking their progress seemed important to Kim, as if she could will someone to follow her trail if she knew it herself.

The jet descended and landed. Five of the girls were taken off the plane and hurried into a container truck. Kim glanced behind but didn't inquire about the missing assaulted girl. No one did. All she knew was that she hadn't been allowed to leave.

As the container truck moved, the girls didn't speak, even though they were alone. Kim was exhausted—more emotionally than physically. She wanted this nightmare to end. Hoping for help was becoming more difficult. Even her prayers had been reduced to two words repeated almost mindlessly, but full of earnest pleading: "Please, God. God, please. *Please!*"

The truck stopped and the back opened. Kim smelled the sea and recalled the wharf of Seattle.

A giant black and white container ship loomed above them in the light of dusk. The girls were corralled together by the Hispanic men, who were approached by an older Asian woman and a younger Asian man, both in suits. The two parties spoke in Spanish. They seemed to be discussing travel or payment schedules, or maybe both. Other Asian men arrived and the girls were escorted up a gangway to the ship. Kim looked back. The Hispanic men paid them no more mind as the men returned to the truck. It was humiliating to be treated like objects—and so carelessly exchanged and forgotten.

The sixth girl seemed to be no more. Kim wondered if she were the lucky one.

Once on the ship, the girls were taken down several flights of stairs. The route confused Kim so much so that she was certain she would never find her way out if the chance arose.

They stopped at a cabin with two bunk beds, obviously meant for two occupants, but all five were directed inside. The door behind them was shut and locked. The girls stood idly about for a few seconds. A small head with a stand-up shower sat at one end of the cabin and a metal desk in the other.

Two girls climbed to the upper bunk and the other two occupied the lower bunk. Kim didn't argue. She didn't care. The floor was fine with her for now. She just wanted to sleep.

She curled up under the desk as far out of the way as possible so she wouldn't be stepped on or in the way if the door opened. Sleep was her escape, but it evaded her troubled mind.

How could God allow this? None of her prayers were being answered. Every hour, she was being moved farther from Texas and farther from Seattle. This couldn't be the point of life, not her life. It couldn't end this way—lost to her father and friends at church and school. There had to be more. What was the point of a life like this?

No, she corrected herself. The Bible taught that God was love. And He watched over those who trusted in Him. Lots of men and women in the Bible had been mistreated. But they wouldn't be mistreated in heaven. Maybe she just needed to wait for that. Maybe this life had little relevance except to find its relation to God's will. Being kidnapped couldn't be God's will, but maybe, Kim considered, God's will would be revealed soon. Patience . . .

Kim jerked awake as the cabin door opened. Her stomach ached. When she lifted her head, she saw the formal Asian woman in the doorway with two men.

"One at a time," she said in firm halting English, then pointed at Kim. "You are first. Come now."

Climbing to her feet, Kim followed the woman up the corridor a short way until they reached another room. It seemed to be some sort of an infirmary. A suited man entered with them and closed the door to others in the corridor.

The Asian woman drew on surgical gloves and told Kim to take off her clothes. She hesitated briefly, embarrassed to disrobe in front of the man, but he seemed indifferent—much different than the leering Hispanic brutes in Mexico.

Kim was examined and documented and photographed, even her forehead stitches. The Asian woman made numerous notes about her findings, then wrote a code number in marker on the inside of Kim's forearm: A27962-V.

"Do not wash it off," the woman instructed. "Those are your new clothes. Put them on and return to your cabin."

Quickly, Kim ducked into underclothes, a smock, and pajama bottoms. No shoes or socks.

"May I ask a question?" Kim asked.

"No. Do not speak. Go."

She followed her male escorts back down the corridor. It would've been helpful to know if food was on its way, but clearly they intended their "merchandise" to stay healthy if they were checking each girl medically. A meal had to be forthcoming.

Back in her cabin, the next girl was taken and Kim guzzled water from the head sink. The water tasted like a lawn hose.

"What'd they do to you?" one girl asked from the upper bunk.

"There was like a lady doctor," Kim said. "She checked my whole body and then they gave me these clothes."

"They didn't do anything to you?"

"No. I mean, it was embarrassing because they took some pictures."

Her assurances that she hadn't been harmed didn't convince them through their fears.

Without much argument, the girls on the bunks gave her one scratchy blanket since she was willing to sleep on the floor. Another girl was taken and brought back, and another, until all had received a physical, new clothes, and a forearm code. Kim glimpsed the other girls' numbers, but hers alone included the V suffix. The other girls didn't mention the difference, but Kim thought she understood what it meant. Her father had raised her to wait until she was married, and now that suffix would change everything. It would certainly determine who bought the girls and how they were marketed in the days to come.

A day passed, then another. Meals were brought, but the girls didn't leave the cabin and no one else bothered them. They showered in the little head and learned each other's names. At first, Kim remained quiet and listened. She was, after all, younger than the other four. But as she discovered their desperate attempts to cope with the situation and their fears, she felt the need to speak up.

"We won't survive this by thinking positively," she said softly, looking at one girl, then turned to another, "and we won't gain their favor by seducing them like you're considering. They're gonna sell us to the highest bidders. That's the truth, and the sooner we can accept it and brace ourselves for it, maybe we can make the best in it."

"No, I'm not going to accept it!" argued one girl. "I only make it with who I want to make it with!"

"Listen, please." Kim swallowed hard, nervous about her own future, but certain she had wisdom for them. "If you act slutty, they'll treat you slutty. If you want to seduce the guys in the corridor, then they'll sell you to people who will line up to visit you all night in some alley."

"So, what're you gonna do?" another girl, Dakota, asked with less attitude than the other.

"Well, I hope . . ." Kim shuddered. "I don't know for sure, but people like these are business people. If you're classy, they sell us to classy people. Maybe they'll treat us better. If we act like trash, then they'll treat us like trash."

"The last one of us you tried to help clean up," an older girl accused, "they probably raped her to death!"

Kim shut her mouth and remained seated on the desk. They wouldn't listen to her. She had learned her place, defined her territory in the cabin, and something about it helped her manage. The older girls remained on their bunks, and she sat on the desk, or lay under it as the days passed.

She listened to their stories and memorized their cities and towns of origin. Two were from Canada. One was from the Midwest and one was from California. One had been forced into a vehicle. The rest had thought they'd found boyfriends on social media. Different lover boys had drawn them in, groomed them, and played them. When they'd finally agreed to meet face to face and alone, they'd been taken by force and transported down to Texas.

But no one asked Kim to hear her story.

The only window in the cabin was a round port window. They were only a few feet above the waterline. Watching the water and skyline—and occasional dolphin—was a favorite pastime for Kim. She preferred that the girls were sleeping rather than talking, which meant they'd be lying down and silent so she could focus on the ocean.

Africa or Europe, she decided. That's where they were going since they were sailing east. She'd been passed from the Texas boss man, to the Mexican bosses, and now to the Asian boss lady. There had been movies made about human trafficking, but no one Kim's age had ever taken them too seriously that she knew of. That sort of stuff happened to other people, not to them.

In the movies, the girls were forced into prostitution—either high end or street walkers. Some were shot up with drugs, something like heroin, then addicted to the habit. Kim guessed they'd try that with her at some point, but she was determined to resist. She wouldn't sleep with men just to get another fix. Drugs were unknown to her, but she hoped she would overcome the urge somehow. And she would resist sleeping with anyone. Maybe they'd kill her, but she couldn't imagine that she would give in willfully just to stay alive. At some point, they'd need to force her to comply.

Prayer. Yes, she needed to pray that she was prepared, that God would prepare her. Maybe He would perform a miracle and she'd be sold to a nice man. It was possible. But she had to be prepared to be sold to a terrible person as well.

It was her body, but no one seemed to care. If no one cared, then she would be treated badly. If she were treated badly, then she would need to cling to that which mattered more than her body. Her mind? Maybe. No, she decided. Her soul was more important than her body, and her soul belonged to God. She'd been baptized at age thirteen because she believed Jesus had died for her sins. As a child of God, she awaited the resurrection. Since age thirteen, she'd wandered away, placing her social standing above her soul. But all that was different now.

Maybe that's why this was happening? To get her back on track with her faith? It seemed an extreme measure for God to do that for her, but she considered all these ideas now.

Curling up on the floor under the desk, she started to pray with renewed gusto. Beyond her fear about the next stage, she trusted that God was still with her. She was still His child.

As Kim tried to sleep, the girls in the bunks wept intermittently through another night.

CHAPTER TWO

Ram Garrity very rarely left his six-man detail behind, but for this biannual meet, he went alone to a five-star restaurant in downtown Dallas. The spire on the Renaissance Tower blinked red in his peripheral vision as the sun set over Elm Street.

He tapped his finger on his phone screen, but didn't turn it on. He wanted to search for her, the young lady whose forehead wound he'd stitched, but the Feds could look into anyone out of state who was doing a search about Kim Ward. She was from Seattle. There was no reason why a Texas shipping executive would search for a missing Washington teen unless he were involved in her abduction.

But he knew she was long gone now, maybe already overseas, depending on how the next parties in the GLOW network transported her. Hundreds, even thousands just like her had crossed his path, but she'd been the one he lost sleep over. Why? Maybe it had something to do with the forty-eight. That was still on his conscience, too. Regardless, he couldn't do anything about Kim Ward without making himself vulnerable. The blood he'd shed and sacrifices he'd made to get to the top would be for nothing if he risked it all for a girl who had asked for his help and promised to pray for him. He was Ruthless Ram Garrity.

This was why he didn't interact with HTVs! How could he keep a clear head with her in his memory—her wide blue eyes, her quivering chin, her clear pleading?

A limo pulled up in front of the restaurant. Ram watched two bodyguards secure the sidewalk and move bystanders back before they opened the back door.

Senator Nicole Mae Pitney always made a grand entrance. He waited until she entered the establishment before he climbed out of his sports car and smoothed down his black hair in the humid Texas air.

His suit with no tie fit perfectly, tailored to his athletic physique that drew eyes as he approached the entrance. His knuckles were toughened and his body was fit from sparring occasionally with Scott and the other security members.

Those who had reservations to eat at the exclusive restaurant waited in line, but not Ram Garrity. He stated his name to the doorman and was immediately admitted.

He was led to a back corner where three tables were roped off just for the senator, though she occupied only one table. One bodyguard stepped forward to confront Ram, but the second bodyguard, a veteran on Pitney's security team, stopped his partner. The newer bodyguard was larger than he, but Ram stared him into retreat, then slid into the booth opposite the senator.

The seventy-year-old woman from Massachusetts didn't look up from her menu right away. Ram guessed her helmet of perfect auburn hair was a wig, and her teeth were all posts—overly white—but she hadn't been able to correct her excessive overbite. The painted skin on her face was stretched tight across pink though sunken cheeks, giving her bone structure a distinct skeletal appearance. And as always, she wore a purple suit.

Finally, she looked up and smiled, but her eyes were just as empty and expressionless as the first time he'd met her. Maybe it was the Botox that hindered her smile from reaching her eyes at all.

"You've had a busy few months, Ram." She set down the menu. "I like what I'm seeing on the border."

Ram sipped from his water and glanced around the restaurant. The bodyguards' backs were to them. He saw no one who seemed to be a federal team of investigators among the patrons.

"I'm just doing what you paid me to do."

That was mostly true, but not completely. He trafficked in people for the money and power. She'd recruited him to undermine the Texas statehood and security at every available moment. It all impacted America's sovereignty toward Pitney's personal aspirations to reimagine the country.

"Then I guess we're all happy." She leaned over the table and held out her thin open hand. Giant diamonds as big as her knuckles glistened on her bony fingers "Why aren't you happy, Ram?"

He hesitated just an instant, knowing what her skin felt like, but placed his hand in hers. Her skin was cold. Her grip was like moist twigs with huge knuckles that closed over several of his fingers.

"I'm happy," he said coolly. "Everything is going my way. Our way."

"Indeed. I can't remember a time when America has been this close to being rebuilt. Just wait a few weeks until I introduce my new bill called *Managed Families*. It'll be so convincing to Congress that it'll pass overwhelmingly. Everyone will be complicit in what happens next."

"What happens next?"

"Loyalty to government leaders is upset by the family unit more than any other entity nationally, with exception to religion. Loyalty to religious ideals hasn't been an obstacle for us for a long time. The family has been more difficult to dismantle, but we're doing it. You're helping. Placing abortion clinics in minority neighborhoods and sexualizing kids across the country? There's hardly a family that exists any longer that isn't confused about the natural order."

"It's not often that success is defined by total chaos." Ram sipped his water. "People don't even know what's true anymore. You're obviously directing the media to go along with your plans."

"Who else will convince the masses that up is down?" She sniggered.

"As long as you're there in the end to come in and rescue their lives, right?"

"You should've been a politician, Ram. I've always promised you a place at my side when all this is over. Maybe you'd enjoy something else, a position before that?"

Ram did his best not to grimace. She'd appealed to his selfishness to use him years earlier, but he hated her for the sinister way she'd manipulated him. This plan to dismantle and rebuild America had seemed so ridiculous at first, but he'd accepted her funding. Now, years later, he could see the wreckage of America everywhere he looked.

"There are signs of impending collapse on the border." Ram withdrew his hand from hers. "The governor is contemplating calling in more National Guard. We're approaching a tipping point I never thought was possible. Border agents are increasingly laid off for any federal reason, and their mandatory social engineering classes remove them from the ports of entry. It's never been easier to bring more people into our stash houses. Fewer illegals are getting caught and more are finding their way in without relying on the legal system or federal aid. Even states up north are talking. Fentanyl imports are up everywhere illegals are being shipped."

"I've told you to call them immigrants, not illegals." She signaled a waiter. "What we're doing for this country requires a shift in demographics and vocabulary."

"My point is, I'm losing control."

"And my point is, let it happen. You're doing fine." She ordered a meal for them both, then smiled an empty smile at him again. "Confidence in local authorities has never been lower. We have you to thank for much of that. We'll bring law and order back soon enough. It'll be done our way. There'll be compliance again. You'll see."

"I see only anarchy ahead." He swore under his breath. "I can't maintain my networks without some sense of order in society. Our banks are collapsing. Inflation is rocketing up from your party's other activities. My wealth will mean nothing if there isn't a stable currency."

"You're focused on all the wrong things, sweetie. Men like you and women like me will be on top, when things implode. We have a platform and power. When who we are is the fortress on which we stand, the new currency program can be determined by us. Trust me, Ram: you're exactly where you want to be—at my side."

"Texas will fall within the year."

"Perfect." She shrugged. "It's just one piece of the puzzle duplicated all around the world."

"Through GLOW?"

Her eyes darkened.

"I've told you not to speak of my specific movement. There is a bigger vision, something complete, being shaped for this planet's future. The environment, our social order, even the government—it's all being reinvented, reimagined."

"How soon?"

"Soon."

"It'd better be months away and not years away."

"Yes, it's only months away. But you've never questioned me like this before. I don't like it."

Ram smirked. So, he'd gotten under her tight skin. He wouldn't have become a Texas-based human smuggler without her connections in the same trade on a global scale. GLOW was the trafficking network that had revolutionized the black market and undermined governments worldwide. There were executives in the network that Ram could only imagine—politicians, bankers, world leaders. That she met with him at all was a surprise.

"Well, I need new assurances," Ram said. "I need them now. You said if I did my part, I could write my own ticket. When the National Guard rolls into Texas, I want a commission that day."

"I don't see a problem with that. You already have your own security team. For what's next, you'll need a little more help from me, but not much."

Their food arrived. Ram had no appetite, but he picked at the chicken parmesan anyway.

"So, what's next?" he asked.

"Acquire more property, as much as you can. Buy up everyone and everything in sight. The cost doesn't matter. Ownership matters. Whatever we own now, we'll control later. The more we control later, the smoother the transition when social unrest boils over."

"I'm already buying up officials."

"Not just on the border. Move into Houston. Expand into Oklahoma and beyond."

"That'll cost more than I can promise, even if I ignore mounting debt from wild spending."

"I have a new expense account for you. It should make the way smooth for you."

He stopped chewing, not appreciating the glint in her eye. She knew she could manipulate him with such enticements. *Power and money?* What man could resist?

"Just because the country is on the brink doesn't mean we can be careless," he said. "It'll cost millions to recruit and buy up what you're talking about. Hundreds of millions. People will notice right away."

"People we don't own can notice all they want. They don't matter." She ate in tiny bites, barely enough food on her fork to chew, only swallow. "The war in Ukraine has drawn unbelievable zeal. Billions have been allocated with very little oversight. It's safe money. Yours is in a fund to fight against human trafficking of Ukrainians by Russia."

"Clever."

"Of course. My peers and I have a saying: 'Never let a crisis go to waste.' We have objectives, Ram, and we'll meet each one. Soon, America will be transformed, and those who've participated will reap the rewards for envisioning the future alongside us. It will be glorious."

"I'll drink to that." He lifted his glass.

"You can drink to this, too: GLOW is close to removing TROAS. How would you like to operate without looking over your shoulder for that ghost?"

"Sladrick?" He frowned. "How'd you find him?"

"It doesn't matter. What matters is that no one can stop us. If you drink to anything, drink to our invincibility, our immortality!"

They visited more, but not about business. She shared her struggles in D.C., the opposition she received daily from even her own party who kept trying to resurrect constitutional rights and traditional family values.

Ram knew himself very well; he was a criminal because he chose to be one. But what sat across the table from him was something so twisted that he realized she couldn't fathom her own hypocrisy through the blackness of her plans to purify the nation or the world. She was too elitist in her arrogance to realize that her use of corrupt people like himself wouldn't keep her new America pure. The corruption would continue and probably grow. It was only human nature that so many bad seeds would grow into bad trees.

"We're nearly there, Ram." She stood in front of him as he helped her with her jacket, then she used his shoulder as leverage to plant a sloppy kiss on his cheek. While her face was close, she whispered so only he could hear. "I want you, Ram. I always have."

He offered a smile as she withdrew, held her hand another moment, then watched her walk away with her bodyguards. Unable to restrain himself any longer, he picked up a napkin and wiped her saliva off his cheek, certain the moisture could contain some sort of venom. Her whisper had been heavy with sensuality. She'd been so powerful for so long, she couldn't fathom, let alone recognize, his disdain for her. Perhaps she was senile, maybe experiencing some dementia, but she was certainly effective in her plans. America had never been so fragile, unpopular globally, or corrupt from internal sabotage. Even the schools and colleges had ceased to teach fundamental tools for practical living.

Though it seemed extreme to bring America down to usher in the rising global interests of the few, Ram had still helped them. Human trafficking in all its horrors had elevated every fear, drug, and suffering a nation could bear—and America was about to bear it no longer.

Ram returned to his sports car and checked the account she'd given him. Many millions of dollars—tax free. He had millions already, but it had to be carefully cleaned and moved. But not this new money. Ukraine money, allotted for a suffering people, but redirected to heighten everyone's suffering.

It was impossible to know Senator Pitney's goals and not consider the spiritual ramifications. Darkness was winning against the light, and Ram hadn't minded that his whole life. But now he saw it in all its rancid putrefaction.

He guessed his father would have something to say about the changes occurring in America and around the world. Maybe at the family reunion next week, Sam Garrity would share some of his biblical insight, but Ram wouldn't argue. He couldn't defend his secret work.

Young women like Kim Ward were scars on his conscience. Something was happening inside him, and it felt that it was beyond his control that he was beginning to hate what he had loved doing for so long. Yet he had nothing else to love in its place, only himself.

❧

Brody Sladrick stretched his stiff limbs while still on his bunk in Tampa, Florida. He was angry with himself for getting injured while in Syria. Who would've thought a bullet to the thigh could make his whole body feel like this? The wound had brought to the surface all his other aches and pains he'd suppressed since his youth.

He rolled off the bunk and put weight on his injured leg. The pain felt like a deep muscle tear, almost to the bone. Not wanting to cause more damage than necessary, he wrapped his thigh in a soft brace and limped through a couple steps.

Greg Rotz's bunk lay unmade next to his own.

"Sister, please confirm my last inquiry," Greg instructed his AI from the living room of their studio apartment. "You're not cooperating with the search parameters!"

Brody smiled as he made his bed to military standards. Greg was awkward socially, but quite comfortable with technology, even though he had a flesh and bone girlfriend down the hall on their twelfth floor. Six months earlier, the young lady of twenty-two had joined TROAS, working under Brody's right hand, Binsa.

"Any word from Binsa?" Brody called to Greg. He used the counter to walk carefully into the kitchen.

"Should you even be vertical?" Greg asked, swiveling in his chair. "Binsa would probably tell you to stay in bed for a couple more days."

The computer expert was thin with barely discernible muscle on his bony limbs, but Brody relied on the youth's spiritual maturity—not to mention his technical genius.

In the kitchen, Brody set a bowl of oatmeal in the microwave and peeled a bruised banana.

"How old are these bananas?"

"Hey, you can't expect me to go shopping for fresh fruit while I'm handling more threats against TROAS than we've ever seen before. I'm playing dodgeball with botnets from every country in the world! And I should tell you, I was never very good at dodgeball."

"Are they new threats?" Brody walked gingerly over to Greg's computer station. "Can you handle it in the digital world or do I need to visit an actual site of origin?"

"I can handle this stuff, Brody. Remember, we have an agreement: you get shot and stabbed so I can focus on dark net threats."

The microwave beeped, but Brody remained at Greg's side, watching the screen as Greg continued working.

"Start with Binsa," Brody said, "and tell me how things are going. What've I missed that's happening in Poland?"

"As expected, the safe house in Szczecin is overrun with Ukrainian refugees, and we're not even close to capacity there. Poland took over Ukraine's infamous trafficking reputation as millions of women and children have fled the fighting. They're fair game for traffickers, and GLOW predators have presumably flocked to the country to take advantage of the displaced population. It's impossible to measure how many thousands have already been abducted and transported out of Europe to different parts of Asia, but that's where I think most of them are being taken."

"How's Binsa coping? Has she asked for me to come help?"

"Here's her latest update." Greg positioned a brief text on one screen. "Let's see. The safe house has one local Christian woman managing forty women and children who have potential safety concerns or have already been approached by traffickers. There's an old Christian man who sleeps or stands at the front gate, but he's the only man in the whole place. Binsa has spoken to two church leaders about helping with safety concerns, but they want money to help staff the safe house. I guess Binsa's still looking for help."

"God, help her." Brody sighed. "She's really in the thick of it there. Did Zayed see this message?"

"You know Zayed." Greg nodded. "He didn't want her to go alone in the first place, even though we've had about six months of relative calm lately. He left last night to join her—since nobody figured you'd be up for traveling for a couple weeks."

"I guess I can't blame him." Brody retrieved his oatmeal, then positioned a chair next to Greg. "If it were my fiancée out there in that hornet's nest, I wouldn't be able to sleep until I was at her side, either."

"So, you can see why I didn't bother you about this earlier. Binsa and Zayed are about to be together. He'll keep her safe."

"Okay, I'm satisfied with Poland. Now tell me about these new threats we haven't seen before."

Greg displayed several news feeds on the screens, each speaking simultaneously. One was a White House press conference. Brody caught bits and pieces from each one.

"What's this, Greg?" Brody leaned closer to the screens. "Are they talking about us?"

"Yeah, they say your name in a minute. Listen."

Brody listened, his body becoming numb the more he realized a White House press conference was being repeated by multiple networks nationwide. After a few minutes, Brody asked Greg to mute the sound.

"Greg, this is serious. They're accusing TROAS of human trafficking, or at least aiding in human trafficking."

"It's just talk." Greg shrugged. "Isn't it? I mean, they've got their facts all wrong. We *fight* human trafficking, not help it."

"They're accusing us of helping traffickers because we have some ex-traffickers working with us now, like Marcy's mom and Zayed."

"We've never cared about what they've said before."

"But this is more than talk, Greg, and this is a lot more than some botnet trying to infiltrate your hardware in Iceland. According to this, they want to start an investigation into TROAS."

"Yeah." Greg's voice was low. "I guess an investigation could shut us down. This one news clip says they want to have a hearing to see if an investigation is necessary. It doesn't seem urgent."

"They wouldn't be having a hearing unless they've already decided to proceed. Who's behind this charge?"

"It looks like Homeland Security is providing undisclosed evidence, hoping to indict you at some point. Some senator on a subcommittee is pushing everything forward, a woman named Pitney from Massachusetts."

Brody stood slowly, set down his bowl, and walked across the room. He saw that Greg had stopped working and was carefully watching his boss, then he followed him to the doorway. In the bedroom, Brody tried to juggle his righteous anger with immense sadness. Government oversight over TROAS could mean the loss of life.

"They've mistaken our Christ-like grace toward offenders for being criminal behavior."

"I didn't think it was that serious, Brody, but it's the first time the US Government has tried to come after us."

"Not the whole government. Just a part of it despises our objection to the cancer of trafficking and our methods to bring sinners to repentance."

"So, what are we looking at?" Greg's voice broke. "Could they arrest us? I mean, do you think they'd try to put us in prison for converting human traffickers? We've done it all legally."

Brody sighed, thrust his hands into his pockets, and turned toward Greg.

"Praise God, Greg." Brody chuckled. "So, they come after us. So, they put us in prison. Wouldn't it be an honor to suffer injustices in this world for serving Jesus Christ?"

"Well, I do kind of like my scar." Greg grunted. "I wasn't really planning on getting any more, though."

"No one plans to suffer, but followers of Christ are always prepared for it, right?"

"I guess. The contingencies we have in place can protect us from this, even though we were guarding ourselves from GLOW, not our own government per se."

"The Bible does give us the liberty to flee persecution. Besides, we can't let the devil's hand distract us." Brody placed his hand on the slender man's shoulder. "Satan's objective is always to get us to focus on ourselves and our safety. But we know better. We aren't ever safe in our own hands. Our safety is found in Christ Jesus. We trust Him to fight these spiritual battles. Six months ago, you and I made quiet preparations after our tangle with Jerome Wessel. Now, we use what God has provided."

"So, we don't worry." Greg frowned as if trying to convince himself. "We don't worry and we stay the course."

"Only if we're guiltless. Have we ever trafficked anyone as they're accusing?"

"Yeah, right!" Greg scoffed. "They're probably bothered more about you converting Zayed than Marcy's mom. They don't believe people can change. They don't believe God can change people."

"Zayed has saved more lives in the last six months than he ever trafficked in his few years in the Carolinas."

"I don't think they care about the facts, Brody. This is about them getting their way, and we know they try to change the narrative at moments like this. This Pitney lady is doing this for ulterior motives, probably."

"Yes, I agree. She's up to something, but we won't be around to feel the heat. We'll let them talk. You monitor closely what's being said. In the meantime, how quickly can we go dark from this moment?"

"Um . . ." Greg looked at the ceiling. "Yeah. They're probably already surveilling us. To go dark safely, it'll take me maybe five hours."

"Okay. Zayed and Binsa are in Poland, so they're out of the way for the moment. Can you take Marcy to our secondary site?"

"Yeah, no problem. And I'll send a secure message to Zayed to let him know we're going dark. He'll explain to Binsa what that means."

"All of our other assets are already undercover." Brody narrowed his eyes. "I guess that's one advantage to being a clandestine organization. We're always in shadow mode."

"So, this is it?" Greg's eyes widened. "We're really doing this? We go underground?"

"Yep. We probably should've already done it—if I'd seen this threat when I'd gotten back. They're calling evil good and good evil."

"They're coming for us."

"We need to disappear."

"They'll file subpoenas."

"They won't have our new address."

"They'll call us fugitives. Warrants will be signed."

"We're not defenseless." Brody smiled, hoping his confidence was contagious. "God's people have often continued to minister while local authorities oppressed."

"You have friends, right?" Greg licked his lips. "I mean, TROAS has made friends over the years. People owe you big favors, right?"

"The Lord has given us powerful tools for this kind of moment. I'll alert them quietly. You focus on the transition of TROAS and our work to save souls."

"There's only one way I can do that." Greg implemented a file transfer. "You asked for a target on the US southern border. I just sent it to your phone. I found stuff on this guy even his own family doesn't know about. He might be a good point of entry for you. His name is Ram Garrity."

"This'll keep me busy." Brody scrolled through the file. "I guess I'm going to California, then probably to Texas."

"And I guess I'm heading up TROAS, Version 2.0."

"Then we're in good hands." Brody nodded sharply. "May God be honored by our service, or if necessary, by our sacrifice."

"Aren't those one and the same?" Greg chuckled.

"I guess they are."

Brody shook his friend's hand, then limped away to pack a bag and a couple of disguises.

❧

Greg "The Rot" Rotz wasn't sure whether his trembling was from fear or excitement. He'd gone undercover in Asia to save Christians' lives, but being wanted in America was a whole new experience. And there was a strange boldness that kept flowing over him every time he rehearsed who he was serving and for whom he might soon suffer. Trusting God in His sovereign omnipresence had never been more thrilling!

After Brody left with minimal gear for California, Greg focused on wiping all traces of recent moves and future plans of TROAS. Since TROAS files and Greg's own scorpion botnets operated in the cloud across multiple foreign nations, he required only his small laptop to run TROAS from a secondary site. Only he, Zayed, and Brody had been privy to the second location, secured for this very type of danger. Someone powerful wanted to shut them down based on fabricated, twisted intel. Binsa and Marcy hadn't been burdened with the reality that such contingencies were necessary and in place.

With the tech in the apartment wiped clean, Greg checked his "go-bag." He'd been taught by Brody years earlier to keep one ready at all times. Now, it was needed. It contained an extra set of clothes, food, water, and a pair of identifications for himself and Marcy. Brody had secured the IDs as legit alternates through his government contacts who he'd kept from Greg. But since Greg was a digital sleuth and naturally curious, he had a good guess that Brody's highest contact was the influential Senator Elliot Madison of New York. The man had benefited politically the most from contracting Brody for many trafficking recoveries over the years.

Government contractors like Brody received resources without traditional oversight. Such arrangements could easily be abused, but Greg knew of no such personal agenda in Brody's past or in his future plans, regardless of Homeland Security's recent finger-pointing. They didn't like Brody's Bible-based approach, and authorities who wanted absolute control definitely saw his faith and following God Almighty as a direct threat to their authority.

Taking one last look around the apartment, Greg slid his mobile laptop into a carrying case and shouldered his backpack. This was it. He was on the run. Brody was on another mission—as if business were normal—but the rest of TROAS was going underground. There was honor rather than selfishness in their flight since they were doing so to continue their important work—not only to protect themselves.

In the hallway, Greg shorted out the reinforced steel door to his and Brody's apartment. It would take more than a battering ram to serve a warrant to search that apartment.

He walked down the hallway two doors to Marcy's apartment and knocked. Every day for the past six months, he'd enjoyed her company. Marcy's father, Cole, was still alive when Greg had asked for her hand in marriage, but Cole had died a short time later from liver disease. That had been just three months ago. But Brody had agreed to walk her down the aisle when she'd asked him, and he'd also agreed to be Greg's best man—alongside Zayed and Aidan Nevins, Marcy's brother.

Marcy opened the door, her scarred face and unruly dark hair adding to what he saw only as natural beauty. She'd begun collecting berets the last few months, so Greg wasn't surprised that she was wearing one even at ten-o'clock in the morning.

"Greg!" Her face beamed and she presented her cheek for his customary kiss. "I was just about to head out the door to the House of Leah so I don't have but a few minutes."

She welcomed him in and leaned against her kitchen counter as she tugged on sneakers. One of the things he loved about her was her practicality. Even her footwear was geared for action, not fashion.

After closing the door, he set his go-bag and laptop on the floor. She briefed him on her day's plans to go to the House of Leah, a women and children's shelter on the outskirts of Tampa. Her mother, Emma, and brother, Aiden, lived and served there under overseers from a local Bible-believing church body. The House of Leah operated autonomously from TROAS, though its boarders came exclusively from Brody and Binsa's trafficking retrievals. The House was blessed to have both Emma and Aiden to care for the residents since the two of them had been rescued from the trafficking world in their own unique ways. They knew the horrors of its trade enough to care for similar survivors and overcomers.

"Marcy, can I talk to you for a minute?" Greg interrupted her.

"Okay, but I only have a minute." She took a bite of toast and swigged a mouthful of orange juice. "Hurry, Greg. My mom is waiting. We're orienting a woman from Romania and a teenager from Vietnam."

"Come here." He took her hand and led her to the sofa which faced a collection of photos on the wall and mantle where most households might have fastened a flatscreen TV.

"What's wrong?" Her eyes searched his face as she sat with him. "Greg, you're scaring me. You've got that look in your eyes."

"What look?"

"That look that Brody and Zayed get when they're going on a dangerous mission overseas. Binsa says they're both walking the line between careless and courageous, and I'm reading that in you loud and clear right now. A woman knows these things about her man."

"And . . . your man . . . has that look?" He couldn't hide his grin. "Wow. That might be the greatest sentence anyone has ever said to me."

"Uh, it wasn't meant to be great, Greg. Hurry, I need to go."

"Not today." He mentally surveyed her apartment. It would be very difficult to place a listening device in any of the TROAS apartments without being seen on the surveillance cameras in the elevator and hallway. "Remember Homeland Security Agent, Jerome Wessel?"

"Of course. He's the one who first turned me on to you and Brody."

"And then he turned on us."

"Yeah, I know. I try not to think of him at his worst."

"His zeal to punish people for trafficking conflicted with Brody's zeal to bring people to Christ. It was an unavoidable collision."

"I remember."

"It seems Homeland Security at least in part has gathered some momentum in Washington, D.C., and they're coming after TROAS."

"Coming after us? What does that mean?"

"They've convinced the media and some politician that we're involved in human trafficking."

"Well, we are." Marcy frowned. "We're involved in fighting it. We fight it with the gospel. That's what Brody always says."

"Right, but they're saying we're *aiding* in trafficking. This is what sinners sometimes do. They tangle good people up in trying to defend themselves. It's how they punish us for serving God. And they use the process of the court system to punish people who don't agree with their viewpoints."

"But that's wrong. This is ridiculous."

"They don't care about what's true, what's right, or what's God's best for others. They're coming for us, and they intend to put us away somehow."

Marcy's face paled. She withdrew her hand from Greg's and looked away.

"I . . . can't be locked up again, Greg. We haven't done anything wrong. They're going to arrest us?"

"The Bible gives believers the liberty to run, if they want to, from authorities who hinder God's eternal purpose on earth. Even though we're just building up the church to be a light in the midst of darkness."

"Then, we can run? What's Brody say? Oh, should I change his bandage again? I wasn't even thinking about that this morning. All I was focused on was getting to the House. Where will we go, Greg? I'm not prepared to go on the run. I don't know how. I'm not a spy like you and Brody and Zayed. I'm just a—"

"It's okay." He reclaimed her hand and she conceded. "Marcy, we're already set up. Brody, Zayed, and I have been preparing for something like this. The danger is real, but we have a place to go."

"What about Mom and Aidan?"

"They don't seem to be the focus right now. Besides, they're ignorant of the TROAS international policies and network, and it's best they stay ignorant for their own safety. If they're targeted, then I'm sure Brody will respond. God has given us powerful friends, but we're not supposed to get caught up too much with fighting for our lives. When Paul was in prison, he retained legal assistance, but his main focus even under oppression was sharing the gospel with the authorities, with people who visited him, and with other prisoners around him. This is gonna be awesome for us all!"

"You—" Marcy halted her objection and tilted her head. "Wow, listen to me. In just a few months, I've grown so comfortable here with you that the smallest pressure has me freaking out."

"Yeah, but we don't need to freak out."

"This is an opportunity?" She smiled. "You're going to tell me that next, weren't you?"

"That's one way to look at it." Greg nodded. "I like that. It sounds better than defining for you my emergency contingency mode."

"Okay, okay." She laughed. "So, what's the big deal? We just run away and continue TROAS from somewhere else."

"I knew you'd get it, Marcy. This is one of the things I love about you. You always find God's will through the problem."

"Not always, but I do have a good partner. Or soon-to-be partner. Oh! What about our wedding now? And Brody? Wait. Binsa and Zayed are in Poland. What're they going to do about this?"

"Zayed, Binsa, and Brody's travels have all been by covert means to avoid GLOW's eyes, so no one's aware of where they are."

"Brody's already gone?" She cringed. "Even with his leg like that? He still has staples!"

"Well, he's long gone. I've sent Zayed an encrypted message, so he knows what's up. You and I need to take care of things here. I've already closed up my apartment. Zayed, Binsa, and yours are next. Can you collect from Binsa's apartment what she'd want to keep? I'll go through Zayed's apartment."

"Binsa has lots of records. And all her photos!"

"Get it all. You've got two hours. Bag it up and put it in the hallway. It doesn't matter how much you collect. We won't be going far with it."

He prayed for God's wisdom before they left the sofa, his hands holding hers, and his sense of boldness grew.

Zayed had lived a spartan existence since Brody had recruited the Saudi doctor-turned-agent. Greg packed the man's clothes and a little gear from his closet, then joined Marcy in Binsa's apartment.

"How can we leave anything behind?" Marcy asked. She had barely started gathering Binsa's belongings.

"Take only what we can't replace or buy somewhere else. Get some of her clothes and shoes. I'll get her photos."

In an hour, they had gathered what they wanted and Greg shorted out each door.

"Is this sad for you?" Marcy asked.

"A little bit." He gazed down the hallway from the elevator. "I designed this whole floor with Brody. The security countermeasures were all mine. But the next place will be just as secure once we're set up, though with a much different view."

"We're gonna need a truck for all this." Marcy shook her head at the bags, boxes, and bundles.

"Okay, you're gonna love this."

Greg punched the elevator button. They quickly piled all the property into the elevator. With barely room to stand, they descended one floor to the eleventh story. The elevator doors opened to an entirely open floor—no apartments or interior walls. Only a few electrical cables hung from the ceiling between load-bearing columns, and a cardboard box sat in the far corner.

"What's this?" Marcy asked.

"This is where we leave everything, but we won't stay here. Brody had me lease this whole floor through a shell company five months ago. Zayed and Binsa can come get their stuff here in a few weeks—after the Feds ransack our apartments upstairs."

They left the property in the middle of the floor, then Greg led her to the cardboard box in the corner. He handed her a gray wig and a ratty gray sweater.

"We prepared for this day," he said.

"Disguises?" She critically eyed the wig and sniffed the sweater. "What're you wearing?"

He held up a derby hat and a cane.

"We'll go out one at a time. You first. People really don't pay much attention to transients around here."

"You're talking like there are corrupt agents outside already waiting for us."

"Brody and I think there are. They probably intended to get us one at a time as we left the building. We wouldn't have been on the news this morning if they hadn't already positioned themselves to apprehend us."

"Did Brody do this too? He wore a disguise when he left?"

"Yep. He's been doing this for years, though not usually in the States. He's already long gone. Now, it's our turn to get safely away."

"Where do I go once I get outside?" Marcy removed her beret and fit the gray wig over her wild curls. "Is there a car for us nearby?"

"No, just walk across the lawn to the bus stop that faces the bay. We'll wait for the St. Petersburg bus."

"Wait? For how long?"

"From right now? The next bus will be here in about thirty minutes."

"So, we wait here another twenty minutes, then go downstairs?"

"I don't think so." Greg handed her the ugly sweater. "The sooner we get out of the building and blend in with the other homeless people, the better."

"What if we're caught?"

"Then we keep our mouths shut and wait for Brody to help us."

"Okay." She faced the elevator and picked up one of her two bags. "Can you bring my other bag? It's heavier."

"Sure, I'll bring it. You can do this. The Lord is with us."

"Yeah. He's gotten me through worse, right?"

"This is nothing."

He kissed her cheek as the elevator door opened. She walked in and got in character—bowing her frame and tucking her chin. The elevator door closed and Greg began to pray as he walked to the window. With a little time on his laptop, he would be able to confirm how many agents were already staking out their apartment, even what their names were. But taking time to do those things didn't matter right now.

A couple minutes later, Greg noticed a gray-haired old woman shuffle slowly out of the building, pause, then head up the sidewalk through the brown lawn to the bus stop. There were a few people with whom she could blend in, and in no time, she reached the bus stop where she sat on the bench.

Greg returned to the elevator and donned his bowler hat. He picked up his backpack, laptop, Marcy's second bag, then his cane. As he descended in the elevator, he felt a rush of joy at how far God had brought him. Brody was even trusting him to transition the physical location of TROAS—not just trusting him with some digital keystrokes!

Not only from Brody, but Greg felt the honor of Zayed's trust as well as Marcy's. Binsa also needed him to triumph that day. Greg prayed that the Lord would guard him against failure so he didn't disappoint his companions.

Outside the building, Greg kept his head down to avoid any possible cameras aimed in his direction. The enemies of TROAS would know by now that Greg knew all their organization's secrets. If they couldn't catch Brody—which no one ever had—then they would certainly settle for questioning the Rot.

True to their façade, Marcy didn't look up or greet him when he reached the bus stop bench. He sat on the opposite end of the bench and relaxed his weary limbs from the burden of the bags. A few feet away, a metal trash bin stood reminding him that he'd sat at that very spot earlier that year and eaten tacos from the nearby taco truck. Though he'd never hit the bin with his taco trash, he believed he could hit the mark of protecting the important work of TROAS that Brody had prepared for him.

After a few minutes on the bench, Greg turned his head to scan the parked cars far across the lawn. Maybe all of this caution was for naught. Maybe Greg had misinterpreted the media coverage from Washington. Maybe there were no real problems they needed to—

Then he saw them. Two men sat in a black car with tinted windows. But Greg could see them through their windshield. They were watching the apartment building. From his vantage point, Greg got the impression the men wore some sort of formal shirts. Definitely Feds. All the other cars nearby appeared to be empty.

Greg looked away before he was noticed. Brody had been wise to initiate their relocation and not a moment too soon!

The bus to St. Petersburg arrived. Greg mounted the steps with three others, including Marcy in her disguise. She sat toward the middle, but Greg found a seat in the back where he could watch the traffic and potential tails. Halfway across the Gandy Bridge to Pinellas Park, he shed his disguise but kept the cane.

"Thank You, Lord," he breathed with relief that they'd made a safe getaway.

Now to change buses in Pinellas Park and return to Tampa's Ybor City neighborhood at the new TROAS site. It would be a long day, but care for God's ministry and ministers was always effort well-spent.

Ram Garrity sipped his coffee as he stood on the rocky shoreline of Lake Tahoe. The serenity of the glassy water almost drew him away from the discomfort of attending the Garrity family reunion. He had a dozen issues to oversee back in Texas, but the cover of a normal life needed to be maintained by attending the week-long gathering. This was about family, even though he felt disconnected from them all.

"Maybe a little glimpse of heaven, huh?" said a man to Ram's right. He'd approached silently across the rocks to stand only ten yards away with his own cup of coffee. "This is my favorite time of the day."

Checking his watch, Ram saw it was just six in the morning. Most of the family were still in their rented cabins. Though it was Ram's favorite time of the day as well, he wasn't about to open up to this stranger, even though he must've been a Garrity relation if he were staying in a cabin.

"The forest looks like it's recovered nicely." Ram gestured at the nearby trees that had endured a forest fire during a recent burn season. "The wildlife certainly returned."

"No kidding." The man chuckled. "Those are some noisy birds."

Ram smiled. Maybe it didn't hurt to let down his guard and enjoy the simple folks from mostly on his father's side. The man next to him appeared to be in his fifties, broad-shouldered and stern-faced, but his friendliness proved he was light-hearted. Yes, he was definitely a Garrity, maybe a cousin of his father, Sam. Now Ram recognized him. He was someone he'd seen somewhere, probably in a family photo.

"You get in last night?" Ram took a swallow of cooling coffee. Yes, this was a moment he could enjoy without hurry. "I heard some vehicles pull in late."

"Oh, I've been here a few days already. I don't know if I'll stay all week, but I figured it was important to come for a day or two at least—get to know everyone."

"I don't know half of them myself." Ram kicked some pebbles into the water and watched the ripples spread. "I've been sort of out-of-touch with everyone but my sister and dad. I'm Sam Garrity's son, Ram."

"Brody." The man shifted his coffee cup to his left hand and offered his right. "It's a pleasure."

"Likewise." He shook the stranger's hand. Firm. Manly. "Dad had a thing for Bible names, so he named me Ram."

"Is the name Ram in the Bible?" Brody asked, settling into place beside him to continue their mutual admiration of the lake and mountain scenery. "Remind me."

"Well, I guess Ram was an ancestor of King David, the second king of Israel."

"Huh. I don't think Brody's in the Bible. Is it?"

"I don't know." Ram laughed. "I remember some of the stories, but I don't know much else about it. It was Dad's thing. And my sister is still a church-goer, too."

"Hmm." The man was silent for a few moments before he spoke again. "Seems like a good Book though—the Bible."

"Yeah. I guess so."

"Probably worthy of more of our attention than we give it in this crazy world."

"Yeah." Ram smiled at the lake. This was real living—a beautiful lake and a simple conversation with a distant relative who didn't pry. Maybe the reunion wouldn't be so bad if there were a few more cousins like Brody to quietly connect with. "It's been a while since I took a vacation. This is pleasant."

"I went sailing a few weeks ago in Tampa with people from work. It's good to take time off occasionally."

"Tampa, huh?" Ram didn't remember his dad saying anything about family flying in from Florida. "Never been sailing."

"Hey, check it out."

He followed Brody's gaze down the shoreline to three canoes.

"The canoes?"

"It's not sailing," Brody said, "but look at that water. Imagine being out there. Come on. We'll be back before anyone's awake for breakfast."

Ram finished his coffee and followed the stranger to the canoes. Brody fetched three wooden paddles from a short box and handed one to Ram.

"Contingency." Brody held up the third paddle. "Just in case."

"Smart."

They flipped over one canoe and Ram stepped through a few inches of water and climbed into the forward position. Brody slid the canoe farther out and hopped in. The canoe glided across the water like ice.

"Oh, this is nice." Brody dipped his paddle from the rear seat.

Ram gripped the sides of the canoe with both hands, the paddle on his lap, and felt the power of Brody's stroke. There was real strength in the older man's frame—character and physical power. Like his father.

A view of the shore was left behind as Ram stared straight ahead and took in the mountains above. It was indeed magical. He rocked to Brody's strokes. The lake was empty except for them. Lonely. Perfect. An eternity away from Ram's suburban cul-de-sac and border pursuits. Hundreds of miles from the forty-eight who'd died and from Kim Ward who'd begged for his help. That was his past. They weren't his problems any longer.

Brody stopped paddling. The canoe drifted sideways. Slowly, the beach, the cabins, and the forest slid into sight. Ram wondered if his sister Carmen was awake yet. He knew she'd volunteered to help with the reunion events—things like scheduled hikes, volleyball tournaments, and maybe canoe relay races. She was always prying into his life, or sharing about the peace and joy she had in her faith. It annoyed Ram that she thought he needed something more than what he already had. No one in the family could possibly be as wealthy or as powerful as he was—even without his security team backing him up.

He guessed his father was already awake, about to prepare breakfast for the nearly fifty Garritys. Sam was so laid-back, Ram imagined him fitting in better in the South rather than in rural California outside Sacramento. Knowing Sam, he'd see the reunion as an opportunity to talk to people about Jesus. People might listen politely, but Ram knew no one wanted to hear about that gospel stuff. Life's struggles nowadays were too prominent to spend their free time thinking about religion and guilt and the threat of hell.

"Thought you should know," Brody said softly behind him, "I'll be returning with you to Texas."

Ram didn't turn in his seat to look back. He barely even breathed. What felt like a chill from the glacier water swept up from his feet and consumed his whole body. *This stranger wasn't family! He was the enemy!*

"You . . . deceived me." Ram took a calming breath. "You're good, getting me out here like this before telling me who you are."

"I haven't told you who I am." Brody paused. "Sometimes vulnerability helps us pay attention."

"So, you think I'm vulnerable? If you do anything to me, my family will report you immediately."

"Oh, I'm not too worried about your family. I've gotten to know your dad and sister pretty well. I might even know them better than you do at this point in your life."

Ram glanced down at the paddle in his lap. Maybe he could swing it as he pivoted in his seat. Like a club, maybe he could pummel Brody before the man could attack him. No wonder he'd grabbed two paddles!

"Someone sent you," Ram stated, hoping for more information, stalling while he decided what to do. Maybe swim for the shore? "Who sent you and why?"

"With some effort, I'm sure you can imagine who sent me."

Frowning at the water, possibilities flashed through Ram's mind. Maybe another cartel had sent him—a single assassin to remove him as a competitor. Or maybe Scott was trying to take over 5TRAY? It had crossed his mind before, but Scott didn't have the brains to run the operations nor the discipline to sacrifice life's pleasures to build such an organization. But if Brody were an assassin, then why hadn't he already killed him on the shore of the lake?

No, the man wasn't an assassin, Ram decided. Or maybe he was, but he wasn't there to kill him right away. Was he toying with him? That could be. Some killers were sadists. He'd met some human smugglers who picked out illegals just to rape and torture every week.

He thought back to the conversation they'd had along the shoreline. Was there any hint as to who he was or why he was there for him? And how had Brody already become close to Sam and Carmen if he wasn't family?

Then Ram realized who must have sent him. *Yes, it had to be her!*

"Pitney—she doesn't trust me?" He sighed. "I'll do my job. I always have—long before she showed up. Now we're supposed to play family—you and I? You're good, pal. Really good. You must be good if you fooled my dad and sister."

"I'm nothing special," Brody said. "I'm just committed to my objective. That's all. Like you're committed to yours."

"And you think returning to Texas with me will help anything?" Ram finally turned halfway in his seat to look into Brody's face. Now he understood the hardness he sensed about the imposter. "I have security protocols in Texas. Visitors aren't welcome."

"Oh, I think you'll find a way to welcome me. You and I will be pretty close after a few days together here.

Besides, your men in Texas will do what you say, won't they? After all, you're Ruthless Ram Garrity."

Ram swore and faced the front. The man had truly done his homework. It was already problematic hiding his secret life from Carmen's prying questions. How was he supposed to explain why one of Pitney's goons was accompanying him around the campfire?

"What's stopping me from dumping you before we get to Texas?"

"Curiosity," Brody said. "You're curious about what'll happen next."

"I'm not curious about anything Pitney's up to."

"Okay, well, there's also your family to think of," Brody stated softly.

As his body stiffened, Ram was glad Brody couldn't see his face. His teeth bared and a growl nearly escaped his throat. The man's threat was clear. Carmen was only twenty-four, naïve to the horrors that Ram committed daily in the shadows of the southern border. Half the women Ram trafficked were about her age. But rage filled him at the prospect of her suffering—or that Sam would learn that his son was responsible for many like her being harmed.

"Message received," Ram finally said, but inside he began to plot the murder of this man sent by Senator Pitney. No one spoke to him like this and lived! And threatening his family? Pitney would pay—though not before he found a hole in the desert to hide this killer's body. Certainly, he had to be a killer, for no one less could be stupid or bold enough to expect to supervise his efforts. Sure, Pitney had given him millions to use 5TRAY to undermine the country's sovereignty, but she had messed up by sending a hitman to ensure her interests were protected. Maybe he would abandon any loyalty to Pitney altogether and use the millions she'd given him to enhance his own fortune . . .

"Let's head back," Brody interrupted his scheming. "We'll enjoy the reunion for a few days, maybe all week, then we'll leave together. Everyone will see how we've become good friends in the meantime. And I have a jet waiting for us in Sacramento when it's time to go."

"Of course, you do."

Ram gripped his paddle and stroked wildly, trying to expel some of his frustration at the water. A simple vacation had turned into a complex security threat that endangered Ram's own autonomy. Not even the cartels made such demands against him anymore—as long as he upheld his end of the border agreements.

He'd rented a car in Fresno after taking a commercial flight—rather than fly his own private jet or drive one of his own vehicles. Indeed, he was vulnerable. Pitney knew exactly where to strike him. Brody hadn't even said what his last name was—or if Brody was even his real first name.

By the time they reached the shore, Ram had calmed his fury to a smoldering level of caution. Brody probably wasn't working alone. Pitney was a strategist. She would layer personnel for her own safety. Maybe he needed to work with this man until he understood more of Pitney's intentions against him.

Hopping out of the canoe, Ram tugged it ashore. Together, the men flipped it over and stowed the paddles in the box.

"How are we supposed to do this?" Ram asked as they approached the cabins. "You're not even family. Nobody here knows, you know, who I am."

"Don't worry about a thing." Brody rested his hand on Ram's shoulder for a few steps. "Your dad and I have a kinship."

"You're kidding." Ram stopped suddenly. "You mean you really are a relative?"

Brody smiled. It was the smile of a teacher who patiently waited for a student to find an answer, and Ram definitely felt like the student in this man's shadow. He and Pitney were five moves ahead!

"It's a long story, but one I'll tell you at the right time. Just be a good son, and we'll be out of here in no time. Smell that? Your dad's got the griddle going. Pancakes probably."

Between the circle of rented cabins, a number of picnic tables had been moved together. Almost fifty relatives—a third of them under fifteen years old—gathered for blueberry pancakes and maple syrup. The air was cool but hearts were warm, and laughter abounded as they ate shoulder to shoulder.

Ram lost track of Brody as the stranger mingled, accepted additional flapjacks from Sam, and participated at the next table in a conversation about the war overseas.

"You're quiet." Carmen elbowed Ram in the arm and stole a piece of bacon off his paper plate. "Nice break from work, huh? Just relax."

She'd studied foreign languages in college, settling on Mandarin after a year abroad in Nanjing. Now stateside, Sacramento kept her on staff as a translator and Chinese culture consultant. And it didn't hurt that she'd passed the bar as a licensed corporate attorney.

For an instant, Ram thought of the Chinese families he'd trafficked that year. He hadn't understood their language, but his sister would have. Carmen could never learn what he'd done to those families. The foreign fathers and sons had been sent to the docks for hard labor—or if their blood type matched, they'd become organ donors by force. The women had been sold to East Coast sex shops and massage parlors. And he'd sold the kids for ridiculous amounts of money to buyers who specialized in the exploitation of minors.

"I am relaxed," Ram said, hoping his frown had been corrected. "That's why I'm quiet."

"Can you stay all week?"

"We'll see. Work is pretty demanding lately."

"Family is more important. Besides, I want to talk to you when we're alone."

"We're talking now."

"No, I mean really talk. There must be a special lady in your life by now. I worry about you being all alone so far away in Texas. You know I pray for you a lot, right?"

Ram stopped chewing. *Praying for him?* Like Kim Ward had promised to pray for him? Why was everyone so intent on praying for him all of a sudden? It didn't help anyone at all. Kim Ward was probably being sold in Europe or Africa, and his sister was practically broke since she spent all her money on charity efforts in various Sacramento neighborhoods.

And prayer hadn't yet helped him. If anything, his life had become more complicated from Pitney's ambitions, and the whole Garrity family was being threatened by Brody—who was probably some deep GLOW spook who took out the trash for the global network.

"Earlier, I saw you out on the lake with Brody." Carmen tucked her blond hair behind her ear. "He seems nice, huh?"

"You know him?" Ram glared at Brody. So, the man wasn't bluffing. He really had connected with his family already. When Brody looked up, he winked at Ram. *Winked!* "He's family?"

"I guess so. He and Dad were here a couple days before everyone else. You should've seen them organizing all this before I even showed up. They were getting the cabins ready and moving these tables together. They were even praying together, so I know Brody's a believer."

"A believer!" Ram felt his anger rise up again. Such a jackal taking advantage of his naïve and gracious family! "Seems nice, yeah, but I didn't take him for a Christian."

"Look at him. What makes you think he's not?"

Ram didn't answer, but he was willing to bet that Brody had at least a dagger on him that had shed the blood of innocents. Pitney was heartless. She wouldn't send anyone but a complete savage into his presence.

The conversation at his table suddenly turned very heavy. Someone brought up the tragedy of the forty-eight illegals killed in the truck near the border. Ram's forty-eight. The pancakes lost their flavor as he listened. They criticized the cartels and cold-blooded coyotes. Carmen seemed to be watching his face until he met her gaze, then she turned away. She couldn't possibly know those were his forty-eight, *could she?* Ram wanted to tell everyone that he hadn't intentionally killed them! There was no money in a dead illegal, let alone forty-eight.

Accidents sometimes happened when 5TRAY hired careless smugglers and drivers. Scott Carrell had said he'd be more careful, but with an ever-increasing surge at the border encouraged by the US Government, more accidents were inevitable.

Carmen graciously interrupted the melancholy conversation with the announcement of the hike planned for that day.

"We'll have lunch on that mountaintop!" She pointed at a wooded peak. "Hiking shoes and long pants for everyone. We leave in thirty minutes."

From the deck of the cabin Ram had been assigned to, he watched Brody clean up the picnic area. While everyone else was tying on proper footwear and day packs, Brody had no need to prepare. Ram noticed Brody's light boots were already well-used, and his cargo pants were faded but in good shape. He had to be special forces. Now that he thought of it, when first shaking the man's hand, Ram had felt the calluses of a laborer. Now he understood those were the calluses of a soldier.

A killer had inserted himself into the Garrity family, and Ram saw no way to escape the stranger's strategies.

❧

Kim Ward believed they had reached the end of their journey. The giant cargo ship had stopped in some

European port. When the other girls weren't crowded around the port window over the lower bunk, Kim had noticed many other ships nearby, most with Spanish-looking names. Or they could be in Portugal, she thought.

For over a week, Kim had kept to herself by sleeping on the floor under the corner desk or sitting on the desk listening to the other four girls talk. During the first couple days on board, they'd ridiculed her when she'd offered some insight to their situation, so she'd remained silent after that. Their conversation had been filled with false hope and delusion about the future. Two of the girls still thought it was in their best interest to seduce whoever came for them and "purchase" their way to freedom by using their bodies.

But no one had come for them after the doctor lady had inspected them. Their only contact with anyone outside the cabin had been with the two Asian men who brought them meals three times a day. The two didn't seem to speak English, and the door had slammed on the girls' attempt to engage them in conversation.

"We're Americans," one girl reasoned aloud for the hundredth time. "We have rights. They'll treat us better than they do girls from other countries."

Kim wanted to shake her head at the young woman's ignorance. They were being trafficked. She knew that the appearance and condition of their bodies was all that the sellers and buyers cared about. Like livestock, they'd be sold. The other girls didn't have a *V* suffix written on their arms, so they might even be sold for their organs. At the least, forced prostitution awaited them all.

But Kim kept this upsetting yet probable news to herself. She prayed for herself, her cabin mates' silly notions, and for the Texas boss. And she prayed for her father. He was probably losing his mind over her. If she could get a message to him, it wouldn't matter. The people who held her were organized, careful, and powerful. No one could help her but God, and she understood that His help would primarily come by way of endurance to weather whatever mistreatment awaited.

The clanging of boots on the metal corridor outside the cabin silenced the girls' worried whispers. Kim steeled herself. This was it. Her body would be taken, but she remained convinced that God held her soul in His mighty hands. No one could take that from Him, no matter what happened to her physically.

The door opened. The two Asian men were backed by the female doctor again.

"Show me your numbers," she ordered.

Kim and the others hesitantly presented their forearm numbers to their captors. The doctor spoke Chinese to her two men, pointing out the two girls on the top bunk.

"You and you," the doctor said. "Come with us."

The men didn't wait for the girls to climb off their bunk or to hop down. The Chinese men entered the cabin and grabbed ankles and wrists. The struggle was short. The girls were dragged off the upper bunk as the two on the lower bunk shrunk as far away from the conflict as possible.

The two chosen girls wailed loudly on the floor where they'd landed. When yanked to their feet, they were forced limping and bruised into the corridor. The cabin door slammed shut. Kim remained still as she listened to the fading screams.

"Why didn't they take us?" asked one of the two on the lower bunk as she clung to her friend. "Why didn't they take us?"

Kim moved to their bunk and sat facing them.

"Shhh." Kim held her finger to her lips, then whispered to them. "We can only guess why. Now, we just need to prepare ourselves for when they come for us. It'll happen eventually. They won't just forget about us."

"How are you not freaking out?" cried Dakota, a nineteen-year-old that Kim had slowly learned everything about while listening to the girls talk.

"To start with, I'm not lying to myself about what's happening to us." Kim felt bolder now with the two others gone and these two so vulnerable. "I'm sorry, but you need to get a grip on yourselves, or it'll be worse for you."

"Do you expect us to just go along with them?" asked the other, a college girl of twenty-one named Felicity.

"No, we can't go along with them." Kim sighed, begging God for the right words. "But I think we can act with dignity. You know, have poise and self-respect."

"You really think that'll help us?" asked Dakota. She was a summer school student from Canada.

"It may not help us escape what they'll do to us, but it'll help us cope and recover if we don't lose our minds. The more we struggle without thinking, the more they'll injure us. We need to resist them without losing our minds. Let's hold in our emotions to start with."

Felicity wiped her eyes, smoothed down her frizzy hair, and glanced at Dakota, who lowered her gaze and shook her head.

"I'm sorry you had to sleep on the floor the whole way." Dakota was a brunette with shining blue eyes on the verge of fresh tears. "We could've made room for you or taken turns."

"That's not important right now." Kim crossed her legs on the bed and folded her hands. "We need to talk about reality and come up with a plan. The more organized we are, the better we'll face whatever they have planned."

"Organized?" Dakota nodded. "You mean, like, to fight back?"

"Maybe there'll be a time to fight back, but we have to wait for the right moment." Kim raised her eyebrows. "Didn't you notice those two Asian guys have tasers with them? We have to be smart about this."

"What do we do?" asked Felicity, clearly the more sensitive one. "I'm so afraid!"

"Fold your hands like this," Kim instructed. "And we pray like this: 'God, we believe You're loving and powerful. We're really afraid. We've been stolen and sold away to people like Joseph was sold to the Egyptians. We don't know what's going to happen to us, but we want to trust You to help us . . . survive, understand, and maybe escape. Please lct our enemies treat us with mercy. But if they don't, keep us sane. Don't let us have hatred or treat them like they treat us. In Jesus' name, amen.'"

When Kim raised her eyes to Dakota and Felicity, they were staring at her, their hands still folded. Felicity swallowed, her lip quivering.

"Did . . . He hear you?" she asked.

"Yes." Kim smiled confidently. "He definitely heard."

"How do you know?" Dakota asked.

"Because He touches my heart with peace whenever I trust Him. That's why I'm not freaking out."

"What do we do next?" Felicity urged.

"We memorize everything important about each other. Chances are, once we're sold to someone permanent, one of us will get a chance to make a phone call. Maybe we'll escape or talk to someone in authority. If one of us can get word out, it'll help all of us. Who we are, where we came from, and when we were last together— that'll help our families find us later."

"I don't know anything about you," Felicity said. "Where are you from?"

"Seattle. My mom is dead, but my dad's name is Jack Ward. Say it."

They repeated his name, then she helped them memorize his phone number. Their eyes dried and hope appeared on their faces for the first time as they shared their families' contact information with Kim and each other.

"Everyone you meet," Kim said, "you tell them about yourselves and me. And everyone I meet, I'll tell them about both of you. It's possible that someone back home will hear about us this way."

"What if we can't ever get a phone?" Felicity asked. "We may be locked up forever."

"Maybe." Kim took a deep breath. "I think they'll make us . . . prostitutes. As horrible as that is, it means we won't be alone. Maybe we can talk a john into letting us make a phone call—or take a message out for us."

The girls shuddered together, agreeing to try everything they could to get word out or escape. And they wouldn't abandon anyone left behind.

"One more thing before we continue to plan." Kim parted her bangs and presented her forehead. "I need you guys to take out these stitches. They're itching like crazy."

Felicity had chewed her nails too short to help, but Dakota used her dirty nails to pull out the stitches and knots. It was slightly painful for Kim, and a little blood trickled from the healed gash, but after thirty minutes, all the threads were free.

"Remember that Texas boss man?" Kim fingered the threads. "He's the one who stitched me up."

"The one who took you out of the cage?" Dakota asked. "I heard Rosa call him Ram."

"Ram?" Kim felt that now knowing his name was a gift from God. "Ram. Ram what?"

"I don't know," Dakota said, "but she definitely called him Ram."

"It must be a nickname," Kim considered. "Wait! Look!"

The ship was too large to feel movement, but the scene outside shifted across the port window. The three girls crowded their faces against the glass.

"They're taking us somewhere else," Felicity said. "What does it mean?"

"It means we have a little more time together," Kim said. "God must want us to plan a little better."

They watched out the window until they could see no more land or ships. Kim thought they were turning north, but she didn't share her guess with the girls to cause them to worry more. All they could do was pray and hope.

CHAPTER THREE

Marcy Nevins drifted along the Ybor City sidewalk with a grocery bag on her arm. The District of Ybor had once been a factory district where millions of cigars were rolled every year. But now the distinctly Latin neighborhood was one of Tampa's street-party locations for every abominable vice the city relished.

Though she and Greg were only a few miles from their old TROAS apartment building, he'd agreed that there was little danger of her shopping for food while he finished setting up cameras and other safeguards around their new warehouse location.

Stopping at a store from which the tech display had spilled onto the sidewalk, Marcy wondered if the merchandise was all legit since most of it looked used, though it was priced as new. The crowded, diverse community seemed like an ideal place for TROAS personnel to hide in plain sight. Pedestrians drifted past without acknowledging her. Greg had commented that they were sort of like Lot's family in the middle of Gomorrah. They were God's precious ones in the midst of the world's lost and blind.

One flatscreen TV in the window was playing a news channel. There was breaking news—a hurricane was hitting Cuba, maybe on track to hit southern Florida. And a manhunt was underway, initiated in Washington D.C. Marcy stepped closer to the screen and used a remote hanging from a tether to turn on the captions so she could read the broadcast.

"Millions of women and children are trafficked in the United States and abroad each year," said the broadcaster, a red-headed woman who wore a frown at the news she had to share. "A nation-wide manhunt is now underway for these three persons of interest—Brody Sladrick, Greg Rotz, and Marcy Nevins."

Marcy ducked her head a little as her driver's license photo appeared next to Brody and Greg's faces. Then the photos disappeared to return to the newscaster.

"Ms. Nevins was once trafficked herself, but she's sought for questioning in regards to a number of children who have disappeared in the last six months. With us today is Doctor Samarantha, a behavioral psychologist who has worked with victims of human trafficking for two decades. Doctor, you are a specialist on this subject. Tell us how someone like Ms. Nevins, who was once trafficked as a young girl, is now some sort of human trafficking ringleader."

"Thank you for having me," said the doctor from India. "Victims of human trafficking are always scarred so horribly and permanently that they remain victims of their pasts. They sometimes return to the only thing they know—harming others and themselves. Ms. Nevins is a classic case of—"

Looking away, Marcy checked the faces of passersby. No one was paying any attention to the news feed, let alone her own appearance. She'd often appreciated her homely appearance, her blackened front tooth, and unruly hair for how it all made her seem undesirable to others. Only Greg, Brody, Zayed, and Binsa seemed to see her for who she was—wild hair and all.

Her photo was off the screen now, but even if it wasn't, Marcy didn't feel she'd be recognized since the photo didn't show her with a beret. The beret—a prop Brody had helped her with—significantly managed her stray curls, altering her appearance so much so that she didn't panic on the sidewalk that morning. Using the remote, she changed the channel to a nature program, then walked away from the tech display.

A block later, where the crowd had thinned, she paused at an intersection as if she were waiting to cross at the traffic light. Casually, she swung back and forth her grocery bag of bread, lunch meat, and fruit, as she allowed her eyes to drift back toward the tech store. Over the months with TROAS, Zayed had made a project of schooling her in the clandestine arts. Though the Saudi had entered the shadow world late in life, he had learned enough to teach her not to panic and how to blend in. Misdirection, he'd explained, was invaluable.

Thus, as soon as she was certain no one was following her, she turned from the intersection and moved briskly off the sidewalk through a chain-link fence. The property next to the new TROAS warehouse headquarters was under modernization and partial demolition. She skirted the construction site of men with hard hats and a forklift burdened with debris. In no time, she reached the next warehouse, which still had the woody smell of cigars, and came to a sudden stop in front of the sliding metal door on the first floor.

A young man in his early twenties knelt over a heavy canvas sheet, perhaps a tent, and used a needle and thread to patch a noticeable tear. He had a thin beard, greasy hair, and his jeans were torn at the knees. A camping-style backpack was leaning against the warehouse wall, with several of its zippers open, revealing clothes and a few hygiene items. The stranger didn't look up at Marcy, so she knew she hadn't been noticed. A young girl of about four stood beside the backpack. She gripped a whole carrot with both hands and gnawed on it with her tiny teeth. Her face was unwashed, but her clothes were in one piece. At her feet was a child-sized backpack, the zipper also open, displaying a coloring book and a coat.

Marcy's first thought was that the girl was a kidnapped child, and this man was here, behind the warehouse and out of sight from the street in an effort to hide his criminal behavior. But she scoffed at herself. Her work within TROAS didn't need to color her views of everyone. Besides, the little girl turned to the man, though not letting go of her carrot.

"Papa . . ." she called.

He spoke Spanish to his daughter, then glanced up to see Marcy standing not ten feet away. Marcy didn't move as he was startled to his feet and backed against the wall. Protectively, he drew the child against his leg.

"It's okay." Marcy smiled and gestured with her eyes at the big door on the warehouse. "I live here. Maybe you want to come inside?"

The young man turned slightly and studied the garage-sized door as if he hadn't realized it was a door at all. Such was the rust on the whole building, which made it a perfect hideout for her and Greg.

The man didn't seem to understand her English, so he probably didn't understand that she'd invited him inside, which had been a natural offer she'd made without thinking. Maybe it wasn't wise, she thought, to welcome people into their shelter, but sometimes helping people stretched beyond what always seemed prudent in the moment. She certainly couldn't sleep inside while the man and his little girl slept outside against the wall in their lean-to that was clearly torn. The nights were warm still, but what about if it rained with the approaching hurricane on its way?

"Have you eaten?" she asked. "Uh, *hambre?*"

"Mucho," he assured with a nod, then spoke more Spanish that Marcy didn't know.

"Well, let's go inside. My boyfriend's inside. His name is Greg. Just pull open the door there. See the handle? Just pull on it. *La Puerta.*"

He pulled the door open, wide enough to drive a car inside, and gasped at the size of the warehouse with its visible and vacant floors that rose eight stories. Many of the girders and beams were exposed to the elements since the roof had collapsed in places, as the floor had as well. But several metal staircases led sturdily up to each story.

"Let's go," Marcy invited again with a wave, and walked through the door. Once inside, she set down her bag to help the man and child bring their belongings inside. Then she slid the rusty door closed herself. Finally, she clapped her palms on her jeans and offered her hand to him. "My name is Marcy."

"Hector Savalano," he greeted, then drew his daughter closer. "Gabriella."

With some prompting, the little girl held out her hand.

"*Mucho gusto*," Marcy had learned to say.

"*Mucho gusto*," he and his daughter responded together.

"Uh, *comida?*" Marcy offered, and picked up her bags. "Let's go upstairs for a little food. Come on."

She led the way farther into the warehouse where the floors and ceiling above was intact. Slowly, she climbed the steel staircase as they followed her up to the second floor. Greg had suggested they sleep on at least the second floor since the ground floor was littered with past flood debris as well as insects where grass grew in patches between cement cracks.

On the far end of the second floor, Greg had set up their new TROAS command center. Nearby, they'd unrolled thin sleeping bags, which they'd slept on top of at night. However, Greg wasn't at the helm of his laptop right then.

"Wait here," Marcy told her guests and insisted that Hector set down his belongings and remain there with them. "I'll go find Greg, my boyfriend."

"Greg?" Hector asked with concern. He spoke more Spanish, but Marcy didn't follow it.

"Just wait here. I'll be right back."

She jogged across the floor and around several splintered plywood walls.

"Marcy!" Greg waved and smiled from the western wall of the warehouse. "Check this out. An escape route!"

Wandering over to him, Marcy formulated her words in her mind to convince him that their guests needed to stay with them.

"Look, it's a fire pole!" Greg showed off his invention. "I anchored it down there on the ground. It's at a slight angle, but we can make our escape through here if we get cornered. Then we can circle the block and grab a taxi out on the street to the Tampa Union Station. It'll take sixty seconds, tops. You think you can slide down that? There's grass down there, so it'll be a soft landing."

Marcy stuck her head outside the wall and acknowledged the platform Greg stood on, an old fire escape exit. The pole extended thirty feet down to a side yard overrun by weeds.

"I could do that," she said with approval. "Hopefully we won't need to use it too soon, especially with house guests."

"House guests?" Greg's eyes widened. "They found us already?"

"Um, no. But there were some people outside about to set up camp against the building. I think they're illegals. A man and his daughter. I . . . invited them inside. They look like they need a home."

"Well, so do we, so I guess we're all in the same boat."

"The same boat?" Marcy frowned. "So is this a boat or a firehouse? Because a minute ago you said that's a fire pole."

"Hey, boats can have fire poles, too!" He kissed her cheek. "How was the food run?"

They started back toward their command center, arm in arm.

"No problems, but I saw a TV screen at a tech store. TROAS isn't just under investigation now. There's a manhunt for me, you, and Brody! I saw it on the news!"

"What?" Greg stopped her. His eyes blinked several times before he spoke again. "Why are you . . . happy about that?"

"I'm not exactly happy."

"But you're smiling. No, you're beaming."

"Well, I think it's silly they think we're criminals. I mean, I don't care what they say about us. We're together, and we're already acting like the people God wants us to be, even without a habitable place of our own. Look."

She turned him to observe across the floor how the little girl, Gabriella, was doing her best to lay out a thin bedroll next to Greg and Marcy's sleeping bags. Hector had resumed his work on the torn canvas.

"If I remember rightly," Greg said, "the Bible is full of believers who have very little yet they're still hospitable. I guess God led them to us, huh?"

"They don't speak English."

"There are apps for that. We'll be just fine. Unless we need to run for our lives. I need to get on my laptop to assess the latest risks."

Greg heartily shook Hector's hand and lightly patted Gabriella's cheek, but he broke away as soon as he could to go to his laptop. Marcy excused him and herself from their guests and joined Greg's side at his makeshift desk.

"They're twisting everything," Greg said as he scrolled down a screen of notices. "They've moved from saying we're connected to human trafficking to saying we're trafficking masterminds. Look here, they're all over the old apartments, searching everything we left behind. It doesn't look like they've found our stuff on the next floor."

"You protected us all." Marcy laid a hand on his shoulder. "We have you to thank."

"How can you say that? We're wanted fugitives."

"Yeah, but we're safe here, right? And now we have house guests to look after. If you wouldn't have prepared this place, we'd be on the streets right now, or in prison."

"As long as my botnets are doing their job and scrubbing municipal databases of our getaway . . ." Greg turned toward her. "Are you sure you're okay? I mean, this is pretty serious. GLOW has to be behind the mobilization of this governmental search for us. They're making us look like criminals while they're the ones actually trafficking humans."

"Brody always says to look for God's purpose even in things that look bad and hopeless."

"God has a purpose in us being wanted fugitives?" Greg sighed. "Okay, let's think this through. All of our work for years is being twisted around to make it look like the opposite thing. Some of our supporters in the ministry are probably jumping ship right now. Human traffickers are despised by the public, so we're being isolated."

"But the TROAS network is still in place, right? Our allies know the tactics GLOW uses against people like us, don't they? Binsa says evil people always accuse others of doing exactly what they themselves are guilty of."

"That's definitely their mode of operation." Greg's mouth suddenly gaped. *"I've got it!"*

"What?"

"God's purpose!" Greg pulled up a map on his screen. "Here's Brody in Tahoe still. He's gone undercover to infiltrate some trafficking group on the southern border."

"So, why's he in Tahoe?"

"The leader of 5TRAY has a family reunion there. This is perfect—all of it!"

"How's it perfect? Brody's a wanted criminal as much as we are. He's in trouble."

"No, don't you see? If he's wanted nationally for widespread trafficking, the traffickers he's with will totally accept him!"

"GLOW thinks they're hurting us, but—"

"But what they intend for evil, God will work out a result for good. They're helping Brody infiltrate their whole network!"

"So, this is perfect." Marcy's grin matched his. "Brody's going to be able to do more than he ever could if GLOW wasn't lying about us."

"That's got to be God's purpose in all this. We just have to avoid arrest until Brody's mission is finished on the border."

"That's it? Don't get arrested? There has to be something more we can do. And how about Hector and Gabriella?"

"Yeah." He watched Hector work on his patching. "We need to do the right thing with them. And for them. They're probably here illegally, but we need to make sure so we can start on their immigration papers the right way."

"Can we use your app to speak Spanish to them?"

"Yeah, and we can pray. We're not the only believers today in America being accused of being criminals, traitors, or social justice problems. Maybe we'll remain underground from now on, but we'll do it with honor and faithfulness."

"So be it." Marcy nodded, tears in her eyes. "I'm so happy . . . to be doing this with you. People might hate us for serving God, Greg, but our Lord knows what the truth is. He'll welcome us home soon."

They sat together a long time, accepting by faith that their lives for God came before their reputations before men.

Department of Homeland Security Agent Jerome Wessel walked slowly through the studio apartment that had once been Brody Sladrick's headquarters. As the agent in charge of the manhunt, he'd been discharged from Washington by Senator Pitney herself, his new boss. He would bring TROAS to its knees one way or another, but since their Tampa headquarters had been evacuated, the job would take longer.

He faced the eastern wall, remembering that Greg "The Rot" Rotz had showed him TROAS' sophisticated scorpion botnets that scoured the net for security threats. The computer flatscreens were still there, but the drives left behind had been sent to the Justice Department investigators. Jerome hoped for clues or evidence of Brody or Greg's whereabouts or crimes, but he knew the drives would be blank—scrubbed by a twenty-three-year-old tech wizard who had outsmarted GLOW for years. Now, Greg was outsmarting the US Government, and it infuriated Jerome.

"Sir?" A forensic investigator approached Jerome. "We found this thumb drive in the other apartment in the night stand next to the bed."

Jerome accepted the drive in the plastic bag and admired it. He passed it back to one of the eight men taking inventory of the four apartments. It had come from Binsa's room so it probably contained only photos. The woman was obsessed with photos of trafficking survivors. Oddly, though, Jerome had noticed that her framed photos had been removed only recently from the walls of her apartment.

"Good work. Keep searching. They must've forgotten something important. Nobody is this clean. We're not leaving until we find a trace of something to use."

He stood over Brody's perfectly-made bed opposite Greg's piled sheet and blanket. It'd been six months since he'd sat in that apartment with the people he'd thought at the time were heroic. But something had changed, and Jerome refused to admit the change had been within himself. No, he'd merely realized Brody and his small band of radicals weren't actually working in favor of the US Government. Their "Jesus" passivity towards human trafficking made them a legal liability. He'd noticed it himself, and then when he'd taken his complaints to his superiors, Senator Pitney had contacted him. Now he was her eyes and ears in the field.

Six months earlier, Jerome had been a DHS nobody stationed in Lincoln, Nebraska. Now, he worked for Pitney directly, hunting down domestic security threats like TROAS. Sure, TROAS did rescue a remarkable number of trafficking victims, but that wasn't the problem. They kept "leading to Christ" and reforming human traffickers instead of aiding the government in their prosecutorial efforts. Of course, Brody hadn't resisted in the prosecution of anyone, but the man's priorities for his religion couldn't compete with the state's priorities. One or the other had to go.

Senator Pitney had determined that if TROAS didn't cooperate with Homeland Security as much as Jerome wanted, then TROAS and all its people must be cooperating with GLOW and other human traffickers. Thus, Brody Sladrick had been labeled a human trafficker—along with all his immediate personnel. Jerome knew that Brody utilized an unseen network of churches and volunteers locally and internationally. If any of them raised their heads in defense of TROAS, they were fair game as well.

Jerome walked to the elevator and rode it down to the ground floor. Outside, he palmed his phone and dialed Pitney. The tips of his shoes brushed the grass where he'd watched Brody and Aidan Nevins play catch a few months earlier. But none of those pleasant moments mattered to Jerome any longer. Brody Sladrick's religion needed to be replaced by loyalty to the US Government's legal and socially acceptable standards.

"I've been expecting your call," Pitney answered. "This had better be good news."

"The fugitives are being evasive." Jerome was glad to be talking to her on the phone. In person, her aged face caked with makeup was a distraction—not to mention her helmet of hair and awkward or untimely smiles. Those may have had something to do with her false teeth. "But someone will slip up. Their photos are going out to every news outlet and social media network. I've seen to it."

"Enemies of the state like Brody Sladrick should've never been allowed such free reign in the first place. I'm not the only one who wants his head. Foreign governments are calling in their grievances as well."

"I understand." Jerome was surprised at the disdain she held for Brody, especially having never met him. Her hatred was principled, though, and Jerome certainly wasn't going to argue in Brody's favor. "We'll cast a wider net. They may have left Florida already."

"Explain to me how they could've slipped through your surveillance. You should've arrested them sooner!"

"Ma'am, we were still procuring Federal warrants when you held your press conference about investigating TROAS!"

"Oh, so it's *my* fault *you* let the suspects get away?"

Jerome's muscled body flexed, as if every fiber in his being was needed to hold back his tongue.

"I'll catch Sladrick. I'll find them all."

"Good. And the two you said went to Poland—I'll send a team for them myself," she said. "Just send me their names and photos. There's more than one way to make this nation's enemies disappear."

He hung up without waiting for more, and returned upstairs to inspect the apartments with a fresh eye. Brody, Greg, and Marcy were in the wind, probably still in the States, but Zayed and Binsa had been tracked to Poland. He didn't mind that Pitney was willing to deal with those two on her own, even if she wasn't familiar with their identities. The last time he'd gone after Binsa, Brody himself had come and rescued her. Binsa was from Nepal and Zayed was from Saudi Arabia. No one in America would miss them.

But right now, Jerome was going to take down the head of the snake itself—Brody Sladrick. And no one would miraculously arrive to help that religious nut!

Ram was relieved to leave Lake Tahoe and board Brody's jet to fly back to Texas. He'd surprised himself by having a good time, despite Brody being there and his sister trying to pry into his private life.

"I've never needed a drink in my life more than I need one right now." Ram helped himself to the cabinet behind the cockpit. "Uh, Brody? Orange juice and water? Where's the—"

"No booze on board." Brody sat in a swivel seat over the wing. He drew out his phone and swiped through several screens. "Alcohol causes nothing but impairments. Men like us need to have our senses on high alert."

Sighing, Ram slumped into a seat opposite Brody. *No booze?* He couldn't figure out this guy or the real reason why Senator Pitney had sent him—except to keep an eye on him. Unless Pitney hadn't sent him after all? No, he decided. That didn't fit. He'd already dismissed anyone else sending the man. At least he was headed home and about to get back to work. Scott could help him watch Brody, and if everyone followed Pitney's business plans, then the US would be overrun and unruly with illegal migrants to the point of collapse. That would put him out of his current business, but Pitney had promised him another position. Thus, he could tolerate Brody for a few weeks or even months, if necessary.

Like Brody, Ram drew out his phone and reviewed messages he'd missed or ignored while in Tahoe. The nationwide abduction of teenage girls was at an all-time high, but due to the "lover boy" scam, most media were referring to the abductions as runaways.

"Naïve," Ram muttered to himself. The media seemed to be coordinating with Pitney. They knew the schemes that traffickers used to kidnap kids or abduct families at the border, but the media kept calling them everything other than what they were. It was remarkable to Ram to witness such an effort in unison to collapse America and her allies so they could rebuild the country in their own way—an elitist, globalist, tyrannical way. "It's not my problem."

"You say something?" Brody looked up.

"Just watching this country fall apart." Ram read report after report of 5TRAY developments along the border. "Your boss seems committed to this nation's collapse. How certain are you that we don't collapse with it?"

"My boss?"

"Pitney." Ram frowned. "Why? Who did you think I was talking about?"

"Well, it may seem like Pitney's in control," Brody said, obviously dodging the question, "but she's not."

"If she's not in control, who is?" Ram scoffed. "She's pulling strings all over this country and around the world. GLOW wouldn't exist without her."

"Why not?"

"You know why not." Ram felt a chill in his veins. He kept sensing that Brody wasn't who Ram presumed him to be. "You know more about her than I do. She's the Executive."

"Oh, that." Brody nodded. "Sure. I get it. Because she's the Executive of GLOW. Right."

Ram continued to watch Brody's face as the older man returned his attention to his phone. Of course, Pitney was the Executive of GLOW, but no one said it so casually. She was the brilliant mover behind expanding the shadowy universal trafficking network. Many GLOW associates were only now realizing that their work was actually meant to be the vehicle for undermining every country's sovereignty—to promote a new government and world view.

Brody napped on the bunk toward the back of the jet, but Ram had to catch up on issues after a week's absence. Most updates were from Scott, and Ram would be expected to make big decisions for his lieutenant to implement as soon as they touched down in Dallas. There were properties to be purchased, officials to be bought or threatened, and an ever-increasing cartel south of the border to appease.

Suddenly, Ram jumped up, nearly bumping his head on the cabin ceiling. Scott had sent him a national fugitive alert. His security lieutenant was often sending him security notifications, but this one was different. Brody's face appeared next to a young man named Greg Rotz and a young woman named Marcy Nevins. They were wanted for human trafficking. Of course, Pitney wouldn't have sent him someone unfamiliar with the trade. That didn't surprise Ram.

What was a surprise was Brody's last name. Sladrick. *Sladrick!* The Brody sleeping not fifteen feet away on the jet was Brody Sladrick? *The* Sladrick? It was a name every serious human smuggler knew. For some, it wasn't a name at all but a legendary figure that veteran smugglers used to scare into line the junior smugglers. Now the man was wanted for trafficking, and Pitney had sent him to Tahoe?

Ram felt sick. He began rehearsing his conversations with Brody since their canoe ride. Brody had revealed little, but Ram had deduced much. Now that he thought about it, Brody hadn't been the one who'd first mentioned Senator Pitney. He'd heard for years that Sladrick was a notorious retrieval expert mainly operating in Asia and Europe, but he occasionally made appearances in the Americas. Had Pitney been his handler all along? She was, after all, a strategist who called things not as they were, but as she wanted them to appear.

But what if . . . Pitney hadn't sent this guy like Ram had thought? This was definitely the infamous Sladrick right in front of him. The only question was—had Pitney sent him or had he come to the Garrity family reunion on his own accord?

Running into the bathroom, Ram vomited into the toilet. This wasn't happening. This couldn't be true! Images from the past week came to mind. Brody had bonded with Ram's father before the reunion had begun. Brody's face had seemed familiar, but now he realized he'd recognized him from a rough sketch of the one known as Sladrick, not because he was a distant Garrity cousin!

Yet, the nationwide manhunt for Sladrick as a human trafficker changed everything. Who was behind this? Ram wondered if he'd been duped into allowing Sladrick, the greatest enemy of GLOW, to infiltrate the 5TRAY network. 5TRAY was autonomous, but that's how GLOW worked—through autonomous entities or cells who shared intel and forces to defend themselves and promote their little empires.

The plane descended into Dallas before Ram had made up his mind on Brody's true origins. Ram had killed a young undercover ATF agent years earlier who'd tried to join 5TRAY. The Feds hadn't been sure where their leak had been, so they'd committed few other attempts to infiltrate his organization. But he couldn't kill Brody if Pitney had actually sent the crafty veteran. Worse yet, Ram wasn't sure he could disentangle himself from Brody without exposing himself—since he'd allowed Brody to get so close. The man had just spent a week hiking, canoeing, and sitting around the fire with his family!

"We're there," Ram announced as he stood over the sleeping Brody. The man couldn't possibly sleep so soundly if he knew he was already in the jaws of death. "My security team is already here to pick us up."

Stepping back, Ram watched Brody sit up and rub his eyes. There was no hint of worry on his face. Either Brody was a master at hiding his fear or he really had nothing to fear because he was too connected to be killed.

The jet taxied into a private hangar where two SUVs waited—Scott, with his tall crewcut, and the man's five heavily-armed men.

After Brody let down the stairs, an airport ground crew pushed over a supplemental staircase on wheels.

Ram followed Brody down the stairs to the hangar floor. The whole time, he watched Scott's face. Scott Carrell was a soldier, not a clandestine operator who could stump a lie detector. At that moment, his lips pressed together until they were white, and Ram knew Scott had recognized Brody Sladrick from the news alert.

Brody approached the SUVs like he belonged in one of them, but Scott held up his hand, halting Brody from reaching the door.

"What's this?" Scott asked Ram. His voice was strained. The men behind him must've read his body language since they spread out, carbines leveled for action. "You know who this is?"

"Yeah, I know who he is." Ram stopped next to Brody who stood almost toe to toe with Scott. "You want to do this here? Let's talk at home."

"You want to take him . . . *in?* Into our neighborhood?"

Ram was rarely questioned and never by subordinates. If ever there was a time to question him, it was now, but he'd already tied himself to Brody, live or die.

"Did you check out the news alert and warrant for his arrest?" Ram asked.

"Of course, I did—because he's a destructive threat to GLOW interests, not because I thought you'd be flying home with him!"

"Is the warrant legit?" Ram pressed. "Or is it a play to sneak him into our good graces?"

"The warrant came from the top, from someone we know, but . . . this is *Sladrick.*"

"Regardless what we've heard about him," Ram set his hand on Brody's shoulder, "I just spent the last week with him. He's one of ours. Pitney sent him. Is that true, Brody?"

Brody continued to look straight into Scott's face.

"No, I'm a special agent with a well-known face who expects you to give up all your secrets to me." Brody cocked his head. "I belong to a brotherhood with such power that even Senator Pitney was inclined to issue a warrant for my arrest to help me expose 5TRAY's entire network and agenda—and bring it all crashing down."

"Yeah." Scott scoffed. "Right. Okay. At least he's got a sense of humor."

"Go wait in the truck for us, Brody," Ram instructed. "We'll get moving in a minute."

Brody brushed past Scott and approached the lead SUV.

"At ease, gentlemen," Brody greeted the five other gunmen. "It's just me."

"It's just me?" Scott swore as he and Ram watched Brody climb into the front passenger seat and close the door. "Is this for real, Ram? We're supposed to ignore everything we've ever heard about this guy—for years?"

"Pitney's a master at misdirection." Ram shook his head. "I don't know why she'd want this top guy suddenly labeled as a trafficking criminal, but she's got her reasons for sending him here. I mean, he's supposed to help us with the next step, somehow."

"Maybe she knows if the press is focused on him, they'll ignore the rest of us. We've had a lot of abductions lately that've drawn Amber Alerts."

"Then while Brody is doing his job," Ram sighed, "I guess Pitney expects us to keep him safe. It's not like he's a beginner. If the rumors are true, he's been in this game since we were in grade school. What's your latest intel say about him?"

"Well, pretty much, uh . . ." Scott scratched his head. "He's Sladrick. We're kidding ourselves if we think we're going to keep him safe. He takes care of himself. You said you just spent a week with him. What's he like?"

"Friendly. Everyone loved him. It's hard to get a line on him, actually."

"What do you mean?"

"After he told me who he was, I suspected him immediately. Then I watched how he interacted with my family. He's scary-good at fitting into an environment as nosy as my family. He even spoke fluent Mandarin with my sister."

"The translator?"

"And he beat everyone in my family at chess. My uncle was something like a grandmaster. He was impressed."

"You're no slouch, either, Ram," Scott said.

"I didn't play him."

"Well, is he armed?" Scott glanced toward the SUV. "He didn't look armed."

"He's got a blade inside his waistband on his right hip." Ram lowered his voice as the airport attendees passed them. "I only know that because he drew it to sharpen sticks for the kids to roast marshmallows. And he can move, too. I thought he had a limp the first couple days, but then that disappeared. I saw him hike to the top of a mountain. He was carrying two of the heaviest packs by the time we reached the top, and the extra weight someone else couldn't carry didn't slow him down. The guy reached the summit before everyone else. Even me."

"You were holding back?"

"No, I was going full throttle, and my legs are still sore from that day."

"So, he's supposed to be instrumental for us with this transition Pitney gave you to handle?"

"I guess so." Ram shook his head. "So much for knowing what's going on in our own house, huh?"

They loaded up and Ram drove his own SUV with Brody in the front.

"That's smart," Brody said as they reached the highway. "You keep your entire security team behind you for overwatch. Let me guess—they have licenses for those weapons? I saw their patches. Bogus border security?"

"You should know all about it," Ram said. "I hear you wrote the book on misdirection. All these years, we've been looking over our shoulder for your shadow. Now we find out you're one of us? I don't even want to know what Pitney's doing with you now—making you into a fugitive. We've got our own work to focus on here."

"I'll stay out of the way, unless you need to hear what I've got to say."

Ram didn't respond. Brody's choice of words was strange, but he was learning that nothing about this man was an accident. Everything he said and did was intentional, purposeful. Though Ram wasn't one to get sentimental, he was glad Sladrick was now on their side!

From the southern end of the Dallas suburb, Ram drove into the cul-de-sac. He identified the uses of the five residences for Brody and briefed him on the security measures that kept the unwalled, ungated neighborhood perfectly safe.

"Let's put our stuff inside," Ram said as he parked in the garage, "but don't get comfortable. We've got to deal with something next door."

As Ram led Brody inside, he pointed out a bedroom that the veteran could use for as long as he wanted. After they dropped their bags off, they walked out the front door together. On their way to the Hispanic HTV residence, Scott joined them.

Inside, Ram waved a greeting to the house mother in the kitchen, who watched the house residents as Rosa watched over the non-Hispanic HTV house and captives.

"We'll be just a few minutes, Judy."

The small woman in her sixties didn't respond. Like Rosa, she rarely left the house. Unlike Rosa, Judy was a wanted criminal in Great Britain—wanted for accessory to murder.

"We excavated this ourselves," Ram told Brody as Scott opened a wall panel in the hallway. Behind them stood the closed doors that led to the captives' rooms. "It's come in handy more than once."

They descended a short flight of stairs to a collection of six large metal barrels. Scott turned on a low florescent light. Ram was used to the odor, but Scott covered his nose with his fist. Brody didn't react, and Ram would've been disappointed if he had.

"He came up on us," Scott said as he removed the lid of one barrel, "when we were picking up a whole caravan scheduled in from Nicaragua. He thought we were a private patrol at first, but as soon as his guard was down, we grabbed him and put him in here. We get him out and question him every couple hours, just to keep him alive."

Ram shouldered his way past the other two guys to the barrel and took hold of the short curly hair of a thirty-something-year-old man bound and wedged inside the container. He'd been stripped of his patrol uniform and bloodied a little, but he was alive and alert. When Ram forced the man's head back, his eyes were wide and full of fear.

"He won't work with us?" Ram asked. "Doesn't he know what happens to those who won't be friendly and cooperate?"

"Guess not. He won't even talk," Scott said. "We threatened his family and put a whip to him. Still nothing."

"Are you too good to work with me?" Ram asked the patrol agent. "This is your last chance, Agent. You work for me, or I put the lid on this barrel and I bring your kids and wife under my roof. Do you know what that means? Anything to say yet? No? Scott, where's the lid?"

"Wait." Brody moved up beside Ram, gently pushing him aside to look in the barrel. "Let me see your face, buddy. Come on."

Brody reached into the barrel and lifted the agent's chin.

"This is Aaron Ridgewood!" Brody exclaimed, then looked at Ram. "What's he doing in here?"

"What? These barrels are for problems that have no other solution." Ram glanced at Scott. "What's the problem? It's necessary. He witnessed one of Scott's pickups. You heard him—the Nicaraguans."

"Get him out." Brody backed away from the barrel. "I said, *get him out!*"

Ram liked to think of himself as a man prepared for anything, but he hadn't been prepared for Brody's sudden reaction to the condemned man in the barrel.

"We're *not* getting him out," Ram stated. He hated to contradict the man Pitney had sent—not on the first day home. "He's got to die, Brody. We have a reputation. There are rules. You know that."

"It's Aaron Ridgewood!" Brody's voice was full of force, but it was his eyes that Ram noticed most—they were full of fire. "Get him out. Now."

"His name *is* Ridgewood," Scott said. "I've got his badge and ID upstairs. I never said his name to you guys."

"You know this guy?" Ram asked Brody. "For real?"

"He's one of mine." Brody crossed his arms. "It's a pretty tight space down here, boys. You really want to find out the length I will go to make sure he's out of that barrel in ten seconds or less?"

Ram nodded at Scott, and together they reached into the barrel and lifted Border Patrol Agent Aaron Ridgewood out. His legs had been folded and cramped under him for over a day, so he was in no condition to stand on his own. Scott drew out a knife and cut the man's ankle and wrist binds.

"Come on." Brody started up the stairs. "Let's get him into the bathroom. You do have a regular bathtub in this house of horrors, don't you, Ram?"

Brody's orders completely threw Ram—under his own roof even! And furthermore, Scott had somehow missed the fact that this patrol agent was actually connected to someone like Brody Sladrick!

He and Scott deposited Aaron gently in the bathtub of a bathroom off Judy's bedroom. Scott turned on the shower head as Aaron whimpered.

"His legs are waking up," Scott told them. "That's why they're all discolored. Bad blood circulation in that barrel. He might be sick for a couple days from it."

"Thank you!" Aaron gasped and lay back in the tub. His eyes acknowledged Brody, and Ram took note. "Thank you so much! I thought I was a goner."

"You know him?" Ram asked the agent and pointed at Brody. "You really know who this guy is? What's his name?"

"Go ahead, Aaron." Brody nodded once. Aaron glanced from face to face. Ram looked between Brody and the agent. "Tell them my name. They just want to confirm you're really with me."

"It's . . . Sladrick. You're Mr. Sladrick. We met last year."

Brody crouched against the tub, not seeming to care about the pattering of water from the shower head.

"How are the brothers in Elm Creek? Is everyone staying the course?"

"Yes, sir." Aaron squeezed his eyes shut in obvious agony. "I'm sorry. I don't understand what's happening."

"He's delusional," Scott said, then called up the hallway. "Judy, this is Aaron. Clean him up and get some antibiotics into him. Food and water right away. Keep me updated. Treat him like he was our own family, because he is."

"I'll take care of him." Judy knelt over the tub.

"She'll do a good job." Ram patted Brody on the shoulder. "Don't worry about him. He'll be his old self in no time. Judy's had experience keeping HTVs alive who're in worse shape than he is. Imagine crossing a desert with no water. Judy takes them all in. Let's give her some space."

Ram led the men into the living room and offered his expensive soft chairs.

"I'll get us a couple beers," Scott volunteered and started back to the kitchen.

"Water for Brody," Ram called. "He doesn't drink."

Scott returned with drinks a moment later. Ram watched Brody sip his water. Brody's face was no longer the picture of serenity. It had hardened, or darkened, and that worried Ram. His man Scott seemed to notice it, too, since he raised his eyebrows at Ram and nodded towards Brody, urging Ram to feel out their newcomer.

"Uh, Brody, Aaron should be okay," Ram said. "He should recover in a couple days."

Brody nodded without making eye contact.

"We'll chalk this up as a lesson learned, huh?" Ram said to Scott.

"Yeah," Scott agreed. "Absolutely. There may be other assets of yours on the border. I'll be more careful. I should've checked aerial coverage of the area to make sure no one was around. It won't happen again."

Ram nodded at Scott that he'd said enough, then gestured at the man to make his exit.

"I'll, uh, check in later." Scott started for the door. "In the morning."

As soon as Scott was gone, Ram noted the irony of how he wanted Brody's approval now, but at the reunion he'd been upset that Brody had been sent to him without warning.

"So, you know this Aaron kid from Elm Creek?" Ram asked. "He works the crossing there? There's a brotherhood or something there? There's more like him—patrol agents—that I don't have on my books?"

"No, they're not on your books." Brody snorted, and Ram was relieved to see his features soften. "It's more like a fellowship of brethren."

"A fraternity. I get it." Ram held open his empty hands. "Sometimes we forget there's a whole generation of assets out there that predates our digital systems today. If anyone but Scott had made this mistake, I'd put the whip to his back, but I hope you understand it was an honest mistake."

"When I most needed forgiveness," Brody said softly, "Someone forgave me. Consider Scott forgiven. You can tell him that."

"I will. He'll be relieved." Ram chuckled. "You had us both pretty shaken up down there when you said you knew that guy."

"Well, I wasn't expecting to find one of my own stuffed in a barrel." Brody shook his head. "That's some tough stuff you guys have been doing around here."

"Yeah, it takes ice in the veins." Ram took a swig of his drink. "I usually don't enter these houses unless I have to. It can get to you."

"Treating people this way for a buck?" Brody asked. "That's some ice you've got in your veins."

"But I'm not all ice." Ram frowned at himself. "A week and a half ago, we lost those forty-eight."

"That was your crew?"

"I went to check it out. The image of all those bodies won't leave my mind. You know, I'm not doing this to cause suffering any more than you are. People's suffering is just an unfortunate side effect."

"Side effect," Brody repeated. "That's one way to say we all try to live with the ugly consequences of our sins."

"The way Pitney talks, she has ten times the body count on her conscience." Ram swore. "Talk about ice in the veins. That old lady is an ice queen. No offense."

"None taken. I'm learning how dedicated she is, and has been, to ruin lives everywhere."

"Yeah." Ram licked his lips, feeling like he could say anything to this man who seemed to sympathize with his situation. In such a short time, he'd gone from wondering how to kill Brody, to now feeling a connection with him. "The day I found those forty-eight, a girl from Seattle came through here. We had her next door."

"Of all your volume, you remember one girl from Seattle?" Brody asked.

"This one was different. She was high-profile, so we had to send her south. Tough girl. She had a cut on her head. The gal next door was making the cut worse, so I stitched her up myself. I should've never done that. Her eyes are stuck in my brain."

"It's normal to be affected by that," Brody said. "I'd be worried about you if you didn't care at all."

"She said she'd pray for me." Ram took a drink. "Can you believe that? She wanted my help, and I just loaded her up in the van and sent her across the border to die."

"You never thought of helping her?"

"I never thought of helping anyone." Ram felt his face warm. "But that one—I thought about it. Just one, you know? But it only takes one. One would ruin me. She saw my face."

"Sometimes it's worth being vulnerable," Brody said, a little light in his eyes again. "They've got no one but you when they arrive here. It's easy to throw lives away."

"You ain't kidding."

"But putting your neck on the line to preserve life? Yeah, there's true power there. Talk about a rush."

"Preserve life?" Ram laughed. "Listen to you. What would Pitney say if she knew you were talking about the opposite of her plans for this country? Or for the whole world. That ice queen knows no boundaries. I guess that's why she's pushing her 'no border' policies so much. Americans are completely duped by her party."

Ram finished his beer and enjoyed the silence in the room. It was night outside. He thought about his rumbling stomach and a frozen pizza he had in his freezer next door, but something inside him told him this was more important. *This was the infamous Sladrick!*

"Why don't you help her?" Brody suddenly asked.

"Who? Pitney?"

"No. The girl you stitched up."

"Nah, she's long gone. A week and a half out there—she could be in Europe or Asia already. Or Africa if her luck turned for the worse."

"You know what I think?" Brody sat forward. "You learned her name—you do know her name, don't you?"

"Brody, you've been doing this too long." Ram swore. "You're becoming psychic. I didn't mean to learn it, but she told me her name and I never forgot it. Like it's tattooed somewhere inside my head. Kim Ward. That was her name."

"Well, you could find her if you wanted to," Brody said. "So what if you sent her south? She's probably still in Monterrey or some hole like that."

"No, not these girls. We sent six all at once. The cartel flew them to the coast, then the Chinese took them—maybe by ship or plane. That's what our contract is with the cartel for high profiles like Kim Ward. Get rid of them and fast. She's gone. Forever."

"But not gone from your memory."

"She's just a bad dream now. Or a good dream maybe? Whatever. I can't dwell on it. Not my problem anymore."

"What if I told you I could find her?"

Ram stared at Brody. Indeed, *what if?* Then what? Kim's face, and her promise to pray, haunted him.

"How?"

"Come on. You think just because Pitney has classified me as a wanted criminal that my network has collapsed? I have people all over Europe and Asia who won't bat an eye at my US warrant. They'll still help. And I have just the tech guy to start sniffing out the trail."

"I don't know. It's careless. We're not those kinds of men. We have responsibilities. And I need to start making acquisitions for Pitney. I shouldn't go against her just for one girl."

"Your guy Scott can make those acquisitions. Your first responsibility is to your own conscience. You have to live with yourself. You remember this girl for a reason."

"It would be hard." Ram grunted to himself, fantasizing about such a moment—*freeing a girl from some sex shop?* "We'd have to hurry, I guess. The Chinese will sell her as fast as the Europeans handcuff her to a brothel bed. But I have no clue what they have in mind for her."

"We'd need to go ourselves," Brody said. "We couldn't trust something this sensitive to anyone else. It's personal."

"What would we do with her?" Ram felt fully sober now. "I mean, she'd see us. What if she turned us in?"

"You said she told you she'd pray for you, right?"

"Yeah, so?"

"Sounds like the kind of girl who might understand forgiveness—and gratitude."

"No, no." Ram stood and faced the dark window that looked toward his own house. "I couldn't run off like that, not with Pitney wanting to get on this new program."

"She's really on you like that?"

"You're here, aren't you? Well, I guess it isn't so bad. I meet her only about every six months. But I know she watches me from a distance. She's the Executive. People report to her. She'll know if I go overseas—and to help an HTV? Yeah, she'd probably have me killed. GLOW has people who put people down. You know that."

"Why do you matter so much to her?"

"I don't think I do. I think she sent you to make sure I put to good use the eight figures she just gave me. And I run 5TRAY operations. I matter in my own way, but the big picture? I'm just small potatoes to her."

"Maybe . . . you put those eight figures to better use," Brody said, "and we find a way to keep Pitney busy with other things."

"How?"

"Well, I can think of a way where she won't notice you overseas at all."

"Yeah, how?" Ram licked his lips. "Tell me how, and I'll consider this."

"Come on, Ram. You just clear your schedule. Leave instructions for your boy, Scott, and I'll line us up an angle on Kim Ward." He held his phone to his ear. "Greg, it's Brody. You staying safe? Good. I'm going to Albany tomorrow, and I don't want any cameras identifying me. And also, Ram Garrity and I are going to look for Kim Ward, a girl from Seattle. The Chinese took her through Mexico to Europe, Asia, or Africa. We want to get her back to her dad. Can you get a line on her? Thanks. I'll call you from the road tomorrow."

Brody turned off his phone.

"Just like that?" Ram asked.

"Just like that. That girl's prayers must be working." Brody smiled. "Things are starting to turn in her favor. And in your favor."

"I'm not sure why," Ram said, "but somehow I believe you."

Kim prayed through her rage as she held Felicity on the lower bunk of the ship cabin. Dakota, the nineteen-year-old brunette from Canada, had just been taken. To her credit, Dakota hadn't gone willingly, but she'd gone with dignity. They hadn't needed to drag her away screaming and crying as they had the last two girls. Dakota hadn't cried. Her jaw had been set in defiance when their Chinese handlers had removed her from the room.

That morning, the three girls had prayed together, knowing their time was short since they'd been once again nearing a port. Kim was learning to read the ship's bearings by watching the sunrises out their cabin window. Nearby ships, boats, land, and birds were clear indications that a port was close.

The waiting had been torturous, but now they knew: Dakota was gone. Kim and Felicity remained, awaiting their own fates.

"God is with her," Kim comforted Felicity. "Remember her faith. She's not alone. And we're not alone, either. No matter what happens, He won't abandon us."

Felicity's cries diminished to whimpers, and Kim's own tear streaks dried on her cheeks.

Dakota's removal probably meant that she'd been auctioned off to the highest bidder. Unless Kim was mistaken, they were in England in a giant shipping harbor. Container ships towered above their port window, but Kim could see down their length to the dock workers moving around immense cranes and vehicles. Much of the writing on signs was in English. It had to be England, but that didn't mean Dakota would remain where she'd been moved.

Kim had immersed herself in memorizing her cabin mates' information, and both Felicity and Dakota had welcomed the distraction.

"Remember, Dakota might get word out now," Kim whispered to Felicity. "She'll do her best. And if she can't, she's counting on us to try for her."

Felicity wiped her eyes and took a deep breath.

"She was so much stronger than I am. I'm afraid I'll be next, Kim. Or even worse—that you'll be next and I'll be last! What if I'm in here all alone? I'll lose my mind!"

"No, you won't." She smiled and petted her frizzy hair. "You're gonna keep your head. You're gonna remember that as much as we know our weakness, God fills in with His strength. Whatever we go through, there's hope, even if it's only in what I told you Jesus did for us so we can go to heaven. We'll be with Him eventually and forever."

"I never cared for all that religion stuff." Felicity sniffed through a sob. "Now I don't know what I'd do without God!"

❧

Ram couldn't stop smiling. He was pretty sure he'd fallen asleep smiling on Brody's jet as they flew to New York. What a feeling to be on the search for an HTV—not to *sell* her but to *rescue* her! For the first time in his life, Ram realized he was going to be someone's hero—Kim Ward's hero.

They landed in Albany, then took a taxi downtown.

"Here we are," Brody announced and climbed out of the taxi.

Sliding out of his side, Ram felt his bare ribs, and wished he'd argued with Brody more about bringing his concealed sidearm. Without Scott and the security team, Ram felt exposed, but Brody had insisted they carry no firearms to a meeting like this.

"Violence is the result of bad planning," Brody had quoted from some ancient muse, then assured Ram they would be smarter than their enemies. Strangely, since they were acting against Senator Pitney's wishes, Ram felt their greater enemies were now within GLOW rather than the US authorities. He'd left Scott with certain instructions back in Texas, but hadn't told his lieutenant what he was really up to with Brody. Pitney, of course, wouldn't approve.

Brody led the way through an open-air restaurant, then entered the restaurant, which had a "Closed" sign on the door. Bustling waiters and waitresses making table arrangements ignored them as they passed through the dining room, beyond the bathrooms, to a closed door where an armed security man in a suit stood. Ram wondered what kind of authority Brody had for the private door to be opened to him, but his question was answered an instant later when the bodyguard didn't hesitate to open the door as soon as Brody approached.

They entered a small card room where cigar smoke lingered. Two more bodyguards flanked a dark-haired man past his prime—the source of the cigar smoke. Brody slid out a chair for Ram, then eased into a chair of his own facing the guarded man across the round table. The bodyguards made their exit and closed the door softly on the room of three.

"The room's clean," their host said. "Swept it a few minutes ago."

Looking around, Ram checked the room visually for vents or windows. He saw nothing that might give an observer easy access, but he didn't know why that mattered or even who this man was. Brody had said he was meeting a friend to help them distract Pitney from Ram's travels, but Ram had thought they would meet with someone underground, not someone who appeared to be a public servant—and out in a public restaurant. Twice during the flight north, Brody had spoken to his man named Greg to make sure the cameras from the airport to downtown Albany were disrupted.

"Your message intrigued me," said their host. He had a strained, raspy voice. "You've got something against Pitney? I'm not sorry to hear that. She's certainly no friend of the people."

Ram's palms were sweaty from excitement mixed with fear. This was exhilarating! High profile cartel or GLOW meetings always happened in Mexico at some cantina or ranch. This was something completely different. They weren't just distracting Pitney, his boss; they were going after her! Though it was more than he'd signed on for with Brody, he guessed it'd be worth it to be Kim's hero.

"Pitney is instigating problems at the southern border," Brody said. "Ram here was tasked in Texas to do her bidding, but Ram and I are on a rescue mission. We don't want Pitney breathing down his neck."

"Not to mention that warrant on your own head?" Their host smiled and tapped his cigar over a glass of water. "I'm sort of enjoying watching you squirm under the pressure, Brody."

"Do I look like I'm squirming?" Brody asked.

Sure enough, Ram looked Brody up and down and found him to appear most relaxed, maybe even too relaxed for such a dangerous meeting.

"No, I guess you're not." Their host frowned. "You're not even here to ask for my help for yourself. This is Ram, you say?"

"Yes, sir," Ram nodded, "if we're just using first names."

"That'd make me Elliot," the man said without rising to shake hands. "Well, Brody, I don't know what I can do for you. Pitney and this administration's use of the open southern border is no secret. They act like they care for the illegals by calling them migrants instead of criminals, then they do everything they can, it seems, to facilitate a disaster from the Atlantic to the Pacific. But no one has really proven Pitney's doing anything more than being totally incompetent as a political leader."

"Pitney's the Executive," Brody stated.

Elliot froze. After a few seconds, he dropped his cigar in the glass and leaned over the table.

"Well, we knew it was a woman, but I never would've guessed it to be her. She's shady enough, I suppose. Can you prove it?"

"I've got Greg looking into everything about her, but Ram here has the smoking gun."

As Elliot's eyes shifted to Ram, Ram took the cue. He was following Brody's lead—who was moving way beyond Ram's own comfort level, but he was committed now.

"She admitted to me herself that she was paying me with funds siphoned off from a Ukraine security agreement."

"It's money meant to secure Ukraine from Russia," Brody clarified. "She sent it instead to Ram to destabilize the border further."

"You're both crazy." Elliot chuckled. "I don't even want to know how you two met. What a pair! How much, Ram?"

"Eight figures."

Elliot took his time lighting a new cigar from his breast pocket.

"We've heard that money meant for Ukraine was being diverted on this end. I've spoken to some commanders in Ukraine who've said they don't even have first aid kits, so I know there's been more than just a supply chain crisis."

"It's orchestrated," Brody said.

"Possible. Even probable." Elliot chewed on his cigar. "This administration did everything they could to keep oversight off those billions, but eight figures going missing isn't easy to hide."

"It's earmarked," Brody said to Elliot. Then he turned to Ram. "Tell him what you told me."

"She said it'll be labeled as a fund to combat human trafficking of the now millions of Ukrainian women and children displaced around the world."

"Yeah, right." Elliot's face darkened. "Meanwhile, she's actually financing the displacement and trafficking? I get it. A lot of us wondered what would happen if that money went to the wrong people, not just political rivals. Too much is going wrong in America and on that border to be an accident. It's intentional. We've suspected it for many months. And now you're telling me it's real."

"It's biblical," Brody said. "The globalists need to tear down old fundamentals to build their new government—

organized around a new currency, new laws, and the new environmental initiatives."

Ram watched both men. He had no love for Pitney, but this seemed extreme, even vindictive, for all he wanted to do was . . . rescue the blond angel who haunted his dreams. How could he assist in the take-down of Pitney and not get burned himself in the process?

"I need hard data," Elliot said. "Get me everything you've got."

"Greg will send you what he finds," Brody said, "but you're to create a smoke-screen for me and Ram."

"You know," Elliot said with a smile, "nobody tells me what to do but you?"

"And don't let her in on Ram's change of heart. Tangle her up in a defense that's so public that her own reputation is under fire. She won't be able to run GLOW if she's on the defense."

"In twenty-four hours," Elliot said, "she'll wish she never targeted TROAS at all. And I'll get to work removing those warrants against you and your people, too. I've already spoken to my coalition about it. We knew it was bogus, but I figured we'd let it play out."

"No one's playing." There was no humor on Brody's face. "I appreciate you stepping up to the plate, Elliot."

Brody stood. Ram joined him as he wondered what exactly this TROAS was. It was a code name no doubt for some powerful tool. Elliot stood and shook Brody's hand.

"You certainly make my life interesting, Mr. Sladrick." He turned to Ram. "And whoever you really are, you've obviously come a good distance from Pitney's company to Brody's. You've got a friend in Senator Elliot Madison. The great state of New York and the United States of America thanks you for your patriotism."

"This isn't about patriotism." Brody moved to the door. "This is a spiritual battle for souls."

Outside, they waited on the curb for a taxi.

"Now where?" Ram asked.

Brody held up his phone.

"We'll start for Europe. Greg found a ship registered out of Hong Kong that left Mexico in our time frame. Kim had to be on it. They just made a stop in London after a stop in Portugal. By the time we catch up to them, Greg might have a lead on who disembarked."

"There won't be any records," Ram said. "GLOW has payment systems that're untraceable."

"Oh, there's always a trace, Ram." Brody didn't look at him when he spoke. He was busy watching the street. "Nothing is invisible. Dock workers see things. Lies are told to harbor masters. Transportation is arranged and observable from satellites. Greg will verify everything. He knows what to look for. You've turned a corner for Kim Ward. You can never go back now. Do you feel it?"

"Are you talking about turning on Pitney?" He thrust his hands in his pockets. "Yeah, I feel it. I must be crazy. I just hope your senator friend here comes through for us. Pitney could ruin me."

"Elliot will have Pitney scrambling to defend herself publicly within hours. She'll be fortunate to even have a political career within a week."

"And this could disrupt all of GLOW," Ram said. "I mean, she's the you-know-what."

"Pitney's days as the Executive are numbered. They'll restructure GLOW and fortify their assets as soon as she's marked for prosecution here in the States. GLOW will go on, but this will still be a win for us."

"Yeah, I guess it's a win." Ram lifted his head. "I've still got her eight figures and no one knows where it is but me."

"Hmm, I wouldn't count on that." Brody stepped toward a taxi that had stopped. "If I know anything about life, you'll be given an opportunity to do something special with that money that has nothing to do with yourself."

Ram climbed into the taxi and didn't speak again until they boarded the jet bound for England. Every time he thought he had Brody figured out, he was thrown a curve ball. Who was going to give him an opportunity to do something special with that kind of money? He was thinking already about buying an island in the Indian Ocean and disappearing for good. Obviously, Brody didn't know what he was talking about.

❧

Per Brody Sladrick's departing instructions, Border Patrol Agent Aaron Ridgewood kept his mouth shut for thirty-six hours as he recovered inside the house where he'd nearly died in the cellar barrel.

When he could stand and walk alone, he was brought new clothes, his phone, and the sidearm he'd lost when taken captive by this Texas smuggling ring. No one apologized to him or explained anything as two armed men drove him into downtown Dallas and opened the car door to leave him on a nondescript city street corner. On Mr. Sladrick's word, he'd been fed and given medication, but he was still trying to figure out why they hadn't killed him and who Sladrick was really mixed up with. But praise God, he would see his wife again!

He checked the date on his phone. It'd been six days since he'd been taken in Elm Creek. Still not trusting his legs, he walked to a sidewalk bench and sat down to call his wife.

"Shawna? It's—" No, it was her voicemail. "Shawna, I'm . . . alive. I'm really okay, baby. I'm in Dallas. It's a miracle, sweetie. I can't even . . ."

Aaron wept through the rest of his brief message, then gathered himself to make his next call—to his captain.

"Ridgewood!" his captain's voice boomed on speaker. He was a hefty black man who preferred an air-conditioned office rather than a dusty patrol vehicle, but he was an honest man of God. "We thought we'd never hear from you again! Where are you? Can you talk?"

"Yeah, I can talk. They held me for a few days after driving me up from the border, then turned me loose a minute ago. I'm still ignorant as to what really happened. All I know is that I was prepared to see Jesus face-to-face."

"Brother, we're sending a plane for you. No, on second thought, I'll be on that plane! Boy, do I have questions. Two days ago, we received a text here at the office with a diagram and details on some buildings. The message said to take down these five houses ASAP, but that you would be able to explain everything to us. We didn't know what to make of it all—except to wait for you to call. Thank God you're still alive!"

"Wait. What five houses are we supposed to take down?" Aaron slowly smiled, remembering the five residences in the Dallas cul-de-sac. He'd known there were illegals being held in the stash houses. "Okay, okay. I'm starting to make sense of all this. I'd better not say anything until we can speak in person."

They agreed on a meeting place in Dallas and the captain sent him some funds to gorge on some fast-food until they could meet.

Three hours later, Aaron was awakened in the fast-food restaurant as Captain Fletter touched his shoulder and slid into the booth across from him. Two other men, armed patrol agents, sat at a table across the aisle. He knew these men better than he knew his blood relatives. As believers, who were also part of the border patrol in Elm Creek, they'd all celebrate his recovery as soon as the captain had debriefed him. It was business first.

"Shawna was starting to plan your funeral." Fletter set his phone on the table and smoothed down the front of his uniform—which needed no smoothing since it was stretched to capacity over his belly. "You talk to her yet?"

"Yeah, right before I started drooling in my sleep on this table."

"You've lost a little weight. I might need to know your diet plan."

"I wouldn't recommend it." Aaron nibbled on some cold fries and offered the captain some. "It began with getting stuffed in a barrel about to be buried in the desert."

"The Lord has mysterious ways." Fletter tilted up his phone. "You want to tell me what this means and who sent us this drawing?"

Aaron squinted at a small diagram on the phone.

"Yeah, I recognize it. That's where I was held—in that second house from the left, there. It was full of trafficked people. Definitely a stash house, boss. I got a look inside one of the rooms. There was a Plexiglas cell in there with lots of women."

"The data sheet we received with this sketch says there may be as many as forty-eight illegals in each of these two houses. Whether they're citizens or not, we're going in to help them before they're trafficked and sold anywhere else."

"You better go armed. I saw plenty of men with guns."

"The data sheet describes what to expect." The captain nodded. "We'll handle them smartly. Any other details you can help us out with?"

Aaron studied a photo that Fletter had taken of the data sheet.

"I don't know, Captain. I was kept inside until this morning when I was let go."

"Let's talk about that." Fletter put away his phone. "What don't I know?"

"It was Mr. Sladrick. Remember Brody?"

"What?"

"Brody Sladrick."

"Brother Brody? The retrieval expert? *Our* Brody Sladrick? You know he's a wanted fugitive right now, right?"

"Hey, Captain, all I know is that he was in there with those traffickers, and they were very organized. I was about to be sealed inside a barrel, and Brody recognized me and made them keep me alive. They released me on his say-so. He said to keep my mouth shut, so I did, and here I am."

"So, he's a wanted fugitive . . . to get where he couldn't go otherwise." The captain sat back and smiled. "I've heard stories of our Brother Brody. Special Forces types call him by a codename: *RefugeGate*. To us few in Elm Creek, he was just another brother in Christ who we met last year. He wanted to encourage us as believers to hold the line for Christ on the border. But it seems he's been busy getting into places none of us could ever access."

"So, he's undercover?" Aaron nodded. "Yeah, that makes sense."

"Brother Brody is private. He can do things we can't. But we can take down those five houses like he asked. Can you remember where they are? We have all this information, but we don't have an address."

"No problem, Captain, but I'm not sure I'm ready for a gunfight. I'm still getting my sea legs under me."

"Oh, this is no longer a border patrol matter. I called in Dallas SWAT already. They're waiting for my call. Those five houses won't know what hit them."

Greg watched Marcy mumble something in her sleep. They'd been sleeping on top of their sleeping bags each night in the humid Florida air. The old cigar-rolling warehouse was missing glass in some of its otherwise dusty windows, and part of the roof had collapsed on the opposite end where doves were cooing. Except for a little exposure to the outside elements, they were comfortable.

He wasn't the only one awake at that late hour. Their two houseguests had been welcome distractions to their lives as Marcy enjoyed doting on Gabriella Savalano. Across the warehouse floor, Hector Savalano was sweeping up glass and bird droppings by lamplight. The Colombian migrant had insisted on earning his keep if they were to stay in the warehouse, and Greg hadn't been disappointed in the man's work ethic.

Guided by the light from his laptop screen, Greg returned to his makeshift desk in the corner of the warehouse. It was nearly dawn in Europe, and Brody and Ram were about to land at London's Heathrow Airport. Greg wanted to be ready to direct or redirect their efforts within the hour. Whatever had brought Brody and Ram together, Greg knew it was God's own appointment, just as the Lord had brought the Savalanos to the warehouse that precise week to keep Greg and Marcy company. The Lord was once again using Brody on the road to create instability in the life of a wicked man to bring him to his knees—as he'd done six months earlier for Zayed.

A human trafficking compound in Texas had fallen that evening. Though Greg hadn't explored the details in full, it had Brody's signature all over it. A border patrol agent had been attributed with the discovery of almost seventy illegal migrants in captivity at multiple stash houses.

Greg was playing catch-up when it came to the six girls transported from Texas into Mexico. It had aided his efforts to learn from Brody's companion, Ram Garrity, that the Chinese had taken the girls from the Mexican cartel. Finding footage of their ship and excluding other vessels or planes had taken hours. The body of a white girl found at a Mexican coastal airport helped Greg narrow his search for five instead of six trafficked girls.

Since Greg couldn't access the CCTV system on the ship, he was limited to watching and searching footage and records in ports after the ship had already come and gone. Two girls had been taken off the vessel in Portugal. It had required a full day to track down the arrival of two supposed "tourists" to Lisbon who had previously been waiting on organ donor lists, one from Indonesia, and the other from France. The girls' blood types matched—though neither of them was Kim Ward. The two girls taken off the ship in Lisbon had been forced to become organ donors—one for her heart, and the other, both kidneys.

That left three more girls on the ship, and Greg was able to get a lead on the ship's manifest after they departed from Portugal. He was only two days behind their stop in London. In minutes, Greg connected the arrival of the Chinese ship with the arrival of a diplomat's jet from . . . Myanmar? It seemed too obscure a location to ignore as coincidental. All he had to figure out was how many girls had been sold by the Chinese and taken aboard the plane to Myanmar.

But the buyers had been careful. No cameras existed in that part of the airport. Even before Brody landed at the same airport, Greg summarized his findings. At least one of the three girls was on their way to Myanmar. And the ship was continuing to the Baltic Sea where Greg would continue to track its business.

With Brody lined up to go to Myanmar, Greg turned his attention back to the Senator Pitney situation. Brody wanted Senator Madison armed with inside intel on the woman's activities. She was the Executive of GLOW, responsible for tens of thousands of trafficking victims.

As Greg's fingers flew over the keyboard, they leaped about in the dim lighting without looking from his screen. This was why he'd become a cybercrime fighter for Jesus Christ. He was saving lives, doing battle not against flesh and blood, but with ones and zeroes on a spiritual bandwidth. He was the Code Fighter, the Code Warrior for Christ, the Code Ninja for Jesus. No, the *Code Spartan!* He was the—

"Greg?" It was Marcy's voice. "Greg, wake up."

He lifted his head at Marcy's hand on his arm.

"I'm awake." He sat up and looked around. Hector had joined his daughter against the nearby wall where they'd laid their sleeping bags. Both were fast asleep.

"You need to sleep." Marcy fitted her beret over her unruly hair. Neither of them had showered in three days, but somehow, she was still beautiful. "Lay down for a few hours before it gets too hot out. I'll watch the cameras."

Rubbing his eyes, he sighed at the second laptop he'd set up, connected to the feed of four cameras with proximity alarms around the warehouse. A thirty-second head start in front of a SWAT team wouldn't achieve much, but at least they could brace themselves for an arrest if the authorities came for him and Marcy.

"I have to get the rest of this stuff sent to Madison," he said and kept working. "Brody's counting on me. We finally have GLOW in our sights instead of always playing defense."

"Let me help you."

"You can help me by keeping me awake."

"Okay, let me find a big stick."

"Stick?" Greg glanced at her. "For what?"

"To prod you in the ribs when you nod off again."

He chuckled.

"Yeah, this is good. Just keep me talking. This helps. Brody wasn't kidding. Pitney has access to all kinds of congressional funding. She's part of several oversight committees—and no one has oversight of them. What a scam."

"But you can't let her know we know about her connection to Ram Garrity. Brody wants him protected from her while he isolates the Texan for spiritual reasons."

"Right." Greg switched to a banking app. "I have a scorpion just for this. And . . . go."

"What's it do?"

"It compares and contrasts financials on someone we're investigating with known GLOW players."

"Don't they hide their, um, money?"

"Oh, they do more than hide it. They clean it through bogus fronts and try to wash it through foreign currency transfers, even cryptocurrencies. And . . . done. Look at that!"

"Over two thousand results?"

"Pitney's been a busy bookkeeper. Wait. Not all of this is for human trafficking. See this trail of transfers? This is the millions she transferred for Ram Garrity's use on the southern border. We know about that, so we can now look for the same repeated process elsewhere. Here's that European anarchist group that's been in the news lately. Twenty million Euros to them? And here's an arms purchase of German weapons for the US Treasury Department. Ninety million."

"Why does our Treasury Department need guns?" Marcy asked.

"Because Pitney and people like her have been preparing this country for a transition into chaos for the setup of a new government."

"Does anyone but us even know about this?"

"Those of us who read our Bibles know to expect this kind of disruption to bring about a one-world government. Conspiracy theorists have warned about it— the pacification of the American citizenry by various means. But it's not just a theory. I'm sending all this to Madison. This'll give him enough ammunition to go after the Executive and keep her off Brody and Ram for a couple weeks."

"But what about all the weapons the Treasury Department now owns? And the money sent to those European anarchists?"

"Those wheels are in motion already." Greg sighed. "I'd say fighting corruption is hopeless—except we know what's going on now. We're taking a stand in the light, exposing the darkness. But only Christ's coming will vanquish all the darkness."

"It's prophecy coming to life. We're seeing it unfold right here in America."

"That's it. God said in the last days a satanic world economy, government, and religion would be established. It's advancing worldwide through the banking systems and the religion of planet worship. But I'd agree with you, Marcy, most Americans are asleep."

"We can't do more to let people know?"

"Well, Marcy, I'd say we're doing something. One soul at a time, we're making a difference. We don't despair when it seems that God allows evil to triumph. Right now, we're fighting alongside Brody. Binsa and Zayed are out there in Poland, doing something amazing for refugees and trafficked survivors. And here we are with the Savalano family. My translation app has helped us communicate with Hector. It seems he was raised to know that God is real. That's a good starting place to keep introducing him to the Scriptures and praying for him and his daughter, like we've already begun doing."

"Binsa always says just to keep helping the simple people," Marcy said, "and not to worry about big things we can't help. I guess God will correct everything you're saying is way beyond us."

"Yeah, Binsa always says stuff better than I can. I was thinking of the two witnesses in the last days. During the Tribulation, the antichrist finally puts them to death, and the whole world celebrates."

"But then they come back to life, right?" Marcy smiled and took his hand in hers. "God wins in the end!"

"It seems that God allows darkness to rise temporarily to prove who are really his own. We'll be okay, even if we die. Brody always says that."

"This is so exciting, but also so sad. I love you, Greg. I'm so glad we're together in all this."

"I love you, too." He kissed her. "But Marcy? I'm going to need your help to continue. The sooner I finish, the sooner I can faceplant myself on that mattress."

CHAPTER FOUR

Dakota Yarlin remembered everything about the day she was kidnapped in Vancouver, Canada. It seemed like it had happened three years earlier, but it was really only three weeks earlier. The boy on social media had seemed so innocent, so carefree. His juggling videos had made her laugh. He'd juggled oranges, carrots, and meatballs, calling it the three food groups.

But when Dakota had lied to her grandparents about where she was going that one evening, she hadn't met that goofy boy as expected. He hadn't even been there. *They* had been there. *They* had learned everything about her from her conversations with the cute boy. *They* hadn't given her a chance to alert anyone before they'd taken her out the back exit of a clothing store and into a vehicle.

"You're with me. You're with me. You're with me," Dakota prayed to God, her hands folded like Kim Ward had taught her in the ship cabin. "You haven't forgotten about me. I believe You still love me. Amen."

At age nineteen, Dakota only weighed one hundred and five pounds. She sat on the carpeted floor of a locked bedroom in a house somewhere in Asia. The air smelled bad. The people didn't wear deodorant. Their food was too spicy, and the water tasted like rust and chemicals.

The plane ride from Europe had been terrifying, but that part was over now. Young men with bad teeth on the plane had laughed and teased her and other girls on the plane. She couldn't understand their language. They hadn't touched her, but only because an older man had shouted at them when they'd tried to.

The other girls on the plane hadn't been white. Dakota guessed that's why she was being held separately.

They had something different planned for her. Someone would pay extra for a white girl. Like Kim had instructed her and Felicity, Dakota didn't lie to herself about what was likely to happen next. She just kept reviewing what Kim had taught her: proof of God's power and love for her was shown in Jesus' death for her. Though Dakota had never opened a Bible, she trusted what Kim had promised her: her soul was safe, even if her body wasn't.

Suddenly, the bedroom door opened. Twenty dark-skinned girls her age submissively filed into the room, then their captors closed and locked the door again. The young women milled about a moment, shyly studying Dakota and her blue eyes, the single bed, and the doorless bathroom.

"Are you thirsty?" Dakota asked, pantomiming drinking from a glass. "Water? Do you need water? Anyone? The water faucet works in the bathroom."

None of them spoke English, but they seemed to settle in with Dakota after she showed them the running water. They washed and drank, though never without furtive glances toward the locked door. There were at least ten young men and a couple older men out there. The girls' fate wasn't in their own hands.

Five girls claimed the bed while the remainder settled on the floor. Dakota was content on the floor next to a girl whose face and head was partially covered under a cloth. Several of them had coverings like the Muslims in Vancouver wore.

"Rohingya," the girl said to Dakota, then gestured to herself and the others.

"Rohingya?" Dakota didn't know what it meant. "Dakota."

"Da-ko-ta?"

She guessed her word was just as strange to them as others repeated it around the room. They were sisters in suffering, even if their language was different.

Dakota flinched from the sound of a gunshot somewhere in the house. The girls in the room who were nearest the door shrank away. The sounds of a struggle ensued out there. Men shouted. Pottery and glass broke. People screamed in pain and another gunshot sounded. Two men yelled at each other in . . . *English?* English! Something about the police. Punches and kicks landed, grunts and shrieks reverberated.

The fight outside the room lasted for several minutes, then there were new sounds—handcuffs clicking and someone in authority speaking in the local language. Then silence, followed by a door being broken through nearby, maybe to a room next door. Then a heavy tool was used against their own door. All the girls scrambled to hide behind the bed or in the bathroom.

Moving to the front of the girls, Dakota's eyes teared up in fear as she allowed the others to use her own body as a shield. They seemed relieved that she offered herself to whatever abuse would happen first. It wasn't much, but she held out her arms protectively, facing the door with a determined gaze and her head down. If this was her last moment on earth, then she would die protecting those God had put with her. Kim had cared for her and she would breathe her last breath caring for others. After all, her soul was safe in God's hands. These girls needed to know they were loved.

The door gave way. In its place stood a white man with a sledge hammer, his face hard and his shoulders broad. His eyes surveyed the room of hushed young women, then his gaze stopped on Dakota.

"Ram!" the man called over his shoulder. "Here she is, but it's not Kim."

"Kim Ward?" Dakota didn't move. "From Seattle?"

"Yes." The man held a phone up and took her photo. He still held the sledge hammer in his other hand like it was as light as a toy. "Kim Ward from Seattle. What's your name, young lady?"

"Dakota Yarlin from Vancouver. And we were with Felicity Torme on a ship up until about two days ago when I was taken from them. I'm pretty sure I was in England."

"It's a pleasure to meet you, Dakota." He leaned the hammer against the door frame and extended his hand. He may have been the strongest man Dakota had ever seen in her life, but his hand seemed very gentle. "You're safe now."

But Dakota needed more than just his hand. This man was from God! And she knew it! She rushed into his arms.

"Is this real?" she sobbed. "Are you real?"

"I'm real. How long have you been here?"

"Just a few hours. These others . . . just arrived an hour ago."

Another white man, younger, entered the room. Dakota could now see through the broken door that policemen were rounding up about a dozen men who occupied the house, some of them from the plane. A few of the criminals lay unconscious on the floor. Her rescuers had fought hand-to-hand combat to reach her!

"The police chief said something about these women all going to China," said the second man. He had a Texas drawl. "From Myanmar to China?"

"They would've been married off," said the first man with the hard face. "Forced brides aren't new in China."

"I know you." Dakota pointed at the younger man. "From Texas. You helped Kim Ward. You're Ram, right?"

He lowered his eyes, then walked out of the room. Dakota hadn't meant to hurt him, but she didn't understand why he was there if he was the Texas kidnapping boss.

"My name is Brody Sladrick." The first man touched her chin, lifting it with a finger. "That man Ram isn't here for you. But I am. I'm going to get you back home. Do you have family?"

"Grandparents. My parents didn't want me."

"Well, I'm not too loved in this world, either." Brody smiled, revealing the heart beneath his hard face. "Sometimes we're mistreated, but we don't need to dwell on that part of life."

"Yes, I know." Dakota wiped at her eyes. "God is bigger. Kim taught me all about Jesus."

"Good girl. You're gonna be just fine. These others in here might have a harder path."

Dakota turned and admired the rescued girls while beside her rescuer.

"That girl called herself Rohingya," Dakota said. "If that's her name, maybe we could help her?"

"We'll help them all, but that's not her name. These are Rohingya Muslims. You're in Myanmar, Miss Yarlin. The Rohingyas are a minority people in this country, so the government rounds them up and persecutes them, pretty much like this."

"So, I go back to Canada, but what about them?" Dakota felt her cheeks redden. "They get sent on to China?"

"Oh, no. The police chief in the other room will work with us. Some of his family are part of the local church here in Sittwe. They'll help these girls return to the refugee camps, probably where they were living before. At least they'll be back with their families, and they'll be given aid packages that contain the gospel message of Jesus Christ."

In a truck with no suspension, Dakota rode between Brody and Ram back to the airfield on the edge of the city slums. Dakota kept looking at Brody who drove, sensing the safety he assured her he'd provide, but she looked at Ram only when she was certain he wouldn't notice. She didn't trust him. He may have helped Kim Ward, but he had loaded up six of them into a van and sent them to Mexico. And at least one girl was surely dead. All of them had been stripped and photographed and handled. No, Ram wasn't like Brody!

Ram sat as far back in the rear of the plane as he could get from Dakota Yarlin. He had participated in her rescue, even fought aggressively beside Brody through the house with the policemen to take down the Asian stash house. But his shame was stirred when he looked at Dakota's face. He couldn't take back what he'd done to her. Nothing he did would ever remove those things—he could see that now in her eyes.

The jet took off, flying west toward Europe. Brody had Greg on video screen, and together they asked Dakota questions about Kim Ward and the other girls Ram had sold, but Ram didn't join them.

There was still no response when Ram tried his own cell phone. For a day now, he'd been trying to check his messages from Scott, but nothing was working. He hadn't told Brody, but he sensed something was wrong in Texas. His cell phone service had never been switched off before. Someone or something was interfering with his communications.

He watched Brody with growing suspicion. No, it was jealousy. The man was so carefree and even joked with Dakota, making her laugh! Brody had been so convincing at the reunion, projecting such authority and dominance. Though Ram had thought the man had inserted himself to protect Pitney's interests, he clearly had an agenda of his own. In fact, Brody had just waged war against Pitney by his use of Senator Madison, and since Brody had involved Ram's own intel, Ram couldn't object. And now he couldn't even find out what was on the news since his phone access had been disrupted.

"What're you guys working on?" Ram asked as he approached them. He sat across the aisle.

Brody signed off with Greg and handed Dakota his phone. Dakota's eyes narrowed at Ram.

"Greg is tracking the ship into the Baltic Sea." Brody folded his hands. "We'll refuel in Paris where we'll drop off Dakota. I have friends who'll make sure she gets safely back to Vancouver to her grandparents."

"That's good." Ram frowned. None of this made sense. He and Brody were supposed to be human traffickers, not retrieval agents. Kim Ward was supposed to be an exercise of power for himself—to track down a girl who'd left an impression on his conscience. "You're good at all this—rescuing HTVs—like you've done it before."

"I try to use my resources where they're most needed." Brody held his gaze "Something on your mind, Ram?"

Ram looked away and clenched his teeth. No, this was all wrong. He didn't know how, but he'd been duped. He didn't know when, but he'd lost control. Brody was running everything!

"My phone hasn't been working. I need to borrow yours."

"Sure. You done with it, Dakota?"

"For now." She handed it to Brody.

Brody gave his phone to Ram.

"Take your time."

Ram settled into his seat to figure out what was happening with Scott, if anything. He tried Scott's phone and received a *"phone disconnected"* message. He tried Rosa and Judy's lines, but received the same signal.

Next to him, Brody spoke in low tones to Dakota about faith and prayer. Brody had had those same kinds of discussions with Ram's family members at the reunion, but Ram had thought Brody had merely been playing a part, fitting into the family environment and impressing his father. But no, he was actually counseling Dakota like Ram's own father might comfort Carmen if she had experienced some terrible experience like being trafficked.

None of the phone numbers Ram tried to dial in Texas were connecting. It was time to broaden his search. He went to a news site in Dallas. It took only ten seconds to scroll through the biggest news stories of the week to find one about a Dallas-based human smuggling ring called 5TRAY that had been uncovered. Everyone on site had been arrested and held without bail after a brief firefight with an overwhelming police raid, coordinated with Special Forces.

His breathing became shallow and rapid. The world had closed in on him and his whole empire had collapsed in Texas in his absence. Those five residences had been the hub of his network! All the other stash houses in Texas and other states had depended on his headquarters. Other connected personnel were probably already regrouping and contacting the cartel to set up new methods—without 5TRAY and without him.

He searched for his own name in the news coverage, but found no mention of himself. None of his people were talking yet, but it was probably just a matter of time before someone made a deal for leniency. They would be coming for him, and not only law enforcement. Pitney was the ice queen. She'd have seen by now that 5TRAY had fallen. In an attempt to cut off any liability for herself, she'd come for him to silence him. It was the GLOW way.

"It's like . . . all of this happened for a reason," said Dakota to Brody. "It was the worst thing I ever went through, but it opened my eyes to God."

"Without Kim," Brody said, "you could've easily escaped in your mind to hang on to a false sense of security to endure the situation, but it would've ended in emotional distress and hopelessness. See how God orchestrates His purposes through tragedy? He didn't make you believe in His love, but He made sure Kim was there with you—starting in Texas and even her humility of sleeping on the floor in your cabin—to show you His love very clearly."

"It's too amazing to imagine." Dakota laughed and wiped her eyes. "How do you even process how big God is?"

"Oh, I don't." Brody waved his hand. "The world tries to process Him, and they diminish God down to a god of their own imagination. But we are believers. We accept Him for who He is as infinite. We express our gratitude for Christ's suffering by living in His light."

"You knew about Dallas!" Ram blurted and watched Brody's face. "Why didn't you tell me?"

But Brody's face didn't twist in horror at the accusation. Nor did he counter accuse to defend himself.

"I didn't want to tell you because I was trying to isolate and shield you from all that."

"Shield me?" Ram started to rise from his chair, but he saw Brody shift his left foot as if to meet him head-to-head. "I don't need you to shield me!"

"Yes, you do." Brody plucked the phone from Ram's hand. "Your life has been a disaster, ruining families, destroying lives, and killing the innocent for more than a decade."

"And what have you done?"

Ram checked his voice. He was on the edge of losing control while Brody was calm and confident. It was wise not to physically grapple with the older man since Ram had seen the veteran fight with skill against the household of Burmese traffickers. Brody had used submission holds and martial tactics in split seconds—moves that Ram had never learned himself.

"Tell me what I've done, Ram," Brody challenged. "Go ahead. Let's have it out. What are you accusing me of? Go ahead. Speak. This is your moment. You have the floor."

"You threatened my family in Tahoe."

"No, I arrived at Tahoe before you to talk to your father and your sister about being there for you. They knew why I was there even if you didn't. Why do you think your dad welcomed me like that?"

"My . . . dad knows?" Ram swallowed with difficulty. "And Carmen?"

"Of course. They were heartbroken, but they were willing to play along if it meant I could help you."

"Help me?"

"To show you a better way, maybe even share the gospel with you."

"The gospel?" Ram's head swam. "But Pitney sent you!"

"No. Somewhere along the way, you came to that wrong conclusion, and I didn't correct you. I've actually been trying to find the Executive of GLOW for years. You're the one who revealed her to me, and it's helping us take her down. She's finished. We owe you for that."

Ram's hand went to his brow. *How could he have been so naïve?*

"GLOW's going to kill me." Ram felt his chest heave in a sob. "I'm going to prison, and they're going to find me. You used me! You don't realize how powerful Pitney is!"

"Pitney's in the process of being removed. I only came to disrupt your 5TRAY network by sharing Jesus Christ with you. As soon as I could, I began to show you a better way. You revealed all your secrets to me voluntarily."

"But Aaron Ridgewood! You said he was part of your smuggling network!"

"Correction: I said he was part of a fellowship of brethren. I implied he was a fellow believer in Christ, and he is. I met him last year at a border security conference for Christians. You mistakenly thought I was a smuggler with a network. My only network—and it is a mighty one— is composed of God's people in churches all around the world. That is a network, my friend, and it is invincible. God says so in His Word."

"You've ruined me."

"That's debatable. I'd say you've been ruining yourself for years, but God used Kim Ward to pierce your conscience days before you and I ever met."

"If anyone has used anyone," Dakota said forcefully, "it's you. You deserve everything you get now. You shouldn't have even taken us girls!"

"But I'm—" Ram stuttered. "I'm the one who— I didn't want to—"

He blinked through his frustration, his mind blank. His way hadn't worked. How could he have been blind to all that had happened the last few weeks? Brody was right. Dakota was right. Kim was right. His father and Carmen were right. This had started before he'd ever met Brody. But how could it actually be . . . *God?*

"Your journey isn't over," Brody said softly. "By the time we arrive in Paris, Greg will know where the last two girls are from the ship."

"Kim and Felicity," Dakota said.

"Yes, Kim and Felicity."

"No. I'm done." Ram crossed his arms and sat back in his seat. He looked out at the dark green far below the plane. They were somewhere over India. "You can go on without me. I'm out."

"Oh, no, you're going to finish what you started with me," Brody said. "We're going to do it together. Kim Ward started all this. I'm a little curious to see how the Lord will use her to finish it."

"I don't want to see her anymore. You can find her. You can rescue her on your own. You're obviously more than capable."

"Kim's not the one who needs rescuing from you." Brody reached out and patted Ram's knee. "She may be the only one who can convince you that you're in need of rescue."

Ram opened his mouth to object, but it seemed futile. Brody had been thorough. He was his captive, now so isolated from all resources that he had to go and do whatever Brody wanted. He definitely didn't want to see Kim now. Looking at Dakota's critical eyes was bad enough.

If only he hadn't stitched up Kim's forehead wound. It was his own fault. He'd been weak. Now, all his associates were in jail. Pitney may have been someone he could've relied on to rebuild 5TRAY, but Brody had already involved him in her own probable demise.

With no heart to hear any more bad news that day, Ram returned to the back of the plane. He meant to sleep away his woes, but instead, he lay on his back with his eyes closed, thinking about everything that had occurred. His life was over. Jail definitely awaited him. Who was he now? What could he possibly become now that he'd met his ruin? Scoffing, he imagined that Brody had an answer for that as well.

When Felicity was taken off the ship, she'd already resolved to accept Kim's advice: she'd cooperate with her captors until she couldn't cooperate. There would be a time to fight perhaps, but not while they were treating her okay.

She stood beside her familiar Chinese captors somewhere in Europe. On the dock where the wind blew against her ship uniform, another party met with the Chinese. One of the men held her by the arm as someone shined a flashlight in her face and her arm number was checked. The Chinese spoke a different language with the newcomers. It sounded like Russian.

They all shook hands and Felicity was taken by the arm by an old stout Russian man, but his grip wasn't harsh.

As Felicity was led away, she looked back at the ship and the Chinese party returning to the gangway. Kim was alone now. Her fate still awaited her.

A car awaited Felicity and she was guided into the back seat. A man sat on either side of her, one of them the old Russian with the stout frame. Both smelled like cheap cologne.

The drive was only minutes long. They stopped at an airfield where ground crews were yelling at each other in something that sounded like German. A large prop plane waited. It had Cyrillic writing on the fuselage.

Inside the plane, no one directed her to a seat, so Felicity guessed it didn't matter. She sat mid-cabin by a window and crossed her legs like she was just another traveler on a normal day. In fact, she'd only been on a plane once before her Mexico flight—a skydiving trip with her boyfriend for her twenty-first birthday.

"You want water?" asked the old Russian in a heavy accent as he sat next to her. "We will serve food soon."

"Yes, please."

He ordered one of the younger men to fetch some drinks. Felicity saw no women aboard, but she did notice a couple of the men were armed.

"You are not afraid?"

Felicity accepted her bottled water and took a long drink. So much better than the ship's tap water!

"I am trusting God through my fear."

She surprised herself with her boldness. When professors had called on her in college classes, she'd always declined to answer.

"God?" The Russian snapped his fingers at his subordinates. Several came closer, sitting in nearby seats as they conversed hurriedly in Russian. "They ask where you learn of God."

"On the ship." Felicity watched their faces. She couldn't tell if they were amused or curious. Or maybe mocking her. They were human traffickers, so they couldn't possibly care what God thought of their evils. "A girl on the ship told me about God. I'll trust God now . . . no matter what."

He translated for the others.

"I am private contractor." He swept his meaty hand at the luxurious interior of the plane. "I buy girls. I say girls are for my son. It is very expensive to buy girls, but I am rich man. You see?"

Felicity wasn't sure what he wanted her to see or say, but now she knew what she was to be used for—apparently for the man's son. She studied the younger men. Which one was his son?

"No, you listen." He tapped her on the arm. "Look. I have no son. You will not go to my son. You see?"

Felicity stared at him.

"No, I don't see."

"Look at us. What do you see?" He was amused, but Felicity wasn't getting the joke. "You see rich Russian oligarch, no? I know you American children. No sense for how do you say, uh, international affairs? You see one bad Russian in media and all Russians are bad, no? We are not bad Russians. We are good. I bought you. I have no son."

He translated for the others, and Felicity waited, barely understanding his English. The plane soared into the night—east again. She was still trying to gauge how much trouble she was in when one of the younger men brought her a hot bowl of red soup. *Hot food!*

"Borsht," said the older man, and received a bowl of his own. "It is Russian staple. Eat, child. We talk more after."

Felicity nearly wept as she sipped at the thick beet soup. The others on board were served next. It had been prepared at the back of the plane. One of the men took out his phone and played with it between bites. Of course, they had phones! This is what Kim had prepared her to do—get to a phone and call everyone she could. The contact numbers for Dakota and Kim were permanently fixed in her memory from days of rehearsal on the ship. She couldn't let her friends down. God was with her!

Zayed Aziz understood that he was being followed, but he wasn't sure how long his tail had been on him. Twice, while exploring the city and suburbs of Szczecin,

Poland, at night, he'd entered a dead-end street. That certainly hadn't helped his evasion efforts. Somehow, he needed to get back to the safe house without anyone tracking him there.

Over two weeks earlier, he'd arrived in Poland to join Binsa to establish and strengthen the safe house in the crime-ridden suburb of Goclaw. Poland was once again ripe with human trafficking, mostly of Ukrainian refugees due to the war, and TROAS was committed to responding to the suffering that attracted selfish and greedy criminals. However, the presence of TROAS seemed to have attracted even worse conflict. Darkness hated the light of Christ!

During the last months, Zayed had traveled with Brody to visit a number of women's safe houses around the world. That had been his training time. Now, six months into his State Department probation, he was allowed to travel abroad with someone besides Brody. Since the beautiful Binsa had captured his heart a few months earlier, he had been quick to join her in Poland. After all, Brody had been recovering from a bullet wound to his leg. It had been a good excuse for Zayed to run to Binsa's side.

But while Binsa was overseeing the safe house needs, Zayed had been in protection mode. He'd served in the Saudi military beside a member of the royal family. His skill in medicine had inclined him to become a physician. However, a fatal misdiagnosis had resulted in exile from the Kingdom. Homeless and wandering, he'd applied his many skills to the trafficking trade in the American Carolinas. Of course, that had been disrupted by Brody Sladrick six months earlier.

Only by the grace of God was he not in prison for trafficking. Because he was grateful for that grace, he believed God was allowing him to serve with an effective man like Brody and accompany a courageous woman like Binsa.

In Zayed's mind was a memorized map of the city of Szczecin. Even if he were dealing with locals who knew the city better than he did, he was happy to be the one choosing where he hoped to lose his tail. From Kolumba Street and the city center, he hopped a fence then a wall to enter the Cmentarz Centralny, the third largest cemetery in all of Europe. Statues and monuments offered plenty of cover for Zayed to sprint west in the cool night air, then double back and watch for his pursuers from a low hill.

There they were—three men jogging intermittently after he'd passed that way. One man held a phone to his ear as if he were alerting someone ahead to intercept their subject.

But Zayed returned to the east wall and exited the cemetery mere feet from where he'd entered. Maybe his enemy had access to the city's cameras, but by the time they realized he'd doubled back, he'd be long gone.

He caught a night tram to the Oder River, then walked to another tram stop to Glowny railway station. There wasn't as much night life in the city as expected, but there were young people about and those who appeared to be transients. From the station he hailed a taxi to return to Goclaw, a neighborhood known for crime as well as its shipbuilding on the riverbank. He would've used his phone to warn Binsa if it hadn't already been the middle of the night. There were women and children in the safe house, and waking them to explain to Binsa that there were enemies about still might've been premature.

Goclaw was one of the only suburbs of Szczecin that tourist brochures warned visitors to avoid, especially after dark. It was an unlikely place to establish a safe house, yet it was where it was needed most. God had placed them there.

Zayed exited the taxi before reaching the safe house, but he could see the monstrous structure in a street light a block ahead. The building, originally designed by Duke Wortislaw I, was an architect's attempt at replicating

Szczecin Castle, which stood across town. The safe house was three stories high with an elevated tower two stories taller on the southeast corner and at the entrance. The enclosed courtyard, garden, and parking space completed the property covering half a city block.

Across the street from the safe house, Zayed skirted a lone street light the best he could as he approached the front gate, his hands in his pockets. There were no cameras in this part of the city. The social element wouldn't tolerate them. Cars along the street appeared empty. Except one.

Walking slowly, Zayed passed the car with two men in the front seat. He stumbled a couple times as if drunk and fell into the garden wall of an adjacent estate. When he reached the intersection, he turned right and away from the safe house. The next street was clear of parked cars or hiding places. He gazed west at the north side of the safe house. He'd never reach the entrance without being seen by those observing unless he circled wide another block beyond their sight.

Instead of calling Binsa, Zayed called Brody.

"We're being watched," he said.

The low hum sound from Brody's phone told Zayed his friend was in the TROAS jet.

"I'm not surprised," Brody said. "Babylon is hunting the faithful everywhere."

Zayed knew they probably could've spoken without codes since Greg's encryption software was un-hackable, but he appreciated that about Brody: the two could speak with or without codes.

"The castle isn't secure." Zayed didn't want to burden Brody with news of the millions of dollars it would take to outfit the safe house with bulletproof windows and security systems, but Brody did need to know there were enemies about. "It'll take weeks to prep."

"If you're in danger, call the police."

"Binsa talked to one of the chiefs. Unless someone is harmed, they don't want to hear about it."

"Then we're on our own," Brody said. "It's not our first time. Maybe Babylon is just watching you, seeing what you're up to."

"No, this is . . . beyond me." Zayed's flesh didn't like admitting his inadequacy, but his inner man who now lived by Christ wasn't afraid of honesty. "It's too soon for me to handle something like this. You should be here. I think they're dangerous. Binsa's already welcomed in a number of refugees—all women and children."

"We're both exactly where we should be right now, Zayed."

"I can't keep the boarders here safe, Brody. And more women and children arrive every day, sometimes at night. Word has gotten out around the city, and they're coming from all over Poland. I think some traffickers are on to us as well. We're being targeted, not just watched."

"You called the place a castle a minute ago, so defend it like one. Binsa said it can hold a couple hundred boarders."

"Except for an old doorman from the local church, I'm the only man here. I need more personnel to defend something this huge."

Zayed waited several seconds for a response. He would've thought he'd lost the connection except he still heard the hum of Brody's jet. It was likely his friend was praying during the silence. That's just who Brody was.

"Cast a big shadow," Brody finally said. "When Israel has been overwhelmingly outnumbered as a nation, which is all the time, they've found ways to give their enemies the perspective that they're stronger than they are. Get creative, Zayed."

"Creativity isn't my forte," Zayed said.

"Involve Binsa and pray about it. You're on site, so you'll know what's best. I can't be there for a few days still.

TROAS is under siege everywhere, Brother, but we still have to shepherd the needy for the Kingdom of God."

"I see." Zayed took a deep breath. "I'm remembering something I've learned from you over the last few months."

"What's that? I actually said something helpful?"

"More than you could ever know. When we are most desperate, we can be the most devoted."

"It sounds like God is already giving you light for the situation. Keep me posted."

Turning off the phone, Zayed chuckled at the fresh courage that seemed to flow from his rising confidence. Brody's faith in what God could provide was contagious. Living for Christ in that day required taking risks. Danger didn't mean they stopped living.

Rather than slink along in the shadows, Zayed returned to the intersection and stopped in front of the vehicle with the two men. From their vantage point, they could see him easily—as well as the east wall and north entrance of the safe house. While gazing at them, he tapped his temple, letting them know that he not only saw them but he knew their intentions. Maybe they were locals, or maybe foreign hired guns. Either way, they were GLOW thugs who meant him and Binsa harm. And they certainly would've loved to get their hands on the women and children inside who had no one else but God's people to rely on.

Zayed crossed the street at the intersection and continued to the entrance of the safe house. Another car with two more men was parked there. As Zayed reached the front gate, the two men emerged from their vehicles and stood next to it. Knocking loudly on the iron gate, Zayed prayed for calm. It seemed that men had surrounded the safe house. Now he understood that when he'd left that afternoon to orient himself with the city, they'd merely followed him since they'd already been outside.

The iron hinges squeaked as the gate opened. The toothless old man had been a volunteer from the local fellowship of believers. He spoke no English, but both men knew Russian. Zayed instructed him to open the gate for no one but women and children, and to be on the alert for more of them who might show up that night. Together, they dropped a metal security bar and a chain across the double doors. At least the previous owners had secured the entrance in proportion to the local crime threats.

"Call the police if anyone tries to force their way in," Zayed ordered, then after an encouraging embrace for the old man, he moved into the courtyard of the castle.

He stopped on the edge of the roughly cut grass and admired the fortress he'd been given to defend. Three of the four courtyard lamps glowed a dusty orange. The fourth needed a new bulb—which they didn't have. The rooms above the first story could house close to two hundred residents. Even the old horse stables on the south wall had been converted into bedrooms, though there were no bed frames in those rooms yet.

The grass had been cut the day before by a couple of ten-year-old boys taking turns with a push mower and its dull blades. Zayed envisioned a time when children might safely play games on that lawn, but now wasn't that time.

Where the grass ended, a gnarled, overgrown garden began. Its tangled plants and vines were thick and dying, the soil pitted and hard.

The rooms above were mostly dark. Not surprisingly, one of the two lights on at two in the morning shone from Binsa's room. True to form, she had insisted that she not board alone but with a couple of younger Ukrainian women who'd been widowed in the war. Another sixty women and children slept in the west side bedrooms, with the exception of one crying infant who was pacified even as Zayed stood there listening.

Since the western rooms were occupied, they were safer. Those occupants could call an alert if someone broke through those outer windows. Though they were just thin single-paned glass, few had shutters or locks. The east side was completely uninhabited and thus more vulnerable.

"Cast a big shadow." He hefted the dud grenade he carried in his trousers pocket. It had been a gift from Binsa, a real grenade, but disarmed. *Of course!* A convincing bluff had worked for him before and it could work again here, at least until they could install better windows and an alarm system. "Thank You, Lord!"

Zayed walked quickly past the only two vehicles in the ten-car lot—an old van and his rental car he'd driven from the airport. If they had to flee the safe house, most guests wouldn't fit inside the vehicles, so that meant they couldn't flee. There was no way Zayed was leaving anyone behind, so they needed to take a stand together.

He ascended the stairs to the second floor, then walked down the balcony to tap lightly on Binsa's door. She opened it, her eyes red but her face shining. When abroad, she usually slept in her clothes like now, being ready for anything.

"Good. You're back." She touched his left cheek with her right palm. Every time she did that, it was like a kiss from this gentle caretaker of many. "I feared we'd lost you to the city's *paszteciki.*"

Paszteciki, he knew, was the Polish dish of deep-fried cake with meat, cheese, and mushroom filling.

"Not yet." He smiled and leaned against the door post. Inside the room, two young women sat on one bed, a single Bible open between them. "You never cease to build up the church, do you?"

She glanced behind her at her roommates.

"The time is short. True? Hearts must be prepared. Besides, we must prepare these people to look after themselves." She nodded. "I'm glad you let me know you have returned, Zayed."

He realized she was ending their conversation, but he instead held up his finger to say more.

"Brody's warnings were warranted. The same pressures TROAS is getting back in America have found us here."

Though he saw her face change, it didn't lose its tenderness.

"What has found us?"

"GLOW operatives. They are most certainly after you, but me as well. If they get in, they'll take advantage of those who rely on us here. Brody may not get here for several days still."

"Brody has his own troubles and work." Binsa lifted her face. "I know you have a plan. I trust you, Zayed."

His heart swelled.

"I do, but I need a few of the older boys to help me, uh, cast a giant shadow."

"Cast a giant shadow?" Binsa frowned. "That's one of Brody's favorite sayings when he's employing a bluff. You're adopting it here?"

"I estimate as many as . . ." He lowered his voice. "Twelve men at least are outside on the streets. They're looking for an easy way inside. They have their orders. I think they'll try something in the dark of night. The front entrance is sturdy, but the bottom floor windows are all vulnerable to penetration."

"Can you wake the boys without causing a panic?" She tensed. "You know what you're doing. The girls and I will be praying in here."

He closed the door and found himself further encouraged by her confidence in him as well as her confidence that God would respond to their pleadings.

Zayed didn't start a panic, but he definitely caused a stir as he woke sleeping rooms to recruit the older boys for the security mission. The oldest boy from Ukraine was only fourteen and spoke good Russian, so Zayed used him as translator for four other boys who spoke only Ukrainian or Polish.

When Zayed explained his plan and showed them his defused grenade, the boys stood taller and sized up one another in a new light. They understood warfare. They knew what it meant to hold the line and defend the home front. Though they had existed as transients for many months, they had mowed the grass in the courtyard, run down the halls beyond the cafeteria, and explored the empty stable rooms of the castle as all curious boys would do.

His war plans were simple, and after a prayer of dedication from Zayed, the boys were dispatched at a run.

Step one: turn on all the lights on the first floor and open the shades if they were closed. Zayed wanted their besiegers outside to get a very good look at what seemed to be happening inside.

Step two: three of the taller boys were to round up three coats and hats apiece. In random fashion, those three were to move from room-to-room, wearing one coat and hat, and make a good show of checking the windows and looking outside. Anything untoward was to be reported to the captain of the guard, Zayed. Every few minutes, the boys were to change coats and don a different hat. Three disguises for three different boys might give the illusion of nine different men within the safe house—nine vigilant men.

Step three: the last two boys were given the task of building more counterfeit grenades. They used Zayed's genuine article as a model. Glue, paint, oatmeal, and paper mâché were applied in convincing fashion. Taking a spool of kite string with him, Zayed hung one grenade in each window on the east wall, bottom floor. The grenade was strung up with tape and line to appear as a booby trap on the window.

Zayed was so theatrical in setting up the mock trip wires that he was certain the men outside were fooled by his antics. And since the boys had begun making their rounds, no one outside could possibly approach and inspect the devices undetected.

By dawn, they'd exhausted their art supplies, but the bottom floor was sufficiently under guard.

Taking the boys together to the two towers, Zayed showed them their vantage points as the sun rose. He even pointed out the vehicles where the wicked men sat in wait on the surrounding streets. The boys accepted their charge as guardians of the castle, and their watches were designated by Zayed according to a four-hour rotation. Two would remain on duty during the days with a third joining them at night when the danger was the highest.

The boys weren't expected to stop an invasion, but Zayed was confident enough to finally get some sleep, knowing that they would sound an alarm if anyone broke in. The alarm was a football whistle one of the boy's mothers had donated to the cause.

Zayed slept in his clothes, knowing the danger had only been temporarily stayed, not removed. And they were out of food. He'd need to leave for groceries with a couple of women before nightfall, but that was a worry for later.

❧

Homeland Security Agent Jerome Wessel admitted to himself that he was off the reservation when his commercial flight touched down in Warsaw, Poland. In a rented car, he drove west two hundred miles to Szczecin. He'd never thought of himself as a rogue agent, even now. First as a Marine, and now as a federal agent, he had the interests of the United States in his heart, and Brody Sladrick wasn't complying with those interests.

His last communication with Senator Pitney had been an order like no other: "Take Sladrick down!" In the midst of her own sudden political upheaval, she was still focused on defending America from evils within. Jerome knew he needed to overlook the media's own angle against Pitney and remove Brody once and for all. After all, Greg Rotz was probably creating propaganda against Pitney in an effort to defend TROAS with a strong offense. One conservative media outlet was even calling Pitney the Executive of GLOW! That was of course ridiculous, Jerome thought, because she was a congresswoman from Massachusetts.

Greg and Marcy were somewhere in the wind in America. Jerome didn't view giving up on that manhunt as a failure. He was merely shifting his attention to where Brody was most vulnerable. Pitney had said she would send resources after Binsa and Zayed in Poland, though she knew only that they were connected to Sladrick and didn't know them personally. They were in an identified location in a suburb of Szczecin. If Jerome couldn't find Brody, then he would make Brody come to him by going after his team.

Jerome parked his car on the street outside a three-story building that his navigation system said was the address Pitney had given him. It was late afternoon in Poland. He'd seen the neighborhood on satellite and studied the area while on the flight over the Atlantic, but he hadn't been prepared for the grandness of the castle. The safe house that Binsa and Zayed were apparently establishing was too immense for two people to defend. The two must've had a lot of help if the building was indeed still secure.

He first walked around the massive square-shaped structure, checking the front iron gate and the windows from his sidewalk perspective. The windows didn't seem to have alarms, but if he wasn't mistaken, what looked like a fragmentation grenade was strung on a trip-wire in every downstairs window. *Grenades?* Zayed did have a history . . .

Next, Jerome studied the nearby buildings for a possible high-wire intrusion from across the street, but none of them were taller than four stories. No cameras seemed to be mounted outside or inside the safe house, yet Jerome noticed at least a few young adults inside who regularly checked the windows and looked outside at the street.

It was during his second time around the building that he noticed several teams of men outside in their cars. These had to be Pitney's people. She had poured a remarkable number of resources into catching Brody. *Catching?* No, Jerome admitted that he wasn't there to catch anyone. Poland was a country growing in unrest economically and corruption politically, and with that came an elevated crime rate at the local level. Jerome knew he could execute anyone he could find associated with TROAS and leave the country on his own credentials. Local criminals would be blamed for the bloodshed.

Jerome tapped on the passenger window of one of the cars outside the entrance of the safe house. Now face-to-face, he found them to be four young Asians, about thirty years old.

Suddenly, from the yard of a nearby residence, two young women darted across the street. One woman wore only flimsy shoes. She lost one running across the pavement, but she didn't return for it. The men in the car piled out and shoved Jerome aside to intercept the women. But the women were too quick. They reached the safe house gate, which opened a few inches, allowing the women to slip inside. The gate closed with a clang, and a chain rattled into place.

The Asian men glared hatefully at Jerome, then they climbed back into their car. The one in the passenger seat lowered his window beside Jerome. The man held a sidearm in his lap with one hand and his phone in the other.

"I'm Agent Wessel," Jerome said. "Pitney sent me."

"We know who you are," the passenger said with an accent. He held up his phone to show Jerome his DHS photo. "Get in the back."

Eying the back seat, Jerome saw that two men were already sitting in the back. Nevertheless, he opened the back door and squeezed into the seat with the other two men. Instead of acknowledging Jerome, the professionals continued to watch the safe house across the street.

"What fool walks in the daylight around the building?" the driver asked.

The men smelled like they hadn't showered in days. Jerome had driven straight from the airport, but he'd had the sense to use the washroom and put on clean clothes.

Jerome ignored their criticism. They didn't know TROAS like he did.

"Sladrick isn't the danger you think he is," Jerome said coolly, "even if he is our enemy."

"We haven't seen Sladrick, but you have shown yourself to those inside the building."

Rethinking his first impression of these men, Jerome decided now that they weren't professionals. No, they were foreigners, maybe mercenaries. Perhaps Malay hired guns. That was smart for Pitney to distance herself, but Jerome didn't appreciate their rudeness.

"If Zayed Aziz is really in there," Jerome said, "then sitting in your car out here isn't fooling him. There are thirteen windows on each side of the castle on every floor. I promise you—he's seen you. If he's in there."

The safe house front gate opened and a blue van emerged. From only thirty yards away, Jerome recognized Zayed's face, his dark brows and rigid jawline. The Saudi looked both ways, then drove onto the street in the opposite direction. Two women and a young man rode in the back of the van.

Jerome's Malay driver started their car after the van while the passenger spoke in a foreign language on his phone. The two men next to Jerome readied their sidearms and two short carbines with folding stocks. Apparently, they weren't there to arrest anyone from TROAS, either. Someone was dying today.

"This is perfect," Jerome said over the front seat. "Why try to get inside the safe house if we can get them when they come out? Zayed Aziz might be going to meet Sladrick!"

The Malays didn't answer. Jerome sat back and drew his service handgun to chamber a round. Their guns would be loud, but this was their opportunity to cripple TROAS by taking out one of Sladrick's right-hand people. The Malays would help him get away if Jerome was the one who actually shot Zayed. After all, the Malays were mercenaries of some sort, but he and they were on the same side.

Only a few blocks later, the van pulled into a grocery market. The parking lot was half-filled with cars. Customers with children moved to and from their cars with plastic bins.

"There are a lot of civilians around." Jerome holstered his weapon. "We'll need to do this carefully. Maybe wait next to the van for when he comes back out."

They didn't answer him, but pulled into the lot and parked a row away from the van. Zayed climbed out with his three passengers and walked toward the market entrance. The boy at Zayed's side appeared to be about fifteen, tall and lanky, speaking excitedly to Zayed as they disappeared inside.

The Malays climbed out of the car.

"Guys!" Jerome called, then checked their surroundings. He didn't like being ignored.

Another car with two more Malays pulled into the lot and parked next to them. It was an army now of six men. They rallied a moment, then started into the store in pairs.

Jerome climbed out of the car and again looked around. The safe house probably needed groceries. Maybe Zayed didn't trust a delivery driver or a truck entering their safe house courtyard, but still, this seemed careless for Zayed to try alone unless he had backup nearby. The

Malays were moving too quickly. It seemed wiser to recon before risking everything.

The six Malays had gone inside. Jerome stopped at the entrance and surveyed the lot and street once more. Then he saw them: a police car, white with red stripes, parked on the curb. It was a long distance away, but Jerome believed he could see two people sitting in the front. Maybe it was just a coincidence that they were so near, or maybe Zayed had called them since he knew the castle was being watched.

Inside the market, Jerome skirted four checkout lines to reach the produce section. He glimpsed one Malay down one aisle before he moved into another row. Jerome licked his lips. His heart beat rapidly, glorying in the hunt. If he could take out Zayed, it would damage Brody's organization and earn him points with Pitney for sure!

One of the women accompanying Zayed was alone near a display case of cereals. The prices were exorbitant because of Poland's energy and economic missteps, but Jerome focused on the woman. She would lead him to Zayed.

He followed her from the cereals. Suddenly, Jerome realized his error. A figure stood alone and still behind the display. Jerome spun and set his hand on his concealed handgun, but he didn't draw. Zayed held a grenade in his right hand and the pin in the other. The Saudi had been waiting in ambush! It was a real grenade, obvious at this distance of only a few feet. Six months earlier, Jerome had seen the man with probably the same grenade.

"You're on the wrong side, Jerome," Zayed stated calmly, his head down and his eyes daring. "Polish prisons aren't too comfortable, I hear."

Two Malays stepped into the aisle. Jerome held up his left hand to halt their advance. They must have seen Zayed's weapon because for once they didn't ignore Jerome.

"Brody wouldn't agree with you using a grenade and killing people," Jerome challenged. "Put it down. You don't want to hurt anyone, Zayed. We just want to talk to you. Come with me and we can sort this out."

"Oh, you just want to talk?" Zayed acknowledged the Malays. "Since when does GLOW want to do anything but maim and destroy lives?"

"I'm not with GLOW. What are you talking about?" Jerome frowned. "I'm still with the DHS, Zayed. Now, come with me peacefully. Put the pin back in the grenade."

"If you're not with GLOW, then why are you with *them?*" Zayed gestured with his head toward the Malays. "They're GLOW soldiers, Jerome. I'm not sure if you're just blind or complicit."

"No, I've spent my whole career fighting GLOW!" Jerome checked the volume of his voice. "How dare you accuse me of being complicit with traffickers. You were a trafficker, not me. TROAS has acted in defense against people like you for years. I have the evidence to support it!"

"I'm a legal US asset," Zayed said. "You know Brody secured my probation, Jerome. Even if you don't like it, I'm on God's side now. I'm here with Binsa. We're helping the Ukrainian people here in Poland—or whoever else needs refuge."

"God may forgive you," Jerome said, "but I don't. Neither does the US Government."

"Senator Pitney isn't working for the US Government, and neither are you if you're working for her. She *is* GLOW, Jerome. Don't you see? She's the Executive!"

"Oh, you bought into that misinformation?" Jerome cackled. "That's just propaganda from Greg, wherever you guys are hiding him."

With a whistle, one of the Malays signaled a retreat. Again, they didn't wait for him. They left down another aisle. But Jerome didn't want to retreat. He was still a Marine at heart and Zayed was right here!

"You're not going to talk me down, Jerome." Zayed's voice was steady, unafraid. His hand with the grenade didn't tremble. "Go join your GLOW friends."

"So, you called the police." Jerome relaxed his arm at his side.

"Binsa's been caring for families in Europe for years. You don't think one of them is related to someone in the police department around here?"

"One day soon, your favors will run out." Jerome backed away. "I'll see you soon, Zayed."

"Then I hope we can talk about your repentance." The Saudi didn't replace the grenade pin yet. "I'll always be ready to talk to you about your conscience, Jerome. So will Brody. We're here for you as much as we're here for anyone else."

Jerome walked away, forcing his way past customers as he exited. This wasn't right. Brody and Zayed belonged in federal prison, regardless of who they had convinced that they were good people. No one harmed America and didn't pay a dear price. Not on his watch!

Outside, Jerome slowed his gait when he noticed the police car had parked next to the blue van. The Malays walked to their cars without looking up. Before Jerome could reach the car, his ride drove smoothly away. As Asians, they stood out in the European neighborhood, so Jerome didn't blame them for wanting to leave—but they'd abandoned him there!

He kept walking out of the lot and along the sidewalk toward the safe house. At least they weren't far away. So much for expecting TROAS to be vulnerable in Poland. It would take some serious coordination with the Malays to plan an invasion of the castle. They needed to send Brody a message. A permanent message.

❧

Brody Sladrick sat in the back of his plane a distance from the sleeping Ram Garrity. For twenty minutes in prayer before God, he laid out his greatest spiritual concerns and needs. First, Ram's openness to the gospel, and second, that he might get an opportunity to testify to the Russian traffickers they were about to confront. Next came his lesser concerns in the physical world: Greg and Marcy's safety in Florida, and Zayed and Binsa's safety in Poland.

After those twenty minutes, he remained in communion with God, but made no requests. He sought to know Jesus in a fuller way, to know completely the power of His resurrection in his own life, and to experience, if necessary, the fellowship of Christ's sufferings in his own body. Brody hardly realized an hour had passed in this state of intimacy until Ram touched his shoulder.

"We landed in Saratov." Ram sat down next to Brody and showed him his tablet. "Look at this. I don't think it's Kim. Does this look like Felicity?"

"Felicity Torme." Brody used his own phone to compare a smiling student photo ID from Illinois to the pale-faced, tired-looking tablet photo. "Yes, it's her. Her hair is darker since it's probably unwashed. And her clothing is drab, the same style we found on Dakota."

"They've already got Felicity up for sale!" Ram returned to the previous internet page that showed a 'student sponsorship' façade. "It says, 'Sponsor today this twenty-one-year-old from America for twenty thousand Euros.' This is a dark net site, one of GLOW's."

"It might say she's for sale for twenty," Brody said, "but it's still an auction. Offer twenty-one."

"Me? I've never bought anyone before. I'm looking for Kim."

"We're here and Felicity's here." Brody rose and changed into a clean shirt from his overnight bag. "Put some of that money from Pitney to good use."

"I was wondering when you were going to bring that up." Ram cleared his throat, then gestured at Brody's torso when his shirt was off. "Uh, not to be nosy, but I noticed . . . Are all those scars from, uh, this stuff?"

"Retrievals? Yes." Brody tucked in his shirt tail. "Plans don't always go as expected for everyone. Any day could be my last. Do you think about that much?"

"We all die." Ram turned off the tablet. "I offered twenty-one for Felicity. Do we wait?"

"If there's to be a delivery for a buy-sell, it'll probably be somewhere downtown. We're not far from there. Leave your gun here."

Ram looked down at his shoulder holster under his jacket.

"Brody, Myanmar was one thing. I get it. We fought hand-to-hand against a few scrawny guys and the police had our back. Now we're dealing with Russians. It'll probably be the mob. They'll be armed."

"And we're buying someone they're selling. We don't need to be armed. Human retailers like to build up a clientele. You're on the wholesale end, so I understand why this makes you nervous, but this is where I work all the time."

Moving past Ram, Brody checked his messages from Greg. Senator Madison was putting so much pressure on Pitney through leaking her GLOW activities to the press that she'd called two of her own press conferences in two days to try to address potential charges for rumored mishandling of Ukrainian funds. As intended, she seemed too busy to keep pressure on TROAS. But she was apparently not too preoccupied to send her number two to Poland. Greg had tracked Jerome Wessel to Szczecin!

Sure enough, a message from Binsa included a few requests to make their castle safe house secure from GLOW agents literally outside on the street, keeping the place under siege. Double-plated windows and a security system around the safe house with other features added would cost several million, not to mention labor fees. TROAS had funds, but usually they relied on local church support to accommodate where the local church served. However, the Polish church was overwhelmed financially and undermanned physically.

"Now they want twenty-five," Ram reported from a new phone Brody had given him. "What should I offer? These blind auctions seem deceptive. There might not even be anyone else bidding. It could just be the seller jacking up the price every time I make an offer."

"Offer thirty, last and final." Brody stood next to Ram as they waited for a response. "If you're going with me, you're leaving that gun behind. We're not killers."

"Sorry, Brody." Ram didn't look up from his phone screen. "I don't share your same morals. I'm not going unarmed because I don't have a problem killing someone who wants to kill me."

Brody was silent for a moment as he trusted God to guide him in the right response. Ram was already on the edge—isolated, wanted by authorities and probably by his own people, and homeless. In an instant of force, Brody could've taken the gun from Ram, but that wouldn't help the man find his own way voluntarily.

"Ram, you're trusting in your own strength," Brody said. "Your own ways have led you wrong. It's time to trust God."

"I'm only here because I believed you about being a hero for Kim." Ram's voice was biting, his eyes cold. "I saw the way Dakota looked at me. I'm no hero, Brody. Don't try to make me like you."

"What's it say now?" Brody pointed at Ram's phone.

"They accepted thirty! Okay, Victory Park in an hour. Where's Victory Park?" Ram started to type the location into his phone when Brody stopped him.

"I've been there. Let's go."

"Is there anywhere you haven't been?"

It was early afternoon in Saratov, Russia, when the two boarded a southbound tram along the Volga River.

After a few minutes of staring out the tram window at the city streets, Ram turned to Brody.

"I don't get it. Where are all the food lines, the poverty, and the protestors the US media are always talking about in Russia? I don't see any of it."

"Mostly lies," Brody said. "America has lost her way and her media may have led that revolt from the truth. Russia is an aggressive war machine, but the West has become an aggressive machine of deceit. Any cause that America's amoral leadership pursues for the UN must be spun to portray herself in a glorious light. Similarly, America's enemies must be shown in a disadvantaged and dismayed light."

"Seems counterproductive. The truth will always reveal liars eventually."

"Good point," said Brody. "But liars don't think about the future. They're blind to everything but getting their way in the present. Look at our own lives. We lived the same way—tunnel-visioned for only getting our own way."

"Can we just stay on Russia?" Ram asked. "I don't need another spiritual lesson."

"Okay, well . . . Russia may be led by a tyrant, but its leadership is pushing against the West's infatuation with abortion, homosexuality, and anti-God education. I think it's ironic that you recognize the truth will one day be revealed regardless of American media deceptions to sway certain populations, even within the Ukrainian war effort. Didn't you know that your own deceptions would come to light someday?"

"This isn't about me." Ram returned his gaze to the window. "Besides, you deceived me into thinking you'd been sent to me by Pitney."

"Don't blame your self-deception on others. Sure, I allowed you to come to the conclusion you wanted. I just didn't correct you. Your past of misleading people shouldn't be stamped onto others. I've never lied to you or hurt you."

"You weren't transparent!" Ram swore. "Now my own dad and sister know about me? I've never been this betrayed by anyone in my entire life! Now I have no one except you. GLOW probably has a contract out for me right now. Pitney probably ordered it herself!"

"It doesn't matter how cruel you've been, Ram. Your father still loves you. Don't concern yourself with your damaged reputation any longer. Your old reputation needed to be damaged. I'm here because you matter to God."

"But you don't understand. I'm nothing without my reputation."

"Ruthless Ram?" Brody asked.

"Exactly. People knew what I was capable of. That's all I've ever been."

"And that's why I'm here. Your reputation is ruined. It's time to focus on your redemption."

"There is no redemption for me." Ram's voice was soft but mournful. "I can't change who I am or what I've done."

"I agree. You can't. But *God* can. Let Him redeem you." Brody nudged Ram lightly with his elbow. "Come on. This is our stop."

Pobedy Park, also known as Victory Park, was a hilltop, open-air museum with World War II Russian tanks and planes on display on either side of the walkway. Crisp Russian flags flapped on new flagpoles above brown grass and leaf-strewn pavement.

"I'm surprised you let me come." Ram paused at a plaque long enough to see it was written only in Russian Cyrillic. "I still have my gun."

"Well, I let you come because I think it's important for you to help Felicity. As for your gun, I was hoping you'd give it up on your own initiative. But I'm not really concerned about you killing anyone with it."

"You don't think I will?"

"Oh, you might be willing." Brody chuckled. "But no, I don't think you *can*, at least not unless you replace the firing pin."

"*What?*" Ram stopped walking in front of a vintage artillery machine. His hand went to his holster. "You removed the firing pin?"

"The first time you took off your gun after leaving Texas. What was that, five days ago?"

"You—?"

Rather than anger, Brody was glad to see Ram's face full of disappointment. Even the man's trust in his own weapon had failed him.

"See that tank up there?" Brody nodded toward the vehicle, its barrel raised as if saluting the nearby flag. "I think that's our party. Go ahead. I'll hang back."

"You want me to take the lead?"

Brody acknowledged a couple lone men scattered throughout the park. They seemed to be admiring the exhibits, but he knew they could be backups for the buy-sell.

"Since you already paid them half the price for the girl, just get Felicity, pay them the rest, and let's go. Otherwise, we probably won't walk out of here alive."

Ram seemed to understand as he surveyed the rest of the park. There were greater dangers around them than the war machine relics.

"What if something goes wrong?"

"Then signal me and I'll move forward. And Ram?"

"What?" He frowned.

"I'll be praying."

For the first time, Ram didn't scoff. He started to walk slowly toward the tank where two men stood near the right track.

CHAPTER FIVE

Brody remained standing next to a World War II fighter plane as Ram walked cautiously toward the human traffickers. Felicity was nowhere in sight, but the two men near the tank may have kept her hidden nearby. The two other Russians off to Brody's left remained stationary and watchful, indicating they were indeed part of this buy-sell as well.

Without moving rashly, Brody drew his phone out of his pocket. In Florida, Greg was monitoring satellite communication in the area. Whenever and wherever Ram transferred the funds for Felicity, Greg would track and trace. Brody only negotiated with and paid kidnappers and traffickers if he could track the funds well enough for locals to make an arrest. Merely paying traffickers without attempting an arrest was literally financing them for future abductions.

Taking the liberty to move a little closer to the tank, Brody was wary about the men to his left.

The two Russians at the tank greeted Ram in Russian. Brody was just close enough to hear their words, though they held their heads low. But they had no reason to speak quietly since civilians were scarce on the hilltop park.

"I don't speak Russian." Ram pivoted and acknowledged the other Russians. "Where's the girl? I have the money ready to transfer."

Ram held up his phone.

"Give us rest of money." The lead Russian was a large man, maybe sixty, and wore an overcoat that could've concealed any number of firearms. "And we will give you American girl. She is very pretty."

"The agreement was half down," Ram pressed, "and half when I get the girl. You're here, so I assume you want the rest of your money."

Brody saw the two on his left begin to close in toward Ram, but that wasn't all that Brody noticed. The lead Russian who was speaking looked familiar. At an angle, Brody walked closer to see the trafficker on the other side of Ram. If there was a scuffle, Brody knew Ram could handle himself in a tight spot, but not if these men had weapons.

"Wire the money!" the Russian demanded.

Taking a step back, Ram noticed the others approaching slowly. Brody prayed Ram didn't draw his useless sidearm. That would only provoke the situation, which was shaping up to be a shakedown instead of a buy-sell. Something was wrong.

"Where's Felicity Torme?" Ram insisted. "This is a joke. I'm outta here."

Ram retreated two more steps when the man next to the Russian leader pounced on him. The other two nearby charged forward as well, but hesitantly glanced toward Brody who remained at a distance.

Since Ram's adversary was a skilled grappler, Ram was subdued on the brown grass in seconds. His hands were cuffed behind his back and his lip was bleeding. They found Ram's sidearm, disarmed him, then turned their attention to Brody.

But Brody didn't advance. Nor did he flee. The three Russians looked to their leader for direction. None of them seemed certain how to apprehend a foe who wasn't reacting in the expected way to their overwhelming number.

Careful to keep his hands in sight, Brody walked slowly yet directly toward Ram and the husky Russian. The other three spread out. One drew a firearm.

"Sladrick!" The Russian leader pointed at Brody's face. "What are *you* doing here?"

"It's nice to see you too, Andrey," Brody said in Russian. He stopped a few feet away from Ram, then eyed the edgy three about to close on him. "Still baiting and abducting traffickers, I see. I had expected more from you, my friend."

"Traffickers, Sladrick." Andrey Khataev raised both hands in defense. "Not you. I don't need the trouble."

"Where's the girl? We've come to take her home."

"Sladrick, I didn't know it was you. We would've let her go. We just wanted to use her for at least one meeting."

"This is the only meeting you'll be using her for. She's leaving with us. Understand?"

Brody's firm words in Russian made the man's three toughs look questioningly at him.

"I understand."

"Where is she?"

"Nearby. With my daughter. You remember."

"How is Helena?" Brody asked.

"She still struggles, but I wouldn't have her at all if not for you."

"Are you working with the police in all this?"

"No." Andrey looked away. "We deal with that scum ourselves."

Brody sighed. He'd retrieved the man's daughter five years earlier, but the oligarch hadn't rejoiced in Helena's return as much as Andrey had spent millions impersonating traffickers to hunt down and kill them.

"The man on the ground is a friend," Brody continued in Russian, "but he needs to be taught a lesson."

"What do you want us to do?" Andrey shrugged. "I don't want trouble with you, Sladrick."

"Help him learn to fear death, but don't kill him. Take us to Helena and Felicity."

Andrey instructed his men to treat Ram roughly. They were finished for the day. Two men dragged Ram away through the park.

"Brody!" Ram called, still cuffed. "Brody!"

"This is their show, Ram," Brody said in English. "I told you to get right with God before you stand before Him."

"You are crueler than I remember," Andrey said in Russian as he and Brody walked side by side after Ram and his escorts. The last Russian followed at a distance, clearly a bodyguard for the wealthy man. "Is there no limit to what you will do to bring a soul to Jesus?"

"Suffering in this life can incline the heart to humility before the cross." Brody set his hand on the broad Russian's back. "Some answer that invitation, Andrey, and some remain stubborn."

"You sound like my sainted mother—always preaching to me!"

At the street to the north, they loaded into two armored Audis and drove north. Ram had been placed in the trunk of the lead vehicle. Brody rode in the back seat of the second Audi with Andrey.

"The world is changing, Sladrick," the Russian said. "I'm expected to take sides in matters that I care little about, nationally and globally."

"God has designed it this way." Brody looked out at the Volga River. "Now is the time to decide whether we belong to the kingdom of darkness or the Kingdom of Light."

"I prefer my own kingdom."

"Then you are lost in the arms of your own powerlessness, old friend. The end is near. Our two nations may be enemies, but it's our choice if we will be God's enemy or not."

Before the next bridge east, they left the highway to park below a complex of high-rise apartments. Ram was hauled from the trunk, hooded, then forced into the nearest building.

"You call him a friend." Andrey gestured to Ram as he and Brody followed. "It's a strange way to treat a friend."

"Sometimes our love is uncomfortable for our loved ones, but it's still love if we intend their best, before God."

They entered the elevator and ascended with Ram.

"My children know no discomfort," Andrey said. "They are spoiled. Even Helena. I have often wondered if it is love. Two of my boys are drunks."

"God's love has taught me to love others in ways that I believe encourages them to live faithfully and morally. Make no mistake, God is watching." Brody nodded at his friend. "Maybe this is the whole purpose of our meeting like this, to talk about this important love that God has for us. You already know what Jesus did for you, Andrey. It's your turn now to accept His outstretched hand."

On the tenth story, they walked down a hallway and one of the men knocked on a door. It was immediately opened by a young blond woman in her twenties. She stood aside as hooded Ram was forced into the furnished apartment then shoved into the corner behind a sofa. He crumbled onto the living room floor and lay still, panting under his hood.

"Brody, it's you!" Helena, the blond, spoke Russian, and threw her arms around Brody's neck as he entered. "It's been so long!"

"This is a nice surprise to find you all living in Saratov now." Brody moved farther into the apartment as the bodyguards went to their own back rooms. The apartment was spacious, two large apartments connected by removed walls. "Are you attending school, Helena?"

Brody noticed Felicity Torme near the kitchen counter where she stood from a stool to see who these newcomers were. Though he was eager to engage her and to assure her she was safe, he hoped to do everything in the right order. There were other souls to consider helping besides Felicity—now that he saw she was safe, clean, and healthy. She wore a Russian university sweatshirt.

"Yeah, I'm going to the Medical University," Helena continued as she moved into the kitchen, past Felicity. "And Dad manages the Privolzhskaya. Did he tell you?"

Felicity sat down on her stool again. Brody noticed she was watching him more than the others as they conversed in Russian, a language she probably didn't understand.

"I bought the railroad." Andrey shrugged as he slumped into a soft chair facing the window and river. "Oil has been too volatile lately."

Helena brought them strong tea, and Brody sipped it beside Andrey in a chair of his own. Ram made no sound except heavy breathing through the hood.

"Did you allow Felicity to call her family?" Brody asked Andrey.

"I told him to," Helena said. "He doesn't need to hold her any longer. You obviously caught a pervert."

Brody realized she was talking about Ram. Ram grunted as he rolled over and sat up against the wall. His hood remained over his head.

"GLOW is very careful, Sladrick," Andrey said. "I needed the girl to appear truly lost."

"The girl's name is Felicity," Helena said. "We told her right away, Brody, what we needed to use her for, but now we're starting to look like kidnappers."

"It's good you're all helping those who've been kidnapped," Brody said, "but you need to treat the kidnappers differently. God's way isn't for you to kill them. Tell them their sins, explain the gospel to them, and give them to the authorities."

"Torture and execution is all they receive from me." Andrey's face hardened. "Besides, GLOW agents pay Russian authorities to escape prosecution. I hear it's the same in America sometimes."

"Those who kidnapped me are still out there," Helena said softly. "You got me back from that whore house,

Brody, but the people who first took me—that's why Dad won't stop."

"Can you blame me? No father would do otherwise, not if he had the resources I have."

Brody could've argued that point, but he'd spoken his heart. Now, he would pray their hearts opened to God's grace, mercy, and forgiveness.

He stood and went to the counter where he set his cup of tea next to Felicity. She faced him with wide, curious eyes. Since Dakota had told him much about this young woman, he felt like he already knew her.

"Hello, Felicity. My name is Brody. I'll be sending you home, back to Illinois."

"Oh, thank God!" She hugged him briefly, then pulled back. "You speak English. I told Mr. Khataev about Kim Ward. You have to help her! And my friend, Dakota. We were on this ship from Mexico together. Dakota was taken days ago, but Kim Ward was still on the ship I was on. That was like two days ago!"

"I know, I know. We're tracking the ship. As soon as I get you on your way, I'll go find Kim."

"What about Dakota? Dakota Yarlin. She's from Canada. We promised each other we'd send help. Her family's phone number is—"

"Yes, Dakota's already on her way home, Felicity. We found her." Brody smiled, then took the girl's hand. "You've been through a lot. Dakota told me a little about what they did to you during your transport. I understand Kim Ward is a follower of Jesus Christ?"

"Oh, yes! She saved my life, my sanity!"

"Many who experience what you've been through, become bitter and they feel ashamed for how others have treated them. Kim may have talked to you about some of this. Do you remember?"

"She did. Basically, she said that our dignity isn't in the hands of our traffickers. God holds our souls."

Brody's hand went to his heart.

"You have no idea how happy I am to hear you say that." He took a deep breath. "You're going to be okay, little sister. You're going to be just fine."

Helena took Felicity to gather a few belongings for her trip home, and Brody shook Andrey's hand.

"It seems gracious of you to help Felicity," Brody said. "You tried to use her to catch a trafficker, but you didn't catch a trafficker. The money you were wired by my friend—that'll be sent to Felicity, I assume?"

The Russian sighed slowly.

"Yes, Sladrick. I can wire it to you. You'll get it to her?"

They made the arrangements, then Brody went to the door with Felicity, a tote bag strap over her shoulder.

"Come on, Ram," Brody called in English. "It's time to go."

Ram lifted his hooded head. Andrey himself unlocked Ram's cuffs and removed his hood. When he stood, Ram steadied himself for a moment against the back of the sofa. He glared at Andrey, then noticed Felicity.

"You got her!" Ram was given his sidearm, which he holstered with some force. "I thought I was about to die."

Brody led the way out and down the hallway to the elevator.

"Well, you did your part. Now we can go."

"Any second, I expected a bullet." Ram wrung his hands in the elevator. "I've never been so afraid. I kept thinking of the people, well, I've treated others that way. But I just kept listening to your voice in the apartment. I couldn't understand anything, but I knew as long as you were there, I still had a chance."

"Sounds like a pretty hopeless existence." Brody gestured to Felicity. "What do you think, Felicity? This guy needs to start trusting God, right?"

"Definitely. You can lose your life, but God'll never lose your soul. Wait a minute . . . isn't he that creep from Texas?"

Binsa bowed her head over a dead young woman. Her tears fell on the still forearm of the poor woman who had suffered for hours. The safe house in the neighborhood of Goclaw in Szczecin, Poland, hadn't been enough to deliver her, but at least she had perished in the presence of people who loved her.

The woman's face had relaxed now, finally still and not twisted in pain or delirium. Binsa didn't want to cover the woman's face just yet.

After a light knock on the door, Zayed stepped halfway into the room. He stood there a moment before Binsa looked up.

"She's gone?" he asked.

"Yes." Binsa folded the woman's hands over her midsection. "We never knew her name, but God knew."

"I'm sorry, but we need you out here." Zayed gestured at the courtyard of the complex. "Four more women just arrived. They barely made it past the men outside after walking all night to get here."

"And what of our besiegers?" Binsa stood before him. "They're still trying to stop anyone from getting in?"

"They're trying, but so far, our doorman has opened the door in time to let them inside. The boys in the tower who are keeping watch said they haven't intercepted any refugees yet."

"Your face . . . What are you not telling me, Zayed?"

"It was a difficult night." His eyes didn't meet hers. "I didn't want to burden you more."

"But I need to know what's going on even if it hurts. The Lord will help us carry it together. True?"

Zayed nodded, still hesitating. Binsa's heart wouldn't recover quickly from the recent loss of the sick young woman. She'd been some sort of prostitute, coerced somehow, whose internal injuries and STDs combined had wracked her body. It reminded her of her own six-year-old daughter in Nepal—dying before Brody and medical attention could reach her.

"Tell me, Zayed. It can't be much worse than the ambulance not coming into this district for this poor child."

"You still think this is the best neighborhood for a safe house? The police won't even help us unless we're attacked. If we're attacked, by then, it'll be too late to help us."

"We must accept what God gives us, where God gives it." She touched his arm. He was so strong, so stoic! "Tell me what it is, my brother. I love your protection, but now it's time to share the truth of our situation."

"More GLOW agents have gathered on the streets around us." Zayed frowned deeply, as if admitting such news made it more real. "They appear to be Malaysian. I don't see how it would be possible to risk another supply run to the market. What we brought in a few days ago will have to last until the siege breaks somehow."

"So, it's the same reason why you couldn't drive this girl to the hospital yourself. You might never have gotten back in here to us."

"It's inevitable—that they test the windows and break in. Or crash a vehicle into the front gate. My grenade bluff will be found out, Binsa, and I haven't thought of any better defense. We have only a few boys running from room to room still impersonating grown men."

"Casting a big shadow." She smiled through her teary eyes. "I'm so proud of you. Weaker men have given up under less pressure."

"Brody is still searching for the girl kidnapped from Seattle." Zayed sighed through his weariness. He appeared to have slept very little for days. "I'm ashamed to admit I can't protect you alone. I wish he were here, but he may be several days still."

"Did you tell him we're about to fall?" Binsa searched his face. "Did you tell him GLOW is setting up to capture nearly one hundred souls here, all women and children?"

"His work is important, too, Binsa. I can't ask him to sacrifice a girl's life to come to our rescue. I doubt he would even do it himself."

"Of course." She nodded resolutely. "There would be little he could do here except to join us in our dilemma. What is it? There's more?"

"During my supply run, I saw Jerome."

"Jerome Wessel? *Our* Jerome?"

"He approached me in the market. He nearly killed me. If the Malays hadn't been concerned about a police car nearby, they would've killed me. Or maybe the grenade you gave me, which I held as a bluff, held them back."

"So, Jerome is helping them." Binsa knew the zealous agent far too well from a torture session where he'd tried to pry intel about TROAS from her. "We need to pray for that hurting man."

"Your compassion never ends." Zayed drew her into an embrace and she clung to him. "I'll check all the windows again—and the front gate. Our tired doorkeeper is afraid to fall asleep since new arrivals keep running in."

"GLOW is trying to kidnap people who try to reach us even while they're trying to kill us." Binsa touched his cheek. "Whatever the situation, I'm going to call Brody myself. I must. Is that okay?"

"Of course." He smiled. "I'm a new friend. You are a long-time friend to him. Ask when we may expect him. Perhaps we can barricade ourselves into one side of the castle until help arrives."

"Help may not arrive." Binsa drew out her phone. "But we will finish well, Zayed. I hope it is beside you."

"I may be helping others if the windows are breached."

"And I would prefer you to do nothing less."

After he left, Binsa closed the door. She was oddly comfortable with the dead woman in the room. Though the four new arrivals needed her outside, she needed the encouragement of the founder and backbone of TROAS.

He picked up after two rings.

"It's good to hear your voice, Sister." Brody's voice was backed by the hum of the jet. He was airborne. "How are you holding up?"

"When was the last time I asked you for help in the field?" She tried to hide her sobs. "We are desperate, Brody. We could be overrun any moment. Agent Jerome Wessel is outside. Zayed just told me. I know you are a wanted man, but without you, I'm not sure we will stand. Maybe you can convince the authorities here to come help us. There are so many souls here, I don't want to lose them like this."

"You're not losing them, Binsa." He was silent for a moment. "We're flying over eastern Europe right now, returning from Russia. I can be there in six hours."

"But Zayed said you're in the middle of the other rescue. Brody, please—"

"No, the trail has grown cold. Kim Ward may be lost. Greg hasn't been able to track the girl as we'd hoped. Her ship stopped in three ports in the Baltics, all close together. There are no records of passengers disembarking. I may need to follow up in person to investigate each port. It's involved."

"I'm sorry." Binsa knew he'd lost other trafficked people before—her own daughter for one. He bore those scars courageously, but she knew he hurt deeply. "You know many people, Brody. And you hold the strings to many resources. Something must be done here. Please hurry."

"See you in a few hours."

She turned off the phone. Brody was coming. Hopefully, it wouldn't be too late.

❧

Minutes after Kim was given by her Chinese ship captors to a group of European men at the dock, she was neck-chained to the wall in the back of a minivan. The sky had been dark. She'd glimpsed it in the brief time during her transfer of custody. The interior of the van was even darker, but while a man's rough hands pinched the lock round her neck, the door was open. She noticed four others in the van with her, also neck-chained—three young women and one small black boy. The boy may have been five years old, but Kim didn't study him too closely before the door closed. All light was blocked out except what little she could see through the front cab.

Her heart beat rapidly, having anticipated this day for many anxious days. She'd been sold to someone in Europe. It was finally her turn. First, they'd come for Dakota, then Felicity. She still prayed for them a dozen times an hour in desperate prayers and fervent pleadings.

The driver and passenger seats were empty in the front of the van. Kim tested the limits of her neck chain. The chain links were small, like a dog's collar. At least her hands were free, but her precarious seat on a narrow bench against the side of the van required her to use at least one hand to hold her back against the wall or she'd choke against her restraint.

"Does anyone speak English?" Kim used her right hand to feel the left arm of the boy next to her. "English? Before someone comes back, tell me where we are, quickly!"

The boy spoke a short sentence, timidly, cautiously. Kim had never before heard his language. It didn't sound European. Maybe African. Whatever he said, it soothed her heart for a moment, and his hand covered hers on his arm.

Two men climbed into the front seats. The van started and lurched forward. Kim's chain tightened against her neck. She used both hands to steady herself now that the van was jostling. Behind the van, a car's headlights pierced the windows that were painted black.

"God is here. God is here," Kim whispered. No one had told her not to speak, but she spoke quietly. "Jesus, hold me!"

Fear threatened her and panic rose. She imagined choking to death in the back of the van during the drive. No one would help her. No one would care if she died. No one—

The van swerved around a corner. Her eyes watered as she was choked against the collar until the van drove straight again. Kim gasped for breath and thought of all the things she should be and do in this moment before she died. She didn't want to die with hatred in her heart, so she turned from any spite she felt against the strangers who now held her. In that moment of surrender to God, she was overwhelmed by His love that inspired her to pity even the man who'd chained her so tightly.

And Ram, the Texas boss, still needed her prayers. Jesus had died for even him, too, so she knew he was worth caring for as well.

A few minutes later, the van slowed and stopped. She couldn't control her imagination even after encouraging Dakota and Felicity not to fear what hadn't even happened yet—or may never happen. Now it all flooded into her mind—drugs, prostitution, abuse, maybe beatings. Strangers would leer and touch.

"God help us!" she sobbed.

Again, the little boy patted her hand. How could he think of comforting her at a time like this? A little boy in the hands of wicked men—her heart broke for him, and for the other women in the van with her. So many lives!

The back of the van opened. The same man reached up and unlocked her neck chain. She gasped with relief and fell against him, then his hands roughly drew her out of the van. She collapsed against another man who steadied her forcefully against the side of the van. He said something in another language that seemed like, "Stand there. Don't move."

The little boy crowded against her side. Kim put her arm over him, her hand resting on his thin shoulder. This might've been the last genuine compassion he received in his life. She had to be brave and offer others her own comfort as she was comforted by God. Her soul was safe even if her body wasn't.

Two other men stood to receive the other women out of the van. One of them was giving the men trouble. For an instant, the men were distracted.

The boy took Kim's hand and pulled her away. Kim looked from side to side—remain with four men in a dark alley, or run in the other direction where there were no men?

Kim held her breath as she slipped away with the boy. He led at a run and she joined his side, never letting go of his hand. Somehow, his little legs pumped faster and drew her along. Instead of relying on her guidance as an older person, he seemed to be urging and leading her!

They took the first street left, only fifty feet away from the van, and ran full out. There were no gunshots or loud voices behind them. Kim knew it had been a miracle to leave like that. One minute they'd stood her there, and the next she'd run away! They'd never give her another opportunity like that again! Her last attempted escape had ended with her head wound and recapture. Somehow, she guessed that her new captors would be much less merciful.

But they weren't her captors any longer. She couldn't believe she was free!

Gasping for breath, she slowed and pulled the boy with her to the cover of several trash bins beside a shuttered building. They looked like warehouses. No, they must be storage units. Everything was so dark! The boy patted her on the shoulder and even on the top of her head, speaking in his strange language, trying to calm her in her trembling. She embraced him eagerly, wishing to be the one who comforted him instead. He was so brave!

"It's okay," she whispered. "It's okay. I've got you."

She peered over his tiny shoulder at the dark street. The blacktop was wet and the breeze had the smell of rain.

In the distance, the sky seemed brighter, like city lights lay beyond the nearby structures she couldn't see over. After so much mental preparation for rape and abuse, she hadn't considered what she'd do if escape were an option.

Whatever country they were in, the police had to be helpful, but finding such authorities wouldn't be easy in a strange city—especially since their captors would be searching for them. She had no shoes or socks, only the course top and bottom clothing the Chinese ship captors had given her.

"Let's find people," Kim said, and led the boy by the hand away from the trash bins. "Anyone with a phone will help us."

With her free hand, she smoothed down her neck-length hair. It had grown some. Unwashed, the blond ends turned up in little curls, but she hoped she wasn't too repulsive or smelly. She had bathed on the ship, but never with soap.

They came to a branching street. Both lanes seemed to angle in the direction of the lights, but with metal fences on both sides, choosing a wrong street could lead to a dead end. Kim hesitated. She couldn't bear the thought of getting cornered. If the evil men came upon them at this point, she'd try to shove the little boy over one of the fences and help him escape without her. Even if they took her, at least the boy would have a chance. It would be more bearable to endure their brutality if she knew she'd been instrumental in the boy getting away.

He suddenly pulled on her hand, spoke in his language, and pointed with his other hand to the right.

"That way?" She gazed skeptically. "Okay, we'll try it."

Checking the street behind them, they hustled to the right.

Without a passport and without knowing anyone within hundreds of miles, she knew they were far from safe, but they had to try to find help.

She prayed aloud as they walked along the side of the road. The boy didn't speak much, as if he preferred her to fill the silence with her own words offered heavenward.

❧

As Ram sat in the passenger seat of the SUV that Brody was driving, he felt defeated, but not only that. Something like light was opening his senses. It seemed to pierce his hopelessness and helplessness. From the moment Brody had shown up at his family reunion, his fate had been sealed. His Texas cul-de-sac complex had been stormed and his people had been arrested. He'd depended on Senator Pitney, but even she was playing defense and losing her place as a stateswoman of power. If she'd tried to contact him, he wouldn't know it because his phone had been replaced by another from Brody. Surprisingly, Ram's millions of dollars from Pitney hadn't been confiscated, but he didn't understand why—except that Brody had expected him to use it for their mission expenses, and Brody was always on mission.

"Have you been here before?" Ram asked the older man.

Both had been reserved since admitting their search for Kim Ward had been stalled. The ship she'd been on was now heading back west, having presumably unloaded its cargo somewhere, including Kim.

"I've been in Poland before, but not in Szczecin specifically." Brody drove through the night across the Oder River to the west bank where Ram knew the Goclaw neighborhood lay. "We won't roll into the safe house tonight."

"We won't?" Ram sat forward. "I thought we were close."

"Yes, we are, but we'll do a little recon out here before we go in—*if* we go in."

"Smart."

From the side, Ram eyed Brody. It sure seemed that the operative had been in the city before since he used no map or navigation system. On the plane, they'd studied a city satellite image sent from his friend, Greg, but that was all. On the other hand, Ram was thoroughly lost in the darkness. Szczecin's streets ran perpendicular only half the time, and spiraled outward elsewhere around a city center.

Brody parked on a curb. Ram looked out the passenger window for landmarks in the night to orient himself. A couple blocks away, a tall church steeple was lit by a single beam of light. It seemed symbolic. Poland was a dark land of corruption, and little light existed, according to Brody.

"You ready for this?" Brody asked. "We'll be outnumbered ten to one by GLOW hired guns."

Ram tasted stomach acid in his throat. He'd been running a GLOW cell in Texas for years. Brody continued to speak harshly about human trafficking, but for some reason he'd remained friendly toward Ram as a person.

"No guns for us?" He had to ask, though he already knew Brody's answer.

"They're the killers, not us." Brody offered him a thin metallic object. "It's a tranq-pen. Click the top to reset the water-soluble needle. It'll puncture a couple layers of clothing and take effect within a couple seconds."

"A tranquilizer? How long does it last?"

"An hour. No more."

"What do you expect me to do with this?"

"We're gonna look around, gather intel. If you get in trouble, use it."

"Against twenty men?"

"Zayed says they're scattered around the four sides of the building. Don't worry. It's dark and the enemy won't know we're not just night strollers or Polish citizens."

"They'll spot you from a block away as a threat. You're Sladrick. Besides, you walk like a predator."

"Would you prefer I limp?"

"How can you be joking at a time like this?" Ram shook his head.

"I'm not joking."

"Like all your plans, this is suicidal. But if we're going to walk together, yeah, I'd prefer that you limped. Maybe they'll pick off the weakest one first."

"Believe it or not, knowing my weakness opens me up to unlimited strength."

"I know that's supposed to mean something spiritual, but I don't get it."

Brody climbed out of the car without answering. Ram wasn't as eager to leave the safety of the car. If there were twenty armed men nearby, it seemed wisest to drive away, not wander closer! This wasn't his fight, was it? A few days ago, he would've sworn it wasn't. Now, he wasn't so sure. Again, something was piercing through his desperation, and he knew it had to do with Brody.

He watched Brody face the street alone, studying the lighting and a few parked cars nearby. Ram envied this man—so confident, so innocent of the blood that Ram himself felt as a weight now instead of a mark of success. After a moment, he joined Brody at the front bumper. There was something honorable about everything Brody did. Honorable? No—selfless, heroic, and . . . heavenly? If Ram was going to die, he couldn't think of a better man to die beside, but he wasn't ready yet to tell Brody his heart.

"The safe house is a block that way." Brody pointed at a nondescript street. "We'll use the left sidewalk. I'll limp and use your shoulder like you're supporting me. We'll circle once counterclockwise around the safe house, then consider our next move. Anything goes wrong, we enter the safe house, or return here to the car, whichever's closest at the moment."

"What about our stuff?" Ram gestured to the car. "No bags?"

"Too suspicious. Let's keep up appearances as if we're locals."

They started off, Ram on Brody's left as he limped, with one sturdy hand on Ram's right shoulder for support. With his right hand, Brody checked his phone messages.

"Zayed knows we're out here. He says any window of the safe house is an entry point if we need it to be one."

"I can't believe you're still alive doing things like this." Ram cursed for the first time that night. "I have the money to buy an army to clear out this whole street of threats."

"What God gives us should be used for God's work, not to settle our fear or anger by destroying others. Leave that to God who can do it justly."

The safe house appeared ahead exactly where Brody said it would be. The windows on the first floor were illuminated in orange interior light. It must've cost a fortune to keep such a building lit like that, but Ram understood the light was keeping the GLOW enemy at bay.

"On our right," Brody warned under his breath.

It took Ram a couple more seconds to see what Brody had identified so easily. As soon as Ram noticed four men across the street, he diverted his eyes. The four stood on the sidewalk behind two vehicles, only their heads and shoulders visible. One of them was smoking a cigarette. It was unnerving knowing the four were studying them. They had to be the GLOW mercenaries. No one else would be out at that hour.

At the street north of the safe house, Ram looked to his left. There was the castle entrance. He could see the heavy iron black gate, but they continued south along the west side of the safe house. Now, Ram knew what to look for on the opposing curb.

"Two more," he said softly, and made a good show of helping Brody walk beside him.

"Yep. It's a good sign to see them like this."

"It is?"

"Absolutely. If we didn't see them out here, still circling the prey, we'd know we were too late. But here they are, sitting like jackals, looking for a weakness to break in. They haven't noticed that weakness yet."

The enemy was more visible on this side of the castle—one standing at the bumper and the other sitting on the hood, facing the safe house. The one who stood was also speaking on his phone. He faced them and then limped slowly past.

Now directly beside the safe house, Ram could look into the lit windows of the rooms on the first story. A young man in a coat gazed out one window for a moment before moving aside. The windows did seem remarkably vulnerable, lit or not, until Ram noticed a fist-sized object hanging on a chord, perhaps fastened to the window by string or tape? Shocked, Ram slowed to look closer.

"That looks like a grenade!"

"Keep moving," Brody urged. "I know what it looks like. Zayed has a thing for grenades. How else do you think he's keeping a GLOW army at bay?"

"I figured you'd say a prayer and an army of angels would protect everyone inside. There are grenades on all those windows!"

"Really? Or does it *appear* like there are grenades on the windows?" Brody chuckled. "Zayed may have a thing for grenades, but right now, he's showing he has a thing for theatrics."

"They're . . . fakes?"

"Whatever they are, they seem to be working, right?"

"Well, until someone tests them." Ram snorted at the boldness of Brody's people. "I suddenly have an interest in meeting this Zayed friend of yours. He must be pretty clever to handle GLOW operators like this."

"He's expressed interest in meeting you as well."

"Yeah?"

"Sure. He was like you not more than a few months ago."

"Like me? You mean a skeptic of your religious ideas?"

"No, I mean he was trafficking people in the Carolinas."

"For GLOW?"

"No, he had his own little network for exploiting Middle Eastern refugees."

"And now he works with you?" Ram felt the light inside him open something even wider, like his very soul was being split in two and that which emerged was for his benefit. Nothing his father or sister had ever said about God had had this impact on him. "Why didn't you tell me earlier that you have ex-traffickers working with you?"

"Everyone has a sordid past, Ram. You shouldn't make your move based on someone else's. You should make your move based on your need of God's healing hand in your life."

On the south side of the building, Brody made a show of having some sort of attack. Ram helped him sit on the curb as both men rested a moment to admire the castle's elevated tower, two stories taller than the other three floors. Knowing they were being watched by at least four more GLOW toughs, they kept their analysis discreet and their voices low as they compared notes.

"All those grenades," Ram said, "probably make these guys think if they set one off, the whole place will go up."

"That assumption is probably the only thing protecting the women and children inside from either slaughter or abduction."

"Zayed must be impervious to panic to withstand a siege like this." Ram shook his head. "He's fortified this place against skilled infiltrators. Maybe he doesn't need us after all. We could still be out looking for Kim"

"Come on. Help me up."

Ram lifted Brody to his feet and they continued their trek to the east side where the windows were just as lit and no less watched by more GLOW men on the street.

At the northeast corner, they paused again. This time, Brody instructed Ram to kneel and untie and tie Brody's boots, as if he were too crippled to do so himself. While Ram obeyed for the sake of their cover, Brody reported quietly what he could see.

"There are definitely more men on this street, probably trying to figure out how to get through that gate. I count maybe six or seven midway up the curb. Zayed said they're trying to catch refugees before they reach the gate, too. We need to think of a way to take care of everyone inside and expel all these guys outside."

"They're gonna get in, Brody. It's just a matter of time. Maybe we could use some of my money from Pitney to convince authorities to round up these characters? I'd be glad to—"

"Wait," Brody interrupted. "There's someone on the north side of the street. They're hiding from the besiegers."

Ram turned his head from his kneeling position to see a lone figure crouched behind a parked car.

"Looks like a woman. She's small."

"She's alone. Binsa said they're coming from all over the city ever since word got out that there's a safe house here. The problem is—getting inside."

"They're desperate if they're willing to risk it like this. What's she doing?"

"She's gonna run for it!" Brody warned. "Look at her. She doesn't even have shoes!"

"They spotted her!" Ram rose to his feet. "They're gonna get her. Should I—?"

"Go! Go, Ram! Get her inside. I'll call Zayed."

Ram responded without waiting for clarification. Whatever had been happening inside him seemed to give him flight right then. He was with the side of right. Oh, the joy to be in the light—even to be with a man of God like Brody! If only his father could see him now!

The woman ran at an angle straight at the castle's iron gate. Three GLOW men ran from the opposite angle to intercept her. In his mind, Ram hoped the GLOW men thought in the darkness he was one of them, and that he was merely there to catch the woman with them. But the woman could run faster than even Ram had expected. She zipped in front of the nearest two, inches from their outstretched fingers. One of the men tumbled to the pavement and Ram collided with the second an instant after the woman passed between them.

The man he'd struck was much smaller and bounced off Ram. Ram used his checked momentum to change course and to run directly after the woman. He had to get her inside like nothing else in life mattered! Never before had he run as he ran at that moment. For her, he ran. And for Brody. And maybe even . . . for God.

A figure passed behind the gate. Someone was manning the gate from inside!

"Let me in!" the woman shrieked—in English, much to Ram's surprise!

Two gunshots blasted behind him, but Ram didn't need to turn around to know they were shooting at him or her or both. The bullets slapped the safe house wall. Men's voices behind him were hollering in a foreign language. Oh, they were made now! He was about to show them all whose side he was truly on.

The woman fell into the closed gate at full speed. She screamed incoherently as Ram rushed closer. Another gunshot and a bullet whizzed past his head. The man inside the gate fumbled frantically with a chain. Ram could see through the bars and mesh that he was older and working in dim lighting. Men were on Ram's heels, maybe ten yards back.

A second before Ram reached the gate, searing heat slammed into his back. Breathless, he collided with the woman. He clung to the bars of the gate over her as the man inside finally threw the chain free and opened the gate. It seemed right to Ram to shield the woman from what came next—another bullet. It spun him sideways, but he still held the gate with one hand. Anger and bewilderment flooded through Ram's mind. *Why now?* Why only now was he realizing how he should've been living his life—at the moment of his death?

A second man from inside, tall and authoritative, appeared in the gate's orange light. He held a grenade overhead.

"Hey!" the man yelled at the gunmen. "Hey, you!"

The gunmen didn't fire. In Ram's agony and fear, he saw his pursuers halt. His legs were weak. He sensed the woman pass through the gate, then the man with the grenade reached for him with his free hand.

"Brody says this is one of ours," the tall man said.

Roughly, the man guided Ram through the gate, then Ram's legs could no longer support himself. He fell into the man's arms.

"Zayed?" He gasped.

The young woman was there, the one whose life he'd saved. Her face seemed familiar . . . even heavenly. A familiar face in Poland? In the dim light of the gateway, he noticed a fresh scar on her forehead—but *it couldn't be!* Not here! Not her . . .

"He called you Zayed? I know this guy!" she cried. "It's him! It's Ram!"

The chain was replaced. Ram lay on his side where his blood pooled under his shoulder. He couldn't breathe. But she was there. It *was* her. After days of defeat, he finally understood Brody's plan. It had been his plan since the beginning. Yes, helping her was indeed glorious!

"Zayed, do something! He's dying!" she pled. "Ram? Can you hear me? Ram?"

Dying? *No!* Ram's mind screamed that what she said wasn't true. He wasn't ready. Brody's warnings of death and judgement stabbed at his conscience. Not death. Not when he was just at the beginning!

❦

Kim Ward woke with a start, gunshots still ringing in her ears. But the bedroom was still. She sat up. Daylight streamed through the window where three other unmade beds lay empty. It was morning. The nightmare from the night before—she still had blood under her fingernails . . . Ram's blood.

She walked to the door and opened it on the second floor of a huge apartment complex. An unruly garden and lawn half-filled the courtyard below and a parking lot filled the other half. Four children ran across the yard. Another child's voice shouted in a strange language— perhaps counting, as if they were playing hide and seek.

Two women with guarded eyes walked past her door but they said nothing. Kim's memory slowly returned. Binsa, the dark-skinned woman in the night, had said this was a safe house for young ladies like herself—a refuge for the lost. And the tall man who'd had the grenade had carried Ram into a barely equipped infirmary downstairs. He'd said his name was Zayed and he was a physician. Kim had stayed with Ram for hours until Binsa had shown her to the bed upstairs where young women her age had also slept.

Leaving the doorway, Kim walked along the balcony to the stairs. More women and girls were gathered on the landing. They spoke in foreign languages, but they weren't unfriendly as they moved aside for her to pass. Once in the courtyard, Kim walked past a van to reach the front gate. She was hungry, but her heart and not her stomach compelled her now.

At the front gate, her fingers fit through the iron mesh plated against the bars. Beside the entrance, an elderly man slept in a chair that seemed far too rigid to be comfortable. Kim gazed out at the street at the cars parked at the curb. Two men stood out there, fewer than she'd avoided in the night, but they were still there. Kidnappers, Binsa had warned. They wanted to take the women and children who were inside the safe house.

But Kim wasn't there to eye the human traffickers laying siege of the building. She was there to make sense of the whereabouts of the little black boy who'd led her here. He'd accompanied her from the van when they'd escaped. Their trek through the night had been ominous, avoiding car headlights and potential hunters, all to reach civilization and help. Thinking back, Kim had to admit the boy had guided her the whole way. While she'd whispered prayers, he'd held her hand, choosing one street over another to arrive here. He had even pointed out the dangerous men on the street, then the gate she needed to reach.

And the boy had been beside her when she had run for the gate. Kim had yelled for entry, but it had been the boy who'd spoken to the old man who slept now in his chair.

Ram had then appeared—covering her body with his own. He'd found her! All her praying had culminated then, in those few seconds, at this mysterious oasis run by Christians in the middle of a Polish city.

And the boy? He was nowhere to be found. No one had seen him. Not even the old man had made sense of her inquiries the night before, though she'd needed to speak to him through Binsa as they tried to find the boy. As far as anyone in the safe house was concerned, the boy had never existed. But Kim knew. She placed her hand over her heart as her tears welled. Yes, she knew. He'd held her hand in the van and all the way to the doorstep of safety. She'd never forget.

"Thank You, Lord . . ."

She left the gate and walked across the courtyard. Binsa had expressed some concern the night before that the safe house was in dire circumstances, but the kids who laughed and darted past Kim just then certainly didn't seem aware of that danger.

Kim could smell food from the cafeteria on the west wall, but she first stopped in at the infirmary. She found Zayed asleep in a corner on a bench, his mouth open and his arms crossed. He'd probably been there all night.

Ram lay on a low table, a wool blanket pulled up to his chin. The Texas boss was shivering, but beads of sweat dotted his forehead. Fever. Something was wrong. From the night before, she remembered that Zayed had said he'd been shot twice, once in the shoulder blade and once in the back beside the spine. The bullet had lodged in his lung, dangerously close to his heart.

She touched the man's pale cheek. It was clammy and cold. This wasn't the man who'd kidnapped her from Seattle, but he'd held her before transporting her into Mexico. He'd sold her to the cartel, who'd sold her to the Chinese. He was responsible. She tried not to imagine what she'd escaped, what many other girls like her hadn't or couldn't escape.

The Chinese had forced her to disrobe and photos had been taken of her body for their trafficking archives. They'd catalogued her and labeled her. Those photos could never be recovered, and that fact threatened her growing faith and joy in God's goodness, but she couldn't blame God for man's evils. Many women were leered at, harmed, and killed in this world. It wasn't right, but it was just her body. Her soul was still safe. God was her refuge not only now but also from her dreadful memories and fears.

As much as she'd been through the last weeks, she looked upon Ram before her with amazement. God had brought this terrible man from a Texas trafficking house to here. It had to be God. After all, she'd prayed for him for days—since he'd stitched her forehead in that kitchen. She couldn't imagine that he was there for any other purpose but to save her. And he had. If not for Ram, she would be the one lying there with a blood bag attached by an IV to her arm.

Zayed hadn't stirred. His phone lay on the counter next to bloody bandages. He'd allowed her to use it the night before, so she picked it up again and quietly left the infirmary for the open air and children's voices in the courtyard.

"Dad, are you there?"

"Kim! Oh, thank God you called back. I've been on the phone all day with Polish people—administrators, I guess. Have you heard anything? They say you're still in lots of danger."

"I'm still with the Christians I told you about last night. We're safe inside this place, but there's people outside who're trying to get in. Bad people."

"No, Kim. The authorities I've talked to over there are saying you're actually staying with the traffickers. You have to get away, Kim! Those people are wanted. You hear me? Get away from them. There are warrants for their arrest all around the world!"

"Dad, I don't know who you've been talking to, but it's the people outside who are the human traffickers. They have our building surrounded. The police won't even help. They're too afraid or corrupt."

"I can't believe that, Kim. You need to get out of there, somehow, and get home. Turn yourself in to the police. They'll get you here. They've promised me."

Kim eyed the gate across the courtyard. The old man was allowing someone else through the gate—three more women. Then he closed the gate. When she thought of her father's words, she couldn't help but see the whole world distorting everything. Good was all twisted up, and evil people were being presented as the answer.

"Dad, I didn't want to tell you this last night, but when I tried to get in here to this safe house, those people outside tried to kill me. They shot at me with guns. These people I'm with saved my life."

"That's not what the people out here are saying, Kim! They're saying you've joined a group of wanted extremists. Radicals! Kim, are you sure there's no criminals sheltering with you in there?"

She thought of Ram—a definite criminal. Everyone else were women and juvenile refugees.

"Dad, you're not here right now. You've got to trust me that God led me here. I don't understand all the lies you've been told about the people I'm with, but I'm with good people—praying people. I guess I could still die, but it won't be by these people. There are killers right outside, and the police aren't doing anything about them."

Her father sighed. She knew this was hard for him. He'd raised her within a conservative household, doing his best to guard her from so much of the world since her mother had died two years earlier. But the world had still found a way into their family to harm them.

"You're in God's hands, Kim." His voice broke. "You're there, seeing what's going on. I'll keep calling people on my end. Maybe it'll help."

"Okay, Dad."

"I just want you home."

"Yeah, I know. I'll try. I don't know how yet, but I'll try."

She turned off the phone and stared at it, praying that God would give her dad some peace. Remarkably, she seemed more at rest than he did, so hopefully he could hear the confidence in her voice. She'd grown from the teenage girl he'd once known just a few weeks ago.

The phone rang. She glanced at the infirmary door. No, Zayed needed his sleep, and Ram didn't need to be disturbed more than necessary.

"Hello?" Kim answered.

"Hello?" answered a man's voice. "Binsa? I thought I was calling Zayed."

"No, this is Zayed's phone. I haven't seen Binsa yet this morning. My name is Kim."

"Kim. *Not Kim Ward?*"

"Yeah. This is Kim Ward. Who's this?"

"My name is Brody Sladrick. I don't know how to make sense of this—talking to you. We found Dakota and

Felicity, but we lost track of you. All they could talk about was finding you."

"I'm here with Zayed and Binsa! I just got here last night. I'm in Poland."

"You were the . . . woman who Ram helped get inside?"

"Yeah." Kim steeled her emotions. "I'd be dead right now if it weren't for him. He got shot up pretty bad. Twice."

"He's still alive?"

"Yeah. Zayed's sleeping now, but he was up all night with him. Ram doesn't look good."

"Is Ram awake? He needs to receive Christ as His Savior, Kim. He may not survive this."

"If he wakes up, I'll tell him."

"Thank you, Kim. I know that about you—that you're a believer."

"I don't know what I was before all this, Mr. Sladrick, but I know now that I'm a believer."

"Then Ram is in good hands. Listen, I'm outside about a block away from you."

"You're here? Outside?"

"Well, I can't get too close—the guys with the guns, you know."

"Right."

"Tell Binsa and Zayed when they wake up that I found a back yard across the street on your east side. I think I can sling-shot small weighted packages into you from there, since you guys can't get out for supplies."

"I'll tell them."

"How are you doing with all this, young lady?"

"My dad's super worried. He's being told I'm staying with criminals."

"Since governments define what a criminal is, anyone who defies a government is a criminal, even if those governments are in bed with human traffickers."

"I sort of tried to tell him that. So, what do we do?"

"Well, little sister, you're in there, so you take care of the people in there. I'm out here, so I'll take care of the people out here. We're followers of Christ, so we don't fuss too much about what it costs us, right?"

"Right." Kim smiled. She might never meet this Sladrick man in person, but he'd called her his little sister. They had a spiritual connection. "I'll remember that."

"Your heart is good? You're staying pure from hatred and offense?"

Kim raised her chin and closed her eyes, holding back a sob. This man *really* understood what she'd been through, and the real emotions and testing she was experiencing.

"I think so. I'm praying like every thirty seconds."

"Good girl. Keep touching lives in there. I hope to see you all soon. Tell Zayed to call me when he wakes up."

"I will. Thanks, Mr. Sladrick."

She couldn't wipe the smile off her face. Kim wished the phone would ring again so she could talk to more of these amazing faith giants! Her dad would *love* to meet all of them someday, especially Zayed—who'd made the bad guys stand back last night by threatening them with a grenade—which she'd learned had been diffused for months!

Although Kim had met only Binsa and Zayed the night before, she was welcomed into the cafeteria and offered a small plate of powdered eggs and sliced, grilled potatoes. No one else received a larger portion. The cooks were all women, probably trafficking survivors themselves. They were rationing the food out of necessity.

Sitting at one long table, she picked at her food. No one she sat among seemed to know English, but she didn't mind. The younger kids were a little fussy and the young mothers seemed a little distant. Kim doubted they were all believers, but they'd fled to those who offered some safety in a migrant-burdened country.

After breakfast, Kim helped in the kitchen by washing dishes for an hour, which she was happy to do without being thanked. With the kitchen clean, she returned to the infirmary to find Zayed still asleep, but Ram was stirring. She placed her hand on his forehead and looked down into his weary eyes.

"Water . . ." he whispered.

She held up his head as he sipped and sputtered. His eyes closed and Kim thought he'd drifted off to sleep again.

"Kim?" His eyes didn't open. "It's really you?"

"Yes." She smiled down at him, petting his head. "I'm right here. You saved my life. I would've died last night, but you found me. You really found me. Remember what I told you in Texas? I told you I wouldn't stop praying for you."

"Brody . . ."

"Brody Sladrick? Yeah, he's outside still. I talked to him on the phone this morning. He said to tell you, . . . um . . ." She glanced at Zayed. She'd only ever told the two girls on the ship about Christ and the gospel of peace. A dying criminal was no different than them. "You need to trust in Jesus as your Savior, Ram. You might die soon. God will take and guard your soul. I want you to go to heaven."

"I know. Brody never . . . gives up."

"You need to trust in Jesus, Ram. You've been a bad man. You need to be forgiven. Can you hear me?"

"Yes." A tear rolled from the corner of his closed eyes. "You talk . . . like my sister."

"Your sister? She's a believer?" When he didn't answer her, Kim took his hand and squeezed it. "God knows what you've done, Ram. God's not happy with you, but it sounds like you know He sent His Son to die for us all. Trust in that now."

She recited John 3:16 into his ear and for a moment she spoke about its promise.

"Do you give up?" she asked. "Do you give your life to God, Ram? Ram?"

"Yes." He lifted his head and opened his eyes. "My phone. My . . . *phone!*"

She searched the infirmary and found his device, blood on its screen.

"Here it is." She placed it in his hand. "You want me to call someone for you?"

"No. My thumb." He unlocked the screen. "My account. See?"

"Your account?" Kim frowned at the screen. *"Whoa!* Is that money? Dollars?"

"I'm sorry, Kim." He shook his head. His eyes closed again. "I'm so sorry . . ."

"No, no. It's okay. I'm okay. We're both here now. I just want to make sure you trust in God for eternal life. I think that's why I'm here."

"Take it." He lightly pushed his phone toward her. "Take it."

"Okay." She accepted the phone. "Ram? Ram?"

"I . . . know, Kim. I believe. Tell Brody that I . . ."

"Ram?"

His face relaxed and his chest deflated. The IV bag continued to drip, drip, drip. But Ram had stopped breathing.

Kim looked to Zayed for help. He was awake, now sitting up on the bench, but he didn't approach his patient.

"There's nothing you can do now, is there?" she asked.

"No. He's just too weak. Even if we'd had a ventilator . . ." He shook his head and looked down at his own blood-stained fingers. "I heard what you told him."

"Mr. Sladrick said to tell him the gospel."

"It sounded like you did."

"Do you think he—?"

"We'll know in heaven," Zayed said, "but it sounded like he believed."

"I don't think people would like it that I told him he could be forgiven after all he's done to, well, you know. People would want him to suffer."

"Jonah didn't want the Ninevites shown mercy, either, but God's love doesn't discriminate between sinners. I'm thankful for that myself. We all deserve to be thrown away forever when we're measured by a perfect standard. I've learned a lot from talking to Brody for the last six months."

"Ram gave me his phone."

"Yes, I saw that."

"He has a lot of money."

"How much?"

She showed him the screen.

"Is it real?" she asked. "I mean, that's *millions*, right?"

"That's . . . millions." He stood slowly. "And that might be just what we've been praying for."

"You think God brought Ram to us?"

"To you."

"Why?" Kim stood up straighter, like a woman much older than her years. "What do we need to buy?"

"Everything this safe house requires to turn it into a fortified compound."

"Real grenades?"

"No, not grenades at all. Bulletproof glass windows and a secure camera system. Maybe an armored transport or two? If we can convince enough workers to come out here together, they might not mind the crime in this neighborhood. Their numbers will be their strength. Our besiegers won't know what to do with all kinds of civilians outside, flooding the streets around us."

"And food," Kim said. "The food here is, well, it's pretty bad."

"Yeah." Zayed smiled sadly. "But I'm not one to complain."

"Me neither. I mean, I've had worse."

"Yeah." He smiled again. "But I can't eat any more powdered eggs, either."

❧

Greg Rotz stood on a Ybor City sidewalk as an electric streetcar passed him. It was early morning in Tampa, Florida. Marcy was still asleep where Hector and Gabriella Savalano had joined them in the new TROAS headquarters building a half-block behind him. He'd been up all night, working through the time difference on Poland's urgent concerns. His heart was swollen with honor at having been the one depended upon to fulfill the needs of so many so far away.

Few pedestrians and cars were about at that hour, so Greg knew he stood out in his tan trousers, bright red t-shirt, and blue baseball cap. He'd worn that t-shirt for a reason—as a test.

Sure enough, after a few minutes, a police car cruised along the street toward him. Greg took off his baseball cap and presented his face to the police car. The car slowed. The officer adjusted the dash cam, and Greg knew his mug was being checked against state and federal databases. Against his tendency to run away, Greg remained still. He even casually waved to remove any possibility that he hadn't been seen by the officer.

The officer nodded in response, then sped away. Greg watched him go. That was it. That's what he needed to know. After almost three weeks as a fugitive for the false charge of human trafficking, the warrants against TROAS personnel had been cancelled. Their "wanted" status on federal sites had been removed, and now Greg had confirmed it.

With his cap back on his head, he returned to the warehouse through the construction site. He was relieved to confirm they were no longer wanted criminals, but that didn't mean their powerful enemies were gone yet. It was probable that Senator Madison had merely convinced the Justice Department that the embattled Pitney warrants couldn't be justified. Occasionally, Greg had checked the woman's own status, expecting her to be arrested any day now for the misappropriation of funds. Her GLOW companions were distancing themselves from her to preserve their own interests, and the media had remained silent about one of the their own lest they'd, too, be shown to be as complicit as they had been.

GLOW wouldn't go under because of Pitney's pending demise, Greg figured, but any stand against sin mattered in the grand scheme of God's purpose. When the Lord came back with all the saints, then GLOW would finally be eradicated. Until then, God's people would just keep standing.

At their upstairs living quarters, Greg checked his computer. Zayed had asked him to order security materials for the besieged safe house in Poland. It would cost millions to retrofit the complex with bulletproof windows, reinforced doors and a heavy gate, and to purchase a number of vehicles for their use. Greg knew the funds Zayed was offering had been given to Ram, who'd given them to Kim Ward. Ram only had them since Pitney had financed him to keep the southern US border fluid. Since TROAS wanted to follow the law wherever possible, Greg had conferred with Senator Madison personally for direction. Those funds had already been earmarked for Ukrainian refugees, and TROAS intended to apply security measures to protect predominately Ukrainian women and children sheltered at the safe house. So, Madison had signed off on the TROAS use of the funds as an NGO. Instead of the funds being misappropriated, they were actually being appropriated as the original congressional bill had intended.

"Everything okay?" Marcy asked Greg as she stretched atop her sleeping bag. Against the nearby wall, Hector pulled on his boots for another day of labor. He'd been clearing the whole warehouse of debris. "You haven't gone to bed yet?"

"Not yet." Greg touched a few keys on his laptop without sitting down. "Just double-checking the delivery of security measures for Zayed and Binsa."

"It's a miracle they haven't been invaded already."

"Well, as long as these Polish construction people don't take their time with installations, the safe house will have better security than we did at our old apartments."

"That's good for them, but what about us?" Marcy sat beside him. She hadn't remembered to put on her beret, but Greg didn't mind her wild hair. "How long do we have to hide out here?"

Suddenly, Gabriella sprang from her sleeping bag, ran barefooted across the floor, and climbed into Marcy's lap where she seemed to fall promptly back to sleep.

"She misses her mother," Greg said. "My app translated a little of their story from Hector. They were split up at the border coming across. The coyotes took the mother, then turned Hector and Gabriella away. He crossed the Rio Grande later and came here. He assumed his wife was dead."

"Maybe she's still out there?" Marcy petted the child's unwashed hair. "We're the people to find her, right? Or at least Brody might be able to."

"I have my scorpions searching for any sign of her whereabouts over the last month." He glanced at Hector as he tugged on work gloves and started for the stairs to the next level. "I might need your help explaining that to him. If I find her alive, well, you can help me present that to Brody for a rescue."

"But if she's dead, would we plan the funeral?" Marcy frowned. "Hector has no one else, but should we risk something like that?"

"It's safe now. The wanted sites have removed our photos." He nodded solemnly. "We're no longer fugitives. I checked."

"What do you mean, you checked?" Her eyes widened. "You went out there to test it?"

"I had to. One of us had to test it."

"So, we can leave now?" She sighed. "No more disguised dashes to the mission two blocks away for the rare shower and a proper toilet?"

"Not unless you like smelling me like this."

She muffled her laughter so she wouldn't wake Gabriella.

"My clothes and I don't smell any better than you and your clothes."

"Hey, I thought this thing was odor resistant." Greg sniffed at his bright red t-shirt. "It's not?"

"Uh, it's a repelling color for a t-shirt. Repelling in appearance and odor resistant aren't the same thing."

"Fine, we'll check into a hotel for a couple days."

Her face became serious.

"I don't want to live too comfortably, not with Brody and Binsa risking their lives."

"This isn't the first time he and Binsa have set up a safe house in a dangerous neighborhood. But this time, Zayed is with them."

"We might be safe here in America for now," Marcy said, "but I won't relax until they're all back here helping us rebuild."

CHAPTER SIX

Brody sensed someone in the room with him as he woke, but he didn't open his eyes. He knew who it was—no one dangerous—so he enjoyed a few more seconds of rest and solitude with his thoughts of God and His provision for the mission that day. The passing of Ram remained on his heart, but Kim Ward had conveyed by phone that he may have died humbly reaching out to God, so Brody wasn't mourning too much. He'd given his life and attention for a couple weeks to the Texas human trafficker, and the rest was in God's hands.

The night before, Brody had received news from Greg in Florida that US Government tensions against TROAS had softened for the time being. That allowed them to place all their attention and resources into establishing a more secure safe house in the Goclaw suburb of Szczecin, Poland.

Agent Jerome Wessel was still out there on the street, along with about twenty Malay mercenaries hired by GLOW. However, Brody doubted that Senator Pitney, the Executive, was directing GLOW's international interests as fervently as she had in the past. Since Greg had used Senator Madison to expose her to the world, she'd certainly lost traction within her organization, regardless of her press conferences alongside a diminishing number of powerful American politicians and corporate leaders.

When Brody opened his eyes, they focused on a brown-haired boy of eight years old, Szymon Nowicki. Brody's bed was a narrow cot in the boy's own room in a small cottage.

"I'm ready," the boy stated in his native Polish language.

"Yes, I see that." Brody spoke his Polish slower and with effort, recalling some of the words with difficulty. He sat up and ran his fingers through his shaggy hair. There'd been little time for grooming since he'd left Florida to pursue Ram weeks earlier. "Are we ready for battle?"

"Mama said breakfast first, then we can fire the missiles."

"Good work, soldier." Brody nodded as the boy stood up straighter. "The perimeter is clear?"

"Perimeter? Oh, no one's come to the house. We can continue our assault as soon as we've eaten."

"As long as your mama is safe."

"She's not afraid and neither am I."

"That may be." Brody drew on his trousers. "But remember our rule as soldiers for Jesus."

"To care for the women and children?"

"Yes, that's right. And your mama is a woman, so we need to do our best to protect her, too. That's what *Operation: James* is all about."

"From the Bible."

"That's right. Now, let's see what your mama has for us to eat."

At the dining table, Brody was served by a one-armed woman nearly thirty years old. Yana was a single mother of Szymon, a scarred woman from a trolley accident as a teenager. Two nights earlier, when Brody had first contacted her for help as a Christian sister in the neighborhood, she'd seated him at the head of the small dining table and fed him *paszteciki*, which was deep fried cake with meat, cheese, and mushroom filling.

Again, Brody sat at the head of the table, not because he wanted the privilege, but because while in their house, Sister Yana treated him as the man of the house and as a servant-guest of their great God. Yana served him first, fresh scrambled eggs with cheese and potatoes, and cottage cheese on the side. She served her young son next.

The boy compared his portion to Brody's then signaled his mother for more of a man-sized portion.

Once Yana had dished herself a portion, she sat down with her hand in her lap. Brody understood from several meals eaten with them that she had given him his cue. He blessed the food the best he could in broken Polish. More than anything, he understood Yana wanted him to be a godly male role model for the boy. Even though Brody would be staying there for only one more night, he knew that even brief role models left important impressions on boys.

After he'd prayed, Brody started to eat slowly. Szymon watched Brody's every move, perfectly mimicking his bites and sips of milk.

"More medical supplies arrived in the night," Yana reported between bites. "And Bibles, as you asked, to weigh down the packages. I have placed them in the back yard."

"They're not packages, Mama," the boy corrected. "They're missiles."

"God's people are alive and well in Poland," Brody acknowledged. "I'm glad they're able to help even in hard times."

"We are very few, but we know a need when we see it. Szymon, eat more slowly or you will choke to death."

"Yes, Mama," he responded with a full mouth.

"The safe house will be a beacon for God around here." Yana refilled Brody's glass. "There is much work to be done for Jesus since the war began."

The lights flickered overhead, but remained on. Brody thought of electricity at the safe house and how a power outage could be just what Jerome and the Malays were waiting for to attack the castle. But he said nothing of it to Yana.

"The whole world is being crushed by satan right now—every community," he said. "But we can't shine across the whole world. We're meant to shine in our own neighborhoods. God looks upon this house with favor because His faithful ones live here."

"We'll fight like soldiers and kill the enemy?" Szymon asked.

"Do not think violently, Szymon," Yana corrected. "Be a good boy."

"We're soldiers of love," Brody said. "We all play a part in the battle to share compassion to a hateful world."

After breakfast, Yana cleared the table. Before Szymon could dart away, she set a thick Bible in front of him on the table.

"Say your prayers and read while I clean up." She moved to the counter, her activity not diminished by having only one arm.

"But Mama, I did that last night!"

"It is a new day, Szymon! Brother Brody?"

"Each day needs fresh direction and inspiration." Brody drew out his own weathered Scriptures and opened the book. "Where are you reading from?"

"I don't know." The boy flipped through the pages randomly. "Wherever it opens."

"The day calls for courage. Turn to the Book of Joshua." He helped the boy find the right book and chapter. "As men of God, we rely on the Word of God to live each day. Go ahead. Read for us."

Brody explained the first few chapters to Szymon, knowing Yana was listening closely as well. She'd recently been laid off as a night janitor at an office building downtown. The church had helped feed them and the land owner was a kind man who required no rent. But Brody had already recruited her and Szymon, and placed Yana on the TROAS payroll to free her for full time homeschooling for Szymon and serving at the safe house. Since she'd met Binsa days earlier and knew several of the believing women under siege, she was a natural fit.

Szymon listened attentively to Brody's explanation of real courage being founded upon God's presence.

"So, we're not afraid of anything?" Szymon asked.

"No evil thing frightens us from doing good," Brody said. "We're safe with God, so we can risk our lives to care for others now."

"Soldiers of love?"

"That's what a real man of God is." Brody nodded. "We would be hopeless without Jesus' sacrifice, but now we have eternal hope, so we don't mind sacrificing ourselves for others. That's how people learn that we represent Jesus."

"How do they learn?"

"We tell them why we do what we do."

"But we can't tell anyone why you're here, right?"

"Just for a few days, then we'll tell everyone how God used you and your mama to save the women and children in the safe house. That's almost a hundred people now. Most of them don't know about God's love."

"A hundred! Mama, a hundred people in the castle!"

"I heard, Szymon. That is a lot of souls who need Jesus."

Brody prayed for their openness to God's will and influence, then the three went to the small back yard of weeds and bare ground behind the cottage. In the center of the yard stood a small catapult with an arm of heavy wood twelve feet in length. The supporting frame stood taller, held together by refurbished lumber, nails, and cables that Brody himself had fashioned over two days.

"Okay, Szymon, take your position."

The boy started to climb the eight-foot fence alongside the property.

"Szymon, be careful!" Yana cautioned.

"Yes, Mama."

Brody dialed Zayed who picked up immediately.

"Safe night?" Brody asked.

"We're still here," Zayed said from the safe house. "Greg sent us an update. He ordered windows and a new gate structure."

"And cameras," Brody added, "but none of that arrives until tomorrow. That leaves us today. Are you ready for packages?"

"The children are already gathered in the courtyard. Try not to break anything today, huh?"

Chuckling, Brody hung up. The day before, Brody had been adjusting the accuracy of the catapult when Zayed had reported one package had gone through the van window. He adjusted the catapult a little more in hopes that the packages would still land on target: the overgrown garden in the courtyard. The vegetation was meant to cushion the impact of the missiles so the contents didn't explode.

Behind the catapult, Yana wrapped a package in a t-shirt, then offered it to Brody to tie with yarn. Lastly, she weighed the bundle of sweets, instant coffee, and a Bible. Seven pounds was the perfect weight for the catapult's counterweight for that distance—to sail over the neighbor's house and property, across the two-lane street, and over three stories of the safe house building. On a table before Yana were medical supplies, toiletries, and more dry food items. Brody didn't dictate what she was to wrap in the packages. She knew what needs existed inside the castle since the besieged women and children couldn't safely leave for groceries any longer.

Brody loaded the package into the catapult sleeve, then raised the counterweight to a locked position. He stepped over to the fence to look down its length at Szymon who balanced on its top thirty yards down the neighbor's property. The boy leaned against a tree and the higher wall that overlooked the street. He looked both ways, then faced Brody. With a smile, the boy gave a thumbs-up sign. It was clear.

Back at the catapult, Brody took a length of rope, stood back, and released the counterweight lock. The arm levered down causing it to drag the precious package upward far too slowly to seem necessary, but then the sling uncoiled and the package launched skyward, the arc so high that the package faded in the blue morning sky.

Yana was at Brody's side with the next package, bulkier in size since it consisted of clothing, but the weight was the same. He loaded the catapult, locked the counterweight in the upward position, then checked for Szymon's all-clear signal. No call from Zayed meant the catapult was still on target. Brody knew that some of the packages the day before had landed badly in the garden where they'd exploded, but Zayed had said that was part of the adventure for the safe house children who rushed to collect the contents before the next missile landed. Any danger was managed by the older boys calling out warnings of incoming packages, and their poor mothers were left to accept the extreme conditions they were under to participate in extreme solutions.

Around noon, Brody called a lunch break and Yana fixed and served a small meal of bread, cheese, onions, and milk. Szymon admitted to seeing men with guns on the street and the same cars driving past repeatedly. But none of them had noticed Szymon or the packages flying high through the air every few minutes.

Together, Szymon and Brody sat on the frame of the catapult and ate like men as Yana continued to wrap packages.

"It's good work." Brody munched on his dry sandwich. "God likes His men doing this kind of hard work."

"I got two slivers from that fence." Szymon held up his palm. "See?"

"Did you get the slivers out?"

"Yes, with my teeth."

"Good man. Scars are good reminders of what God has brought us through."

"Like Mama's scars?"

Brody noticed in the corner of his eye that Yana had frozen. She had tried so hard to present herself as a normal functioning woman, but her appearance was now the subject of discussion.

"Exactly like your mama's scars. My best friends all have scars from suffering and hardship. They've learned the value of life. People who've suffered and still walk with God have something special. Hold those people very closely, even if they don't talk much about what happened to them."

"But Mama has only one arm."

"You just wait a few more days. You'll see when we go into the safe house. Those women and children will treat your mother like a queen."

"Why?"

"Because she has suffered loss, but she is still willing to give to everyone. She has riches from Jesus that money can't buy. Her character makes her wealthy."

Szymon turned and admired his mother with this fresh perspective. Yana had continued working, but Brody recognized a barely discernible smile reach her scarred face.

"You know what I think?" Szymon asked, then opened his palm. "I need more scars."

That night, after Szymon had gone to bed in the back room, Brody sat down at the small table where Yana was using her teeth and her one hand to let out Szymon's jeans.

"Yana, you've raised him well," Brody said softly.

She spit loose threads into her lap and started on the next pant leg.

"You have taught him more in two days than I have in two years." She didn't look up from her work. "He needs a father."

"He's not the first boy in this world who will become a good man even without a father. You've been keeping him in the Bible. The Lord is the best Father I've ever known. I lost my father when I wasn't much older than he is."

"And now you will leave. After he becomes so attached."

Brody folded his hands. Sometimes this happened. People received a glimpse of him when he visited their homes and they thought he was the answer to their woes. But he also understood Yana was deflecting; she liked having him around, too.

"You haven't known me long enough to discover that I'm a man with many flaws, like other men."

"I do not believe it. Two days is long enough to know someone."

"The things you may like about me aren't things that come from me," Brody said. "It's Christ in me. There are good men out there still—who are your age."

She dropped the pair of jeans as she stood abruptly and faced the window.

"You are only making this worse."

"I'm sorry, Yana." Brody stood. "I need to go help my friends while it's still dark out."

"Will you be coming back?"

"Yes, early in the morning, if that's okay."

"Of course. I will have breakfast ready." She faced him and wiped her wet cheeks. "I knew you would be leaving after the packages were thrown over the fence. It has just been so . . . helpful having you here."

"For Szymon."

"Yes, for Szymon." She smiled softly. "I am just a silly girl."

"No, you're not. You're a strong Christian woman who wants what's best for her son—and for herself. There's nothing silly about that."

"Working at the safe house will be very special." She took a deep breath, recovering her emotions. "Thank you for that job and all you have done."

"So, you'll be okay? You and Szymon?"

"Yes." She held up her head, her smile making it clear she was touched regardless. "Thank you for caring, Brody Sladrick."

"I'll be back in the morning to say goodbye."

Brody walked contentedly from the Nowicki cottage and into the Polish night air. His purpose in life seemed more fulfilling when he could remain near people who enjoyed the peace and security his presence provided. But he was also a man who enjoyed the spiritual battlefield. The Lord was his Champion and Shepherd. In such moments, he pitied those who sided against him—such as the Malay mercenaries and Jerome Wessel, if he was still local.

North of the Szczecin Old Town and Middle Town, Brody walked with his back to the moon for three blocks before he turned west in the Goclaw neighborhood. Sinister characters were lurking in groups—young members of gangs—around cars with expensive sound systems. Their music throbbed violence and vulgarity in Polish, Russian, and German. But once Brody approached the safe house street, the locals were scarcely seen. It was as if a proximity alert had been broadcast for civilians to stay clear of the operation underway to squeeze, pressure, and take over the castle where foreigners had found refuge.

Because Brody wasn't paying attention to any such danger, he walked within twenty feet of where he knew the Malays had parked to keep watch of the front gate of the castle.

He left the sidewalk and hopped into a neighbor's yard of sparse weeds. Now crouching, he approached the hedge alongside the sidewalk where at least three Malay thugs stood beside their vehicles. They were mere feet away. Brody could smell a cigarette and hear their quiet conversation.

Through the hedge greenery, Brody counted two more men to the left, both seated inside vehicles, their doors open. Across the street, the safe house gate was closed and quiet, but not dark. The gate was well-lit, along with the windows at street level. Much farther to his left, about fifty yards, Brody noticed another party of Malays, perhaps three men, who probably intended to intercept women or children before they reached the safe house gate.

Brody drew out two tranq-pens and held one in each fist. He closed his eyes to focus on his priority. The Malay toughs had been brought in by GLOW superiors. They were responsible for the trafficking, molestation, and rape of countless women, girls, and boys that year alone. Their presence declared their effort to remain steadfast in the exploitation of Ukrainian refugees—millions of them.

But for Brody, this wasn't about revenge. It wasn't even about justice. He knew he could trust God to deliver both in His own way and timing. Rather, what he was about to do was to humble and even bring fear to the hearts of wicked men.

He sprang from his crouch and dived over the hedge. His shoulder hit the sidewalk pavement, then he rolled to his knees. His arms were like windmills as he tranqed one man on his left, one on the right, and then pivoted around to stab another tranq-pen into a third. The cigarette settled on the sidewalk as Brody rose slowly to his feet to face the last two inside the open car doors.

His attack had been so abrupt, Brody saw the last two men freeze inside their car. He clicked both pens for new needles then kicked at the first open door as the Malay in the front seat scrambled to pull it closed. But Brody reached him first, then climbed on top of him to reach the second man in the back seat who was tranqed as he clawed for his sidearm.

Returning to the sidewalk, Brody studied the three men who were fifty yards away. They still weren't paying attention since the tranqing of these five had occurred without a cry of warning. Brody dragged the first three unconscious men between the two cars and left them in a heap. From each of the five, he took their footwear and locked all five pairs in the trunk of the first car. He knew that in the darkness, the other sentries wouldn't be able to see who he was or what he was doing. And though he hurried, he wasn't overall concerned about who might glance his way at that distance.

Next, he gathered phones, wallets, and food. He placed the items in a blue backpack he found in a back seat. Finally, he gathered their weapons and carefully disassembled them, removing key components and slipping them into the backpack as well.

With the backpack over his shoulder, he popped each hood and removed the spark plug wires to disable each vehicle. Since he'd spent enough time sabotaging those five, he climbed over the hedge into the adjacent yard again and retreated up the street to the nearest functioning street light. There, he sat on the curb and uploaded the contents of each phone to Greg's remote server in Iceland. Once decrypted, the phone contents would be instrumental in GLOW investigations, which TROAS would share with any agency actually interested in shutting down trafficking.

Brody dropped the phones into an overflowing trash bin, then returned to the street west of the castle. As he had walked with a limp days earlier with Ram, now he walked purposefully to let the remaining Malay besiegers notice that he was studying them. They probably didn't know who he was, unless Jerome was amongst them, but Brody wasn't relying on his identity to harass the culprits. All he wanted them to do was get nervous, call one another, and remain awake all night. The more tired they were for the following day, the better. Greg had big plans for the castle!

After circling the safe house for visibility, Brody returned to the cottage and slipped into the room he shared with sleeping Szymon. He set the backpack next to his travel bag. As he fell asleep in his clothes, he thanked God for the safe night and another day ahead to serve the needy in His name.

But he wondered if it would be his last day alive in Poland.

Jerome Wessel felt for a pulse on the neck of one of the downed Malays between the two vehicles. The man was still alive. They all were. The nearest street light was out, but the light coming from the safe house helped him survey the scene. Five men lay unconscious. And they wore no boots. *No boots?*

"Brody!" he hissed the name as if it were a curse.

It had to be Brody, even though Jerome hadn't seen him yet. This was one of his stunts, meant to demoralize the adversary.

After a late-night food run downtown, Jerome had returned to this. He called over the three men from the far left as he holstered his sidearm. Somehow, they'd missed the tranquilizing of their companions.

The three arrived at a run and pushed Jerome aside as they checked their buddies for signs of life. They spoke in Malay, ignoring Jerome. He'd been treated with disdain by them since he'd arrived, but he seemed to be the only one who knew what they were truly up against.

Crossing his arms, Jerome stood against the sidewalk hedge, returning the scorn of the mercenaries as they discovered what he'd already surmised: besides their boots, the phones and wallets of the unconscious men were gone as well.

"He's just trying to intimidate us," Jerome informed, but they wouldn't listen.

The unconscious men slowly woke. Jerome's food was taken and dispersed without gratitude. He thought about leaving Poland, but that wouldn't satisfy his hatred for Brody's undermining of American justice. Brody had to be stopped! Killing Zayed and even Binsa along the way now would just be bonus blood spilled in the name of honor.

The five recovered their senses, though not their boots. Jerome guessed their footwear was in the trunk, but no one could find the keys. Several men shouted curses at the castle, but Jerome doubted anyone inside was listening, or cared, or could understand Malay.

Checking his messages, Jerome still found nothing from Senator Pitney. Politically-based media were discussing her potential resignation, but Jerome knew this was much more than a political situation. GLOW was fighting for traction, and he'd had to admit to himself that Pitney and GLOW were indeed somehow connected. The Malays were definitely working for GLOW, which he'd concluded when they'd spoken to him in English about taking the castle occupants back to Malaysia to sell. Though Jerome hated GLOW, his own ideals paralleled theirs against TROAS. He might have been in Poland with them, but he was standing up for America by killing her enemies like Brody. *This was a war!*

As dawn neared, the mercenaries gathered to debate an assault on the safe house in response to the assault they'd endured overnight. Their plan had been on hold for days, hoping those inside would grow hungry and give up or slip up. Somehow, the women and children had enough food. The Malays' plan was to avoid the first floor windows entirely, which appeared to be booby trapped, and use a tall vehicle to access a second story window. All twenty of the besiegers could climb through a window in seconds. Any consequence after entering the safe house was dismissed by their impatience and rage that they'd been attacked, and their boots and phones taken. They were willing to risk more grenades inside rather than wait on the street another night outside.

A couple men went for another food run. Jerome had an appetite for the city's pizza, not that he expected the Malays to include him in the next food-sharing.

The storming of the safe house was scheduled for that coming night. Two men were dispatched to steal a semi that they would drive up and park under the second story windows on the west side. With little to do but wait out the day, Jerome walked back to his rental car on the east side of the castle to catch a few hours of sleep. Since the neighborhood was plagued with crime, he set his sidearm on his lap and fell asleep in the front seat.

He blinked awake only minutes later. Several utility trucks drove slowly past his car, their engines rumbling. Then three semis laden with glass windows parked on the north street.

After climbing out of his car, Jerome holstered his sidearm under his blazer. More utility vehicles and even a small construction crane paraded up the street. Who were all these people? Then the workers arrived—a bus full of men with tool belts and measuring tapes. These weren't people who lived in Goclaw, nor worked the Goclaw shipyards. These were city workers and construction crews, at least seven crews that Jerome could count from their truck emblems.

Drawing out his phone, he intended to report this invasion of utility workers, but he didn't know who to call. Very few people even spoke English in Poland. And who would he call in the US? No one remained at his side. Not even the Malays knew what to do. They stood watching in shock as dozens of vehicles and even more men directed their crews to work on the exterior of the safe house.

The front gate was open! But no Malay approached, and Jerome didn't step closer, either. It was likely someone from TROAS who knew his face would be near the front gate. Maybe if it had been dark, Jerome would've risked approaching, even blending into the scene of workers to sneak inside to finish the job . . .

A Polish man yelled at Jerome and waved him away from where he stood in the street. Jerome looked back in time to see the front axle of his car rise behind a tow truck.

Five more tow trucks cruised past and lined up to tow away the vehicles of the Malays. Then came a government highway painting crew. They painted lines against the curb and poured cement for poles with signs that indicated in Polish that there was no more parking allowed on that street—all around the castle.

Jerome searched on foot for a policeman. Someone needed to stop this! But no authorities seemed to be present. The siege was broken. The Malays were arguing with one another at the next intersection. They'd been paid to do a job—maybe hoping to take women and children into their own custody for brothels in Malaysia. But all that was over now. There were dozens of construction workers, far outnumbering the mercenaries, even those who still had functioning firearms.

Someone had convinced the workers to arrive, even in crime-ridden Goclaw, and Jerome knew who was behind the invasion. The Malays were killers, but Brody had shown complete disregard for the lives of the dozens of civilian laborers. Brody had brought in no security forces, and the laborers were ignoring the mercenaries entirely. That couldn't be safe!

Brody's apparent disdain for human life further enraged Jerome. The veteran operative needed to be put down like the self-righteous dog he was. Jerome discreetly drew his sidearm to make sure a round was chambered. He needed to use the chaos around the castle. If he watched for the right moment, he could get inside and put a bullet into Brody's skull. TROAS would die with him. America would be safe and Jerome could return home victorious.

For this reason, he moved to stand alone with his back to the hedge where he'd found the unconscious men in the night. By this time, all the parked vehicles had been towed away, and though bystanders from the neighborhood had arrived to look on, they were mostly gathered at the intersections where no traffic flowed on account of the army of construction vehicles. From Jerome's vantage point, he could see directly into the safe house courtyard through the now-open gate. Children milled around the garden as laborers came and went from their trucks outside. Women farther back in the complex could be seen walking on the second-floor balcony where Jerome believed the bedrooms lay.

The Malays regrouped near Jerome, but for once he had no intention of joining their number. Any attempt to work with them the last few days had blown up in his face. Now, he wouldn't involve them in his plans to get inside. The fact that they were still there led him to assume that they thought they might still complete their objective as well. After all, none of the laborers appeared armed or to be a threat.

Jerome guessed that since he was a lone man, even a dark-skinned man, he'd have a better chance getting inside than the Malays—all of whom appeared to be Asian and distinctly not Polish, let alone European.

One by one, the glass windows on the front of the safe house were swapped out. Jerome watched as first, second, and third story windows were changed in rapid succession, since so many men were concentrated on the single job. Other crews appeared to be doing the same on the west and east sides of the building, working away from the front. Maybe another crew was already starting on the back!

It was some sort of secure window glass. Jerome could tell by the way the light didn't travel straight through them. And once the windows were in place, the castle's dark interior hindered him from seeing through those windows at all. The glass wasn't only bulletproof, but tinted as well.

Then Jerome noticed a work crew operating the crane. They functioned separately from the window crews. The crane crew was installing cameras on the edge of the roof facing outward. At every interval and corner, two cameras were installed inside transparent glass domes—probably bulletproof as well.

The safe house was rapidly becoming a modern-day fortress. If he didn't know any better, Jerome would've thought Greg Rotz himself was involved! If Jerome was going to do anything, he'd need to act now, before that front gate was fortified and closed again!

Before his plan was fully formulated, Jerome started walking. He saw his moment and he reacted. A utility truck door had been left open. A vest and tool belt lay on the seat. Acting like he belonged, Jerome picked up the vest and slipped his arms into it, then draped the tool belt over his shoulder.

Seconds later, he was walking toward the front gate. Workers came and went, fetching tools, windows, or other equipment. He joined a procession of window couriers and even helped support two laborers through the iron gate itself.

He was inside! When he glanced back, he noticed the Malays were still on the sidewalk. They glared after him, perhaps wishing they'd thought to impersonate a worker before he had.

Jerome wished he had a hat to help cover his face, but he could only lower his head and hope he didn't come face to face with Zayed or Binsa before he found Brody. Whether he was alone or not, Jerome's cause was a righteous one. It was moral. It was justified. Brody would now die, and he would leave the castle without further incident. Well, Zayed and Binsa would be consolation prizes, if he could kill them on his way out. Where the Malay mercenaries of GLOW had failed, he would succeed as a federal agent of the Department of Homeland Security of the United States. This was his destiny. He could feel victory within his grasp!

❦

Kim Ward handed out the last parcel of toothbrush, toothpaste, and a tiny shampoo bottle to a woman with two young children. She was Ukrainian, so Kim told her "God bless you" in her native tongue, the only phrase Kim knew. The others in line dispersed, seeing that the table was now empty. Provisions from Brody's hurled missiles had brought the safe house hope and entertainment, but the items hadn't lasted long. At least everyone who had wanted a Bible had received one.

The siege, though, was in the process of being lifted. Kim had heard Zayed and Binsa talk about a man named Greg in America who'd used the money from Ram to pay with convincing amounts of funds for workers from all over the city to come and secure the castle. The overwhelming number of civilian laborers at once was meant to push the criminal element outside back into the shadows. But Kim wondered if she'd ever be able to look at strangers on the street in a casual way again, without suspicions, even back home. GLOW was everywhere, hunting in every neighborhood, stalking every child, marketing every captive . . .

She left the cafeteria and stopped on the edge of the courtyard to watch men with construction tools enter the front gate. Some carried large glass panels. They mounted the stairs and entered the bedrooms or lower levels for installations. Maybe the besiegers outside would see now that the grenades on the windows had been fakes all along, but with so many civilian witnesses around, it was too late for the traffickers to do anything dangerous.

Binsa and Zayed appeared on the second story balcony, observing the bustling activity of the laborers who'd clearly been instructed to coordinate their efforts with other crews around the city. The windows were replaced so rapidly that Kim guessed their work would be finished in a few hours.

She started to wave at Binsa to share their joy about the Lord answering their prayers, when Zayed suddenly drew Binsa away from the balcony and they disappeared together into one of the rooms behind them. Kim searched the courtyard for an idea of what had alarmed Zayed. All she saw were workers, none of whom seemed suspicious. But the gate was wide open. That had to be the problem even though the old gatekeeper stood monitoring the activities. Zayed must have recognized someone dangerous among the workers!

Kim retreated to the doorway of the infirmary and spied on the courtyard from the safety of— No, there was no safety. This was an evil world. God had promised spiritual safety in His arms, not at all in this physical realm where satan ruled for a little while longer. With that reminder of courage, she stepped away from the doorway when a firm hand yanked her backwards and spun her around.

It was Zayed, who must've descended to the cafeteria using a back stairway. His eyes were normally dark and frowning, but now they were wide with obvious concern.

"What is it?" Kim asked. "Who is it?"

"Look." Zayed remained cautiously behind her. "See the dark-skinned man going up the stairs? He's not carrying a window. Look at him. The guy doesn't know where to go because he's not one of the workers."

"Who is he?"

"He's hunting for me or Binsa. But he's not GLOW. He's a US federal agent. Under his jacket is a gun. That man is here to kill us."

"Why? I don't understand. Where's Binsa?"

"She's hiding. I need to—" His face softened as he interrupted himself. "No, Brody would take advantage even now. This might be our last chance to reach this man's soul. His name is Jerome Wessel. Remember how you spoke boldly to Ram Garrity?"

"Yeah. Why?"

"Jerome won't listen to me, but he'll listen to you."

"But I've never even met him. He won't know who I am, will he?"

"No, he won't know who you are. Tell him the Lord sent you. That's no lie. You're here for a reason, Kim. Jerome is one of those reasons. He may not listen to anyone else. If he won't listen to you, then convince him to leave."

"But . . . he's armed, you said!"

"Yes, I know." Zayed set a hand of reassurance on her shoulder. "He's not here for you. Maybe if you can get him talking and get his attention, I can get behind him. Either way, we need to protect Binsa from him. He's tortured her before."

Kim followed the killer with her eyes. He did walk like he was stalking someone.

"I'm . . . just a girl, Zayed. He won't listen to me!"

"No! You're not just a girl. You spoke to Ram. I heard you. He listened to you. And more importantly, the God of heaven and earth listens to you."

Nodding, Kim tried to sense his same courage. She had seen God do amazing things the past couple of weeks, preserving her when others had been harmed or even killed.

"If he kills me," Kim said, "I guess it'll be worth it if I die while sharing the gospel, right?"

"That's not something a girl would say. That's something a giant of faith understands."

"Do you recognize anyone else?"

"No, not yet. The GLOW agents outside are mostly Asian, I think. We'll be able to spot them easier."

"Okay, so I just tell him about Jesus?"

"Nothing else. I'll be close by, okay?"

Kim's heart was racing. She licked her lips and reflected again on all the drama God had preserved her through.

"It would be awesome to turn his heart, right?" she asked nervously.

"It would be a miracle."

"Okay." Kim started out, then looked back at the Saudi. "You've got my back, right?"

"I do. You're not alone."

Nodding again, she knew a million things could go wrong before he could fully protect her, but at least if she died now, she wouldn't die without purpose or without anyone knowing why or where.

Children dashed around her, several playing catch with a foam ball sent over from Brody. She reached the corner stairwell and ascended with several workers, but her eyes were on Jerome, the killer. No, not a killer. A potential child of God. Jesus had died even for him. That's all she needed to know and communicate. Somehow.

She reached the second-floor balcony and started toward Jerome. The man was muscled, easily more than twice her body mass. He was trying to appear casual as he looked into open doors and slipped into rooms for a moment. Maybe he thought he blended in with the other workers, but not to Kim. Not now that Zayed had pointed him out to her.

As Jerome entered a room, he reached inside his jacket. Kim didn't turn to search behind her for Zayed, but she instead trusted that he was somehow nearby. She followed Jerome into the room.

Two workers were fitting a secure window into the frame while two others carried away the old glass. Jerome peered into a closet, then opened another door that joined that bedroom with the next. Binsa could be in any of those rooms, so Kim knew she needed to speak up now. She put her back to the wall.

"Jerome!" she called before he passed into the next room. She was surprised by the authority that came from her voice—something older, something not of herself.

He spun and searched the room for danger, but then his eyes settled on only her. His hand partially withdrew his gun from its holster. Kim could now see it. The workers ignored them. She didn't blame Jerome for seeming confused. After all, she was just a seventeen-year-old blond in hand-me-down jeans and blouse, someone he probably already noticed and dismissed as a Pole or Ukrainian.

"How do you know me?"

Kim took a careful step toward him, then another. She remembered what Zayed had told her to say—what her purpose was.

"Jesus has sent me to be here at this time to meet you."

His eyes narrowed.

"Where's Brody?"

"I haven't seen him."

"He's not in here?"

"No. If he were, I'm sure he'd be here to talk to you himself."

"You're lying. I know he's here. He's left his mark all around the streets."

"I wouldn't lie to you. From what little I've heard about you, you need to know the truth and nothing less."

"So? What's the truth? Where is he?"

"I don't know about Brody. I guess he's out there on the street like you say. The truth that I know is that you're lost without God. He's been waiting for you to come to Him."

"He's not waiting for me." Jerome chuckled, his hand still on his sidearm. "Where's Zayed?"

"Probably nearby. Jesus died for you, Jerome. He wants you to trust in Him for your forgiveness of sins."

"*Forgiveness?* Why? So I can become like all of you, forgiving every criminal at the expense of national security?"

"I don't know anything about national security," Kim said. "But I think what you're doing right now is criminal. Don't you think your sins will catch up to you?"

"Oh, I'm not worried. I'm a federal agent. The bad I've done isn't as much as the good I've done. It'll all work out."

"Who decides that?" Kim shook her head. "I'm just a girl, and I know that's not the way God judges us. You can't rely on yourself for that kind of chance. You need to rely on God's mercy for—"

"Shut up!" He lunged and grabbed her by her collar. "Just shut up! Zayed's nearby? Call out for him. Zayed! You're stalling for him. I know it!"

"No, I'm not. I'm trying to—"

"You're coming with me. You want to play games with me? I have some friends outside who'd love to get their hands on you!"

"What?"

His hand moved to her arm, directing her whole body. He was so strong! When she resisted, he slapped her, just hard enough to knock her down. Then he drew out his sidearm and she felt the muzzle in her ribs as he wrestled her back to her feet.

"March!"

She couldn't breathe. He forced her from the room and onto the balcony. There was Zayed!

"Stay back!" Jerome pointed his gun at Zayed, then back at his hostage. "I'll shoot her, Zayed. You know I will."

Zayed backed away as Jerome forced Kim toward the stairs. Several workers moved aside, obviously not understanding the scene since they spoke no English.

Kim knew not to fight her captor. Her mind screamed for a way out, but with a gun against her ribs? By him holding her up with his strength, Jerome kept her from falling as he marched her down the stairs. Zayed didn't run away, but he kept his distance. Kim hoped he didn't do anything to get himself shot, but she didn't like the idea of being handed over to someone outside. Who could that be? The besiegers? Or had the people she'd run from joined the scene as well?

They reached the courtyard. Several workers identified the danger and an alert was called out. Jerome rushed her toward the gate, but the gatekeeper was on his feet, his hands on the gate. Just then, a commotion out on the street divided the gatekeeper's attention.

Then Kim saw them. Asian men with guns. *The besiegers!* They ran toward the open gate. The gatekeeper started to swing the gate closed.

"No!" Jerome yelled. "Open it. Let me pass!"

The Asian men with guns shouted something in another language, clearly wanting to get inside. The besiegers were finally getting the nerve to attack the castle, but the moment couldn't have been worse for Jerome.

Two Asians fired wildly at the gate and gatekeeper. Kim fell to her knees, covering her head, as bullets zipped past. The gunshots were so loud! And behind her, she heard the screams of women and cries of the children as they ran for cover.

The gate finally slammed shut, but Kim could still see through its mesh and bars. The gunmen's charge was cut short. Construction workers inside and out stopped to watch.

Jerome's hand on her arm weakened. Kim turned on her knees to see blood pouring from his neck. *He'd been shot!* His eyes were wild. He dropped his gun but Zayed was there to catch him and lay him on the pavement, cradling his head.

"It's . . . not fair." Jerome gasped. "I was always right. I deserve . . ."

"Hang on, Jerome!" Zayed held the man's neck wound with his palm. "Jerome, come on! Not like this!"

Jerome faded quickly and his eyes closed. Blood pooled all around Kim. The Asians peered through the gate mesh to see what damage their bullets had caused, but no one had been struck except Jerome.

A shout in another language outside brought the Asians to attention. Construction workers, led by Brody Sladrick, closed upon the Asians faster than they could think to respond. In seconds, they were disarmed and their wrists were bound by electric wire or tape.

"There's no joy in this death." Tears ran from Zayed's eyes. "He's finding right now the terrors of sin and death. God has rescued us, but Jerome chose everything besides rescue."

Kim nodded, her head bowed. The dread she'd felt as a hostage melted away in the sadness she had for this poor stranger. Women and children gathered from all over the courtyard. Some wept. Though Kim knew they didn't know who Jerome was, their crying was appropriate. He'd died in his sins, rejecting his Savior. The way Zayed held him, perhaps others thought he was a close friend of the Saudi's, but Kim knew Zayed was just a man of God anguishing over the death of a foe.

The gate was opened by the keeper, and Brody slowly walked in. Kim stood and embraced him, finally face-to-face. These were real heroes, giants of the faith. Though she was young, she was proud to know such men whose equals she'd likely never meet anywhere else.

An ambulance arrived and the police finally came. The many laborers on the scene made the authorities' neglect of the neighborhood impossible.

When food trucks arrived, Binsa spoke Russian to order the workers to line up for pizza and sandwiches. Kim was willing to serve, but other women from the castle took charge. It was their way to thank the workers for breaking the siege. Some of the Ukrainian refugees carried their new Bibles as they mingled with the workers.

"This whole neighborhood will change now," Brody said next to Kim as they watched the courtyard transformed into a picnic area. "Even in this seemingly godless world, the Light continues to shine in darkness. You're part of that, Kim."

Kim didn't trust her voice to speak. She was so happy, so honored, so heartbroken—all at once.

As if a call had gone out to the whole Goclaw neighborhood, more members of the community arrived, poor and needy, curious and lonely. A one-armed woman, perhaps a local believer, drifted through the crowd, smiling and greeting everyone. Kim almost wondered who was paying for everything, but then she remembered: she was! The money that Ram had left her, she'd turned over to Binsa and Zayed. It was God's money now, and it was obviously going to good use.

The founding of the Polish safe house had been successful, though not without tragedy, suffering, and hardship. Kim was learning this was the path of the faithful in this world.

Marcy picked up Brody at Tampa International Airport's chartered flights section. The car she drove was a new leased town car, much better than her old blue car from Iowa, which had disappeared during the Justice Department's assault on TROAS. Though Marcy was still leery about moving freely around the city, Greg had assured her that they were no longer wanted for human trafficking. The fact that Brody was openly returning home was definitely a good sign.

After Brody filled out shipping orders for Ram Garrity's body to be returned to California, he carried his sole backpack across the tarmac to where she waited.

"I don't know how you fit your whole life into one backpack." She embraced him, then held her beret on her head through a gust of wind.

He smiled down at her. She thought she could see new lines on Brody's weathered face.

"I never found much use in many possessions. There's a rumor going around that we can't take it with us anyway."

Once in the car, she shared her hopes for things to return to normal.

"No, I don't foresee normal on the horizon," Brody said. "We can trust the Word of God when He promises tribulations in these last days, but we know that Jesus has overcome the world. We're safe in Him."

"Well, I was hoping for a return to normal at least for TROAS operations."

"Senator Pitney's assault on us won't be the last. The movements against our Lord are spiritual, and they've not disappeared. The next assault may be even worse than we've experienced thus far. GLOW is still out there, even if Pitney has been unseated as its Executive. We won't be out of the woods until we graduate to glory."

In Tampa's Ybor City, outside the rundown warehouse where TROAS had been moved, Brody climbed out of the car and surveyed the neighborhood. Marcy joined him, but said nothing as he took in their new environment. His eyes surveyed the storefronts of perversion a block away as well as the provocatively-clothed young men and women who loitered outside. Homeless people abounded, as did their night shelters constructed from wood or cardboard scraps, raincoats, and tarps. Any remnants of grass or bushes were brown. Garbage lay heaped in the gutters, cluttered around storm drains and piled against building walls. Half of the buildings nearby were uninhabited, remnants of the cigar factory era, now molding, unpainted, and partially collapsed from the last hurricane.

"Seems perfect for us," Brody finally said.

"That's what Greg said." Marcy smiled. "It's not the old apartments high above Tampa, but we're closer to the people here."

"I can imagine no better upgrade for TROAS, but we still might want to consider some security protocols."

"I think you'll appreciate what we've been doing while hiding for our lives."

They weaved their way through the construction site next door, then mounted the warehouse steps to the second story. Brody heartily embraced Greg and laughed off their challenging time apart, like family happy to see one another again. Marcy counted herself blessed to witness their closeness. Neither the danger of the past nor the dilapidated environment of the present could dampen their reunion.

Greg introduced Hector and Gabriella, and Brody spoke in broken Spanish to their guests, welcoming them as Greg had already done, but Brody also asked about the immigrant's faith in God. For a few minutes, Marcy and Greg listened in as Brody shared the gospel with the single father in ways that Greg hadn't been able to do well through translation apps.

Brody finally brought them all close, even Gabriella, so they could pray together. It was a short prayer by Brody, whose voice broke when he mentioned Zayed and Binsa. The two had remained in Poland a few more days. He also spoke of Kim Ward who had flown home to her family in Seattle, and of Ram Garrity's family who would soon receive his body. Theirs was a work that not many heard about, let alone joined in to serve, and Marcy sensed that such loneliness brought them even closer as servants.

Marcy trailed behind Greg and Brody as they walked through the warehouse and Greg showed him his plans for walls and new TROAS apartments. Hector returned to work on other floors above. Greg offered Brody a breakdown of expenses necessary to establish themselves as a fixture for Christ in the community of Ybor.

"This is good, Greg." Brody returned the tablet to the young man. "But we're just three of the five who'll be living here permanently. We need to hold off on some of these plans until Binsa and Zayed get back tomorrow night. Right now, we can set up a few things, but we also have a wedding to plan, if I'm not mistaken. You two will need an apartment of your own eventually."

Marcy blushed.

"Not to mention," Greg grinned, "whatever's going on with Binsa and Zayed!"

Though Marcy was inclined to celebrate their recent victories a little longer, she'd learned that God's people didn't gloat over their enemies or live today in the triumphs of yesterday. There were new challenges to prepare for.

With that in mind, Marcy was tasked with organizing a list of household items to order once the apartments were fabricated within the warehouse—they would need bed frames, mattresses, towels, and cookware to start with. Her job was to turn their new location into a home, however temporarily. Greg set about implementing security plans, digitally and on site, and Brody joined Hector to plan the repairs needed, and set about calling plumbers, electricians, and builders. With Brody around, nothing was done halfway.

Due to supply issues and other manmade problems intended to create government reliance, Marcy sometimes had to search on the internet for simple everyday items until she found them in stock somewhere. For her this was a reminder that as permanent as they set up this new home, the world under man's rule was rapidly deteriorating. It wasn't just man's evil deeds that were breaking down all of society, but man's attempt to reign supreme without the God of the Bible ruling as sovereign. Everything on earth was temporary and trials in this life couldn't be taken too seriously, she knew. Eternity awaited them.

Binsa and Zayed arrived the following night. Joined by Gabriella, Marcy attached herself to Binsa, and led her older sister around the warehouse floor, describing the plans that Binsa herself would need to perfect. The Nepalese woman was especially thrilled to learn that the new TROAS headquarters would double as a shelter for local needs. It would make them less secure as an organization, but they knew God's purpose would prevail through any vulnerabilities they opened themselves up to as servants of Christ.

The next morning, Marcy woke to find Brody and Zayed had left while it was still dark. When Marcy asked Binsa where they'd gone, she said they'd left on a sudden mission from Greg. When she asked Greg what was happening, he took her hand and sighed, clearly nervous.

"I don't want to say anything yet." He glanced toward Hector and Gabriella against the wall. "Let's just pray God steps in as only He can."

He let go of her hand to return to his computers, but Marcy remained staring toward Hector. Why all the secrecy? Something was wrong. Brody and Zayed wouldn't leave like this unless something terrible had happened. But it couldn't involve Hector. The Colombian refugee had been nothing but pleasant as he'd worked hard in the building and cared for Gabriella. Brody wouldn't have left them with Hector if he were dangerous.

Marcy didn't like to be kept in the dark, but she tried to trust her friends to do what was best, even if it meant she remained ignorant. She trusted Greg, and above all, she trusted God to work out for good whatever was happening.

Brody stood motionless as he looked out the window behind the curtain in a dark hotel room. The room he'd rented for one night was on the second floor of Sunset Inn off Interstate 20 in central Texas. Behind him, both beds remained undisturbed and he'd brought no luggage. This wasn't a vacation.

His phone rang. He answered it immediately.

"I have three women down here," Zayed stated. "They say another is upstairs cleaning rooms."

"Antoneda?" Brody asked. "Is it her?"

"The women here call her Maria. But I think it's her. They were all given new names when they arrived."

"Their employer?"

"Rory Azalea." Zayed's voice was muffled as he conferred with the women downstairs. "They think he's from South America judging by his Spanish. He's upstairs with her."

"Okay. Call Captain Fletter and stay with them until he arrives."

"I'd rather join you upstairs," Zayed pressed. "Rory might be trouble."

"I'm counting on it. Keep them safe, Zayed. I'll be down as soon as I'm finished up here."

He turned on his phone to record and gather evidence. They'd already alerted Captain Fletter to be on standby with his border patrol personnel and trusted INS contacts to treat the undocumented women with mercy and understanding once they were recovered.

Brody left his hotel room and paused on the balcony of the U-shaped hotel. Below in the courtyard, a pool reeked of stagnant water. Several diapers floated in one end. Lawn chairs lay scattered nearby, their frames broken and their material torn from misuse or abuse. Less than half the rooms appeared occupied in the rundown establishment.

Keys jingled to Brody's right. A dark-skinned man in a tank top opened a door.

"Housekeeping," he announced. "It's checkout time. Come on, people. Time to go."

A husband and wife ushered their two young children from the room and along the balcony toward the stairs. On their way, they passed a woman in her mid-twenties pushing a housekeeping cart. Her uniform was wrinkled and she kept her head lowered as the family moved past. Brody noticed her hair from her ponytail was pulled over to cover the left side of her face, deliberately it seemed.

He walked slowly toward the man with the keys. Rory Azalea appeared to be in his forties. If Brody hadn't been in a hurry, he would've had Greg run the man's name to find out everything about him. But for now, what he could see of him would have to do. These women needed to be set free.

Rory's gut spilled over his belt buckle and tested the limits of his stained white tank top. His oily black hair was in a perfect bowl cut, though messily parted on the left side. A faded tattoo on one biceps identified him as some sort of military serviceman, probably foreign. But he was long past his prime.

The housekeeper approached and Rory stepped aside so she could park her cart in front of the doorway and enter the now-vacant room. From the balcony railing, Rory watched the room where the housekeeper disappeared from Brody's sight. From his pocket, Rory drew an e-cigarette and puffed on it. But it seemed to be dysfunctional. He shook it and tapped it on his thigh as Brody moved up the railing to stop beside him.

"Maybe it's a sign," Brody said with a nod. "Those things are terrible for you."

"Yeah." Rory glanced up, cursed, then tossed the e-cig over the side where it plunked into the rancid pool water. "It wasn't mine anyway. You want past?"

"Nah, just killing time." Brody leaned against the wall.

"Is your room okay?"

"It'll serve its purpose."

The housekeeper came and went from the cart.

"I noticed you're alone," Rory said. "A man away from home—maybe you'd like some company for a couple hours?"

Brody glanced at Rory who jutted his chin toward the housekeeper.

"That depends."

"Depends on what?" Rory frowned. "Either you want company or you don't. It's not a difficult decision. She's too chubby for you? I've got a few others downstairs."

"That depends," Brody repeated.

"Depends on what? Look, what's your problem, *hombre?*"

"May I speak to her first? I think she's just the person I'm looking for today, but I want to talk to her first."

"She's not here to be talked to. She's here to earn money."

"Talking never hurt anyone. Come on. You're right here. You can listen."

"She doesn't speak English."

"Then I'll speak Spanish."

One side of Rory's mouth twisted as he studied Brody. The prospect of a paying client won out.

"Maria, come out here," Rory ordered in Spanish. "This man wants to talk to you."

A few seconds later, she appeared in the doorway, her head and eyes down. She gripped a toilet brush in front of her with both hands as if she would use it to defend herself if necessary. And she may have already fought for herself. Brody noticed a swollen lump on her brown face only partially concealed by her loose hair.

"I live in Florida," Brody said to her. "Not long ago, my family welcomed two people into our home. The man's name is Hector. His little girl's name is Gabriella."

Her head lifted and her eyes widened.

"Gabriella?" she whispered, then eyed Rory. "They're in Florida? I was told they're in California. When I'm finished paying for our immigration, I can join them there."

"What is this?" Rory shifted his body away from the balcony railing. "Who are you talking about?"

"I think you've paid enough for your immigration," Brody said to Antoneda, "though you should've entered this country the legal way. Are you ready to join your family?"

Rory reached to the back of his waistband and drew out a weighted baton. He snapped it to its full telescoping length and pointed it at Brody's face.

"She's not going anywhere! This is where she belongs. She has a debt to pay!"

Brody used his foot to slowly roll the housekeeping cart away from the doorway until it stopped directly between him and Rory. He did it so casually and intently that a look of complete disbelief came over Rory's face.

"Come on, Antoneda." Brody held out his empty hand to the woman. "It's time to go."

Antoneda took one last look at Rory, then she darted to her left—past the cart and beyond Brody. Brody sensed that she stopped, turned, and stood close to him as he continued to stare down Rory.

"Are you a cop?" Rory lowered his baton to hold it to the side, ready to swing. "You didn't identify yourself."

"Is that what you use on the girls to keep them in line?" Brody gestured at the baton. "I'm going to need it for evidence."

"Evidence?" Rory's face hardened. "I'm not—"

Brody used both hands to shove the cart hard into Rory. Rory tried to retreat and keep his balance, but in the process, he dropped his defense. With a sharp twist, Brody yanked the baton out of Rory's hand. Then Brody swung low and hooked behind one of Rory's knees. With all his strength, Brody lifted and pushed.

The pimp's eyes bulged and his mouth opened in a soundless scream. His arms flailed in the air as he went backwards over the balcony railing. The splash in the murky water below made Brody grimace. When Rory surfaced and sputtered for air, diapers bobbed in the water next to his head.

Police lights flashed from the parking lot. Brody collapsed the baton and turned toward Antoneda.

"Don't be afraid. The police will ask you some questions, then you'll leave with me. We'll be in Florida with Hector and Gabriella before midnight. You ready?"

"I've been ready for weeks!" Then she rushed into his arms.

When Brody and Zayed brought Antoneda into the warehouse, Marcy wept and regretted that she'd questioned Brody's secrecy at all. She understood now that even Greg had protected the operation by not confiding in her or Hector, in case Antoneda wasn't really at the Texas site.

Three exciting days of homecoming passed, interrupted only by meals and hot summer nights. Then Brody called them together for a meeting. It was evening. The water utilities had finally been installed along with the hot water tanks, so everyone had enjoyed their first hot shower. Whatever news Brody had to share, his eyes were beaming.

"The Lord has given us another special mission." Brody bowed his head as if praying, but then Marcy realized he was simply emotional. "Zayed and I will need to leave immediately."

"You're leaving already?" Marcy glanced about the warehouse floor. "But everything is still . . . such a mess. And you guys just got back."

"The Lord's calling precedes our living quarters." Brody's barely contained emotions seemed to grow until he clasped his hands together to stop them from shaking. "Our most ruthless human adversary to date needs our help, whether she knows it yet or not."

"I thought we won against everyone," Marcy said. "Even Jerome died in Poland."

"Yes, Jerome has passed on," Brody said. "But I'm talking about the Executive."

"Go where you must go, Brody," Binsa said, taking Marcy's hand. "We'll manage just fine here, won't we?"

"*Senator Pitney?*" Marcy asked. "We're going to help that woman? She hasn't been arrested yet? I thought our other government friend was bringing her to justice."

"Greg?" Brody invited. "Why don't you fill in the details for everyone?"

"I'd wondered what GLOW leadership would do since their head, Senator Pitney, has been compromised. Media reports have said she's withdrawn from public and state responsibilities, pending certain investigations. Her retirement announcement a few days ago was expected, but I looked deeper. The senator's own network went after her. They've taken her overseas, probably to protect themselves from anything she might disclose under interrogation here in the States."

"Maybe she has just run away, true?" Binsa asked.

"Except, I have footage," Greg said. "She was taken by force. One of her bodyguards was even hospitalized during her kidnapping. The media is doing what it does best: censoring the real story since it doesn't fit their narrative. Pitney's been a champion of globalist ideals for years. Now exposed, everyone, including the media, are all distancing themselves from the story by shifting public attention."

"Make no mistake," Brody said, "GLOW won't be permanently weakened through Pitney's removal. And it may be time for us to stop calling her Senator Pitney. This is now a rescue mission. I'll be using her first name, which is Nicole. She's a seventy-year-old woman who's now the victim of her own lieutenants fighting for control of the multi-billion-dollar trafficking organization."

"How do we know she is still alive?" asked Binsa. "If she is such a liability to them, she would be better off dead to GLOW, true?"

"Normally, yes," Brody said. "But she held the war chest for GLOW for so long, Greg thinks they're holding her prisoner for a few days or weeks until they're sure they have all the resources she controlled."

"She's in Bangkok," Greg said. "And it won't be easy going in, Brody. They know you there."

Marcy watched his face to see if his popularity in Thailand would diminish his willingness to risk his life for such a woman, but he merely nodded.

"Yeah, we'll take precautions. If there's a chance to bring Nicole out of the darkness she made for herself, we have to try. Most people in this situation would leave her to die or try to kill her themselves. But we're serious about our lives in Christ and His life in us. We have to do this. TROAS has the resources and expertise. This may be our biggest moment yet. Even Nicole's soul matters."

Though Marcy had objections, she kept them to herself now. As mature as she thought she'd become, she realized her natural inclination to offer forgiveness, compassion, and grace wasn't as unconditional as she'd thought. She'd forgiven her own captors who'd held her as a youth, but evil people far away who'd tried to hurt her, people she'd judged but never met, were suddenly difficult to love. Nicole Pitney was one of those people. It seemed that God was using Brody's intentions of mercy to flush out Marcy's own hidden animosities.

Their work still continued in the world, and it seemed God was still sanctifying them in the world as well.

❧

Kim Ward stared at her face in the bathroom mirror, not recognizing the woman she saw. It wasn't only her forehead scar that seemed to have changed her appearance so profoundly. No, it was something deeper, something inside. She'd aged, but not on the outside. Maybe it was her eyes? No, she decided. It was her soul.

She took a deep breath and turned from the mirror. In her bedroom she picked through hanging outfits. What to wear? One of her mother's oldest friends worked at a local radio station in downtown Seattle and she'd asked for an interview. Anne wanted to hear about her experiences as a trafficked "victim." But Kim didn't feel like a victim. And she didn't know what to wear that afternoon to speak to her newfound confidence in life. God hadn't protected her from being harmed, stripped, or trafficked, but He *had* protected her from being lost. People in the world were still as lost about their identity and purpose as before she'd been kidnapped. But now she was seeing life and its meaning more clearly. To her, that didn't sound like a person trapped in victimhood.

That weekend, Kim had attended morning services at their small chapel, but only because she'd heard her father call the elders ahead of time. He'd told them not to make a big deal about Kim's kidnapping, only her return. When she'd asked him how he'd known that's exactly what she needed, he'd said he'd spoken at length to Brody Sladrick by phone.

"What did he tell you?" she'd asked.

"He reminded me that we're followers of Christ. We accept everything that's happened to us as a gift. People want gory details of abuse and wickedness to satisfy their own morbid curiosity. Some offer condolences to survivors only to make themselves feel better, yet they leave survivors still feeling like victims. Brody seems to know about what you went through, doesn't he?"

"Yeah." Kim had smiled. "Binsa spoke frankly to me when I was in Poland, too. Since she knew I was a believer, she expected me to see my trauma from the right perspective. That helped."

"From the right perspective?" her dad asked. "You pushed it all down?"

"Oh, no, nothing like that. I just see it all from God's perspective now. I can't imagine a better path for my life than what He's allowed to happen. I understand how to categorize what's happened."

"People won't understand that. Most professing Christians in America certainly won't."

"I have to try to help them understand. I wouldn't have ever met Dakota or Felicity, or led Ram to Christ, or worked with Binsa and Zayed. Poland isn't this terrible place in my mind. Terrible things happened there, but I witnessed God's hand every step of the way. Dad, people are going to heaven because of me. How can that be anything but a happy ending? I see the results, and the results make the journey worthwhile."

Kim chose a skirt that was her late mother's and a dark blue blouse. The people in their church fellowship hadn't treated her like a victim, but she guessed she wouldn't receive that kind of understanding from a worldly radio station, even from her mother's old friend. But she'd accepted the interview to try to reach someone.

Her father waited for her in the living room. She'd never seen him so proud of her. Now she understood that he'd worried about her mediocre participation in Christianity as a girl. Indeed, she'd gone to youth groups simply because it was her way of life. But no longer was she a mere participant. God had offered her something personal, and she'd accepted it wholeheartedly.

"Ready?" Her father, Jack, stood and took up his car keys. "You look nice. It's not raining. You want to walk?"

"No, the car is fine."

The radio station was only eight blocks away. Kim sensed her father's nervousness, but she felt no such concern. She knew how wicked and misguided the world was, so she expected all the wrong questions to be asked by Anne, the interviewer. All she prayed about was that she gave the right and true answers.

At the station, Anne Vorkin embraced Kim and her father. They hadn't seen the middle-aged woman since the funeral two years earlier. Anne explained that due to the subject matter they were about to talk about, the station manager wanted to record and edit the interview rather than air it live.

"We really want to know how you survived and what brought you home," Anne said. She wore too much makeup, Kim thought, maybe to cover up her perceived flaws and a few wrinkles. But Kim wore no makeup. "We're so glad you accepted our request, Kim. People are going to be listening to this all over the world!"

They set up Kim in a small booth with a headset. A makeup tech applied powder to her nose and forehead since a wall camera was filming for a podcast.

"Just speak naturally and from the heart," Anne coached. "Are you ready?"

Kim smiled at her dad who nodded from an adjacent lobby.

"Yeah, I'm ready."

"Okay, this is Anne Vorkin with seventeen-year-old human trafficking victim, Kim Ward. Kim, we're so glad to see you back home. What an ordeal you've had! You're a local girl here in Seattle. How are you coping with everything that's traumatized your life so horribly?"

"Thank you for having me, Anne. I think I coped during my experience of being kidnapped because I'd been taught beforehand to trust in God's love no matter what happens to us. And I think I'm coping now because I was trusting God while being transported by van, plane, and ship around the world to be sold to strangers in Europe. I was so scared, but God kept me calm."

"Yeah, that's what we really want to hear about. Maybe we'll edit out that God stuff, just so you know. But let's keep going. You were kidnapped at the stadium here in Seattle, right? That's what the police reports say."

"So, do you want to hear about the girls I was with? How one of the human traffickers died in my arms? And how they abused me?"

"Yes! That's what our listeners are into. Can you talk about all that?"

"Yeah, I can talk about all that." Kim smiled patiently. Through the glass, she saw her father shake his head, as if he thought she was making a huge mistake. "Let me first tell you about Ram Garrity, one of the worst human traffickers our country has ever known. Then I'll tell you about Felicity and Dakota, two girls older than me who survived as well."

"Awesome!" Anne licked her lips. "Let's start with that Ram Garrity person. What did he do to you?"

Kim spoke slowly and without interruption about her abduction in Seattle and her initial fear about what would happen to her. She described her panic and attempted escape during transport, then how she'd been recaptured and wounded on the head. Anne listened wide-eyed to Kim's account of the holding houses in Texas and meeting Ram Garrity. In detail, she shared about her desperate prayers for help and rescue which didn't seem to be answered at the time.

She told of her transport into Mexico, the girl they never saw again from the plane, and her transfer to the Chinese ship. Next she described about sleeping on the floor of the cabin, then her time with Dakota and Felicity and her counsel to them to endure with dignity and to trust God regardless. Kim told Anne—the first time she'd told anyone—about the little foreign boy who escaped with her in Poland, and about their flight to the Goclaw safe house for Ukrainian refugees and those also trafficked. And that the little black boy had disappeared after delivering her to the castle refuge.

Then she'd met Ram again, and she'd told him about Jesus, and he'd died in her forgiveness—and in the forgiveness of his Savior, Jesus.

"And now, I'm thinking about graduating high school," Kim said, "and getting back in touch with Binsa and Brody Sladrick again. I want to go back to Poland to serve God there."

"Go back?" Anne shook her head. "But what happened to that little black kid who led you to the safe house?"

"I don't know." Kim shrugged. "The Bible does talk about angels that God sends us sometimes. All I know is that God was with me the entire journey, even though bad people did bad things to me."

Anne stared at her for a few more seconds, then seemed to collect herself and looked at her notes.

"Two hours of interview," she said, "and I don't think I can use any of this. This isn't a religious program."

"Did you want me to lie?" Kim prayed for Anne in that instant—especially if she were the only one ever to hear the interview! "Everything I've told you is true. You can talk to Felicity and Dakota or Brody or Binsa."

"No, no." Anne's eyes were downcast. "I'm sure it's all true. It's just useless. I mean for us. You talk about God too much. You talked about Jesus the whole time. We can't use any of it."

Kim waited in silence for a moment before the right words came.

"Maybe the station can't use what I've said, Anne, but you can."

Kim took off her headset and left the booth. Her father embraced her and chuckled.

"You had me worried, you know that?"

"I know. But I had to do this interview. Just this one. That's it."

"Kim?" It was Anne. She'd left the booth. Nervously, she picked at a cuticle for a few seconds. Then, she rushed forward and wrapped her arms around Kim. "Thank you."

Kim embraced the older woman tightly, then held her hands as they drew apart.

"You have my number," Kim said. "Call me when you want to talk. God will help you through it."

Anne sniffed and nodded, then turned and walked away sobbing.

CHAPTER SEVEN

Nicole Pitney flinched as steam pipes in the ceiling suddenly rattled. They rattled every thirty seconds. She'd counted. So there was no sleeping.

The door to her bedroom clicked then opened. A man in a black suit and tie set a bag of Thai food on the floor, then closed and locked the door. Nicole didn't rise from her unmade bed to recover the food. She couldn't eat it anyway. It was too spicy. A couple decades earlier, when she'd been a junior GLOW leader, she'd enjoyed spicy red shrimp wrapped in a spring roll and dipped in fried garlic. But she was seventy years old now. Her years of indulgence were no more.

Not only could she not stomach the food, she couldn't resist the treatment by her captors. She knew all of them — all younger men and a few women. Without her, they wouldn't have risen to the status and wealth they now enjoyed. They were powerful while she couldn't even attack the single suited man who delivered her food three times a day.

Her holding room was uncomfortable, but it wasn't a traditional cell. She'd visited this exact room somewhere under a Bangkok university over twenty years earlier when she'd replaced her predecessor. He'd lost his throne and she'd become the Executive in his place, quickly modernizing GLOW and securing it as the leading global trafficking network it was meant to be.

But now she was the one who sat there, waiting to be replaced. No, she'd already been replaced. She was really just waiting for the formalities. A peaceful transition of power was expected from her. If she participated willingly, her death would be swift, even though it would be public.

If she didn't submit willingly, well, she didn't want to think about that. The rules were clear, and she'd known going in that she might be replaced someday. This is what happened to leaders who failed within GLOW, and she had definitely failed, nearly exposing GLOW on the world stage and their worldwide ambitions with it.

This was evolution, natural selection, survival of the fittest. She didn't appreciate her end, but she understood it. It wasn't about ambition, but fitness to lead. There was nowhere for her to go now but to the grave. Her successes would become the ground for growth for the organization's next cycle.

The floor toilet in the corner gurgled. She'd used paper towels to clean it up a little, but it was still disgusting and smelly. Twice, she'd fallen backwards onto the rancid opening, her legs too weak and unfamiliar with the squat-style of the Far East. At least the faucet still ran, though only with tepid water.

Any day now, they'd come for her, then the sacrifice would occur. She couldn't bear imagining their eyes upon her once the knife cleared her throat. They wouldn't even blindfold her. The ritual demanded that the others participate by observation. By being complicit in her death, the GLOW leadership would be bound to each other. Loyalty came above all else, even over money or life.

Her purple pant suit was the only clothing she had since that is what she was wearing when they'd taken her from her doorstep. The driver and two bodyguards she'd trusted for years hadn't been able to help her. They knew the rules. This was the way things were done.

The door clicked and opened again. Nicole stood and buttoned her jacket. Even though it was a little wrinkled, she thought she still appeared poised. She still stunk like the toilet she'd fallen onto, but GLOW had always been about appearances.

A tall black man in a silk shirt entered. He wore a gold ring and diamond earring.

"So, it's to be you, Bosco?" Nicole raised her chin. "I suspected as much."

He sneered at her as he strolled confidently into the room. The prime minister of the Democratic Republic of Congo had always been her critic. Bordering on insubordination, he'd used his influence within GLOW to push her to extremes, perhaps hoping she'd make spontaneous errors. In response, Nicole had held back trafficking contracts from his country, hindering his climb up the ladder for power. The feud had lasted for years.

"The accommodations suit you." His African accent was sharp. He planted his large frame inches from her and crossed his arms. The fifty-year-old was tall and muscled, and he looked down at her with pure triumph in his eyes. "I've picked out the perfect gown for you tomorrow. You understand your place?"

Her gaze fell from his face. There was no sense in remaining defiant. Bosco had won.

"I know what will happen," she admitted softly.

"You're not answering my question. I want to hear you say it."

When she'd claimed the throne of GLOW, she hadn't humiliated her predecessor like this! He was gloating.

"I'll relinquish my position."

"And?"

"And die."

"Good." He chuckled. "If it were up to me, the ceremony wouldn't be so formal. I'd treat you like the cheap whore you've been your whole life, selling yourself for favors and money."

She swallowed at the threat. He would give her to his men, even at her age, just to humiliate her further. It was his right as successor if he could show the others she wasn't cooperating. His attitude now was the product of the years he'd spent as a sadistic junior trafficker in his own country.

"I'll pass the scepter to you, Bosco. Consider it done."

"You know you've hurt us all, and you didn't even take out Sladrick like you assured us you would."

"He's part of your inheritance now. Be careful or he'll bring you to ruin as well."

His smile faded. He turned and stalked out the open door. Before the security officer closed the door, Nicole glimpsed a white gown that hung in plastic on the wall in the corridor. *White*. She hated white. Purple had been her color since a child. Bosco certainly knew her profile better than most. This was just another way to goad her in her final hours.

She sat gently on the bed. Just six months ago, she'd been enlarging GLOW, bringing the world to its knees through the undermining of international policies and misappropriation of the UN's money machine: the US Government. Just two months ago, she never would've imagined she'd be here now, defeated and about to be executed. There was no one to stand beside her, no one to defend her, no one who'd care about her passing. There wouldn't even be a Massachusetts gravesite. To the world, her death would be a mystery. An anonymous death. That had never bothered her before, but it did now.

Her vision of global rule beside her peers now seemed so pointless. Everything meaningful she'd accomplished was just passed on to Bosco!

Now she was alone, and this was just the way things were. The rules said so.

Brody Sladrick wore a disguise as he flew from Stockholm to Bangkok. He was now William Holms, statesman and philanthropist in the foreground, but GLOW mastermind in the background. The real William Holms had been quietly arrested and held in a Swedish safe house by sympathetic police officers, and they'd agreed to hold the criminal until Brody's mission was completed in Bangkok.

When Brody landed at the airport north of the city, he was met by two Thai escorts, young men he guessed were associated with the 14k Triad organization who were often used as soldiers for GLOW. Brody was an inch taller than the real William Holms, and he didn't think his blond hair coloring or fake larger nose matched the real article, but Zayed had assured him he was a close twin.

After checking his identification, his escorts then took his two pieces of luggage and loaded them into a limo. Brody climbed into the back and silently stared out the window as they reentered the city. He hoped Zayed was having the same good fortune playing the part of a Hungarian named Miklos Csak, another GLOW somebody in his country.

The last few days had been a hurried blur of details and trusting against unknowns as Greg had found two GLOW men Brody and Zayed could impersonate. Infiltrating a high-level GLOW meeting was simple enough, but rescuing an elderly woman and getting out alive was another matter. They knew plenty about their doubles, but they knew very little about what they were walking into.

The real William Holms and Miklos Csak had confessed to a bare minimum for what awaited Brody and Zayed in Bangkok. But they didn't have time to stick around Europe to wait for more intel from the arrested men. The most important intel seemed to be that they'd need adhesive fingerprints, fake contact lenses for eye scans, and even blood vials for DNA checks.

Since Brody had performed so many rescue missions in Bangkok—even just six months earlier for Aidan Nevins—he noticed they were approaching the horse track at the Royal Bangkok Sports Club. It certainly helped to have his escorts show him the way instead of troubling his Bangkok contacts for leads to Nicole's whereabouts.

East of the sports club, they pulled into the remodeled Grand Hyatt, complete with a rock fountain out front that depicted certain Buddhist figures in its containment wall. The water, like everywhere in Bangkok, was brown.

His escorts carried his luggage through the lobby to the front desk. In the plush lobby, with an adult-sized white elephant statue at its center, Brody noticed a familiar face. Zayed didn't look up from his phone as he sat on a flowery upholstered sofa with tea before him on a coffee table.

The attendants took Brody's visa and checked him into the hotel, then they led him to the elevators. They ascended to the twelfth floor where they used a pass code to let him into his room. He was given a phone, then they bowed slightly, offered him the *wai* gesture, and left his room.

Now alone, Brody went to the room window which faced west toward the track. To the north was the Erawan Shrine, the figure seated on its ungodly throne. Farther west was the massive Chulalongkorn University complex. The US embassy was a few blocks southeast of the hotel, but Brody wasn't trusting too many diplomatic avenues these days. Zayed had shown himself to be in the city already, so they had each other to rely on.

Binsa had contacted the local church, which would be on alert locally, but Brody hoped they wouldn't need to place anyone else in harm's way. After all, they weren't trying to take down a local GLOW thug. They were entering the lair of GLOW itself. Two hundred of the most powerful members had been invited for what Brody thought would be the transition from Nicole to a new Executive. Such was GLOW's arrogance and power that they were coming in person, daring anyone to interfere or challenge them.

Brody was tempted to call Zayed and ask if he'd found out anything since he'd arrived first, but they needed to remain incognito. Their rooms had been assigned, maybe even bugged.

To complicate matters, the humidity was causing havoc with Brody's nose epoxy. He'd reapplied the nose in the bathroom on the flight into Thailand, only two hours earlier. Two hours of epoxy time? It wasn't long enough, but he didn't have much epoxy left, and going without a facial disguise was out of the question. His face was too recognizable among corrupt Thai officials as well as GLOW administrators.

He climbed into the shower and pulled the glass door closed. After searching the showerhead and tiles for cameras, he peeled off his fake nose and washed his face several times, removing any natural oils. When he turned off the water, he dried while still in the shower, then applied fresh epoxy. Using a mirror from his travel kit, he adjusted the nose just so, hoping it would now stay on far more than two hours.

In his room, he dressed in loose trousers and a light cotton shirt. His footwear were dress shoes made of tough mesh, with no socks.

The GLOW phone rang. He picked it up. Thumbprint identification was required. Brody slipped his hand into his pocket and drew out William Holms' print adhesives in a metal cannister. He had three copies of right and left-hand fingers, but he quickly applied only the right thumb. The screen unlocked. A text appeared: *eleven o'clock tomorrow night*. Brody waited for more, like a location, but apparently, he was expected to know that already. The real William Holms hadn't cared to reveal such intel. Regardless, he had more than twenty-four hours to wait now—and that with a failing facial disguise.

Taking his personal phone, Brody typed a message to Zayed:

Brody: *We have 24 hours. Let's get N now.*
Zayed: *Where?*
He paced the room a few minutes.
Brody: *Must be near. Maybe here? Let's look.*
Zayed: *I'll take bottom half floors.*

Brody agreed and left his room. The hotel had sixteen stories, which meant eight apiece to search for signs of someone being held prisoner. That was, of course, if Nicole was even still alive and was being held at that location.

Starting on the top floor, Brody walked slowly down the hallway of suites and doors, considering every food tray left outside a door or any "Do not disturb" signs on handles. The hotel was definitely a five-star, but its tech wasn't fully modernized in regard to cameras, so Brody couldn't simply ask Greg to scour hotel footage for signs of Nicole.

By the time Brody reached the twelfth floor, he realized how ineffective his plan was to find Nicole this way. There were no GLOW security officers stationed outside any room. Like always, GLOW was maintaining appearances. She might not even be held in the high-priced hotel. Nevertheless, Brody finished a survey of his eight floors before he texted Zayed again.

Brody: *Negative.*

Zayed: *Negative.*

Brody: *Thot it was worth shot, but we're too much in dark. Better wait till tomorrow night event.*

Zayed: *See you there.*

Though Brody was tempted to ask how Zayed knew where to go, he decided against it. Cryptic communiques were best. Besides, the following night would see many officials leaving the hotel for wherever they were supposed to go. Hopefully, Brody could merely join the flow of traffic, or GLOW would send escorts again to ensure everyone arrived on location. By now, his thumbprint had confirmed that William Holms was indeed on site. He would be expected.

Back in his hotel room, Brody did what he found most difficult to do—he waited. The instant he felt anxious and considered touring the city for something to do or someone to help—he knelt and prayed. Right now wasn't the time to visit old contacts or recent friends around Bangkok. He'd come to do a job and he needed to see it through. It was possible that the grace he hoped to show Nicole would touch her heart. Then he would give her the gospel message of Jesus Christ. From past, personal experience, God's grace was that impactful.

When the sun fell across the haze of Bangkok, Brody was standing at his window, looking down at the troubled city. For many, this was a playground for sinful indulgence, but he knew it was a spiritual battleground. Souls were in bondage in that city—physically and spiritually. Its corrupt authority structure made the perfect backdrop for a GLOW meeting.

Brody tried to sleep late the following morning, but ended up waking early and ordering room service. He dreaded waiting all day with little to do, since anything he might do outside the room might reveal his identity. Someone who knew the actual William Holms could expose him—since he wasn't a true lookalike. Or his fake nose would peel off from perspiration, showing everyone he was a fraud and intruder. Then word would go out, and Brody would have to run for his life. Coming to Thailand as himself over the years had been dangerous, but coming now to infiltrate GLOW was a potential death sentence. Death didn't concern him as much as the possibility of failing Nicole, or endangering Zayed more than necessary.

He napped, prayed, and ordered more room service. Finally, evening arrived. As eleven o'clock approached, he showered again and carefully re-applied his nose in the secrecy of the shower stall. When he emerged, he dressed in a light suit and jacket, pocketed two tranq-pens, then left the room.

In the hotel lobby, he stood admiring the white elephant figure until he noticed Zayed emerge from the elevators. The Saudi accompanied two other Westerners. Brody watched him guardedly as they walked through the lobby. Zayed glanced at him and gestured with his head just enough that it communicated volumes. The supposed Hungarian had connected with other GLOW advocates, and Brody was to join them.

This was one of Brody's prayers being answered. Outside the hotel, several vans pulled up to transport the meeting attendees to the location. Before entering a van, each attendee's thumb print was checked by an armed suited man. Brody pressed his forefinger against his thumb print to secure it for use. The epoxy on his nose was questionable, but at least the adhesive on his fingers was holding. He chose a seat in the rear of the van behind his friend, Zayed, who was visiting in French. Since the van's interior was dimly lit, Brody hoped he could remain unobserved even as two women joined him at the rear. They spoke Portuguese and conversed about another wildfire that raged across the Spanish border.

Four vans departed the hotel and drove north then west, past the Royal Thai Police Headquarters. A moment later, they turned onto Henri Dunant Street and stopped in front of Siam Square. Brody leaned down to see out the window at his elbow. They'd traveled only a couple of blocks. The hotel was still in sight straight ahead. Siam Square was bustling with tourists, sex peddlers, and drug pushers.

The van doors opened and Brody was the last to disembark. He touched his nose plaster, hoping it remained sealed as the humid night air caused him to sweat.

Instead of entering Siam Square, a walkway lit by candles led into the buildings of Chulalongkorn University. Brody trailed behind the procession that seemed to know from past visits exactly where to go.

The candles weren't the only items standing along the sidewalk. As they neared the buildings, Brody counted nine security personnel who stood like statues. Their short Chinese machine guns were hard to miss—slung across their chests and gripped by both hands. He recognized this as the point of no return. Zayed was ahead but he didn't look back. Anyone who didn't belong in that procession should've fled, but Brody wasn't there to think of his own safety.

The crowd narrowed to a single file line at the outside access to basement stairs. Here, suited security men required a retinal scan to continue. Zayed passed through without trouble. A few people later, it was Brody's turn. A red light scanned his right eye from side to side. He was waved forward to where he was required to surrender his phone. It was the GLOW phone he'd been given, and now he returned it. Since he'd left his private phone in his hotel room, he was cleared of any broadcast frequency when his whole body was scanned an instant later.

Before he descended the stairs, Brody looked back toward Siam Square. Four more vans had arrived, and another parade of attendees was joining them, maybe from another hotel.

The darkness below lasted only until Brody reached the first landing—a linoleum hallway beneath a university building. A suited Hispanic man stood at an open door where the others passed, and Brody followed them through.

Naked orange ceiling bulbs lit a steep and narrow staircase deep underground. The walls were wet stone, the handrail icy cold. Brody felt a jolt of confidence as he thought of Psalm 139. Even here, as he descended into the bowels of the earth under the control of wicked men, God was with him. Thus, he couldn't fear the talons of satan's henchmen on earth, nor the threats of violence to bring him into compliance. He prayed that Zayed was no less stoic even though they were entering the lair of something dark and unexpected.

After descending about three stories, the passage opened to a long corridor supplemented by cement doorways and wall engravings of multi-limbed creatures—beasts or spirits. Between the engravings, water dripped down sweaty walls and pooled in clogged gutters that smelled like mildew.

The flow of people poured into a natural cavern of which the dark ceiling was too high to see. Brody imagined bats along the ceiling. Fire torches instead of electricity burned black smoke at intervals on the walls. One hundred people already stood idly in the room the size of a full court gym, with a four-foot-deep natural stage of limestone at the far end. Upon the stage stood a low, gold altar. Drifting through the small groups of people, Brody reached the edge of the stage.

At the stage, he noticed firelight shimmering off a wall farther behind the stage and altar. Another passage! But did that mean there was another exit? He couldn't imagine trying to escape with a prisoner up the narrow and guarded way by which they'd arrived.

The next crowd of attendees arrived, then a heavy boom sound shook the air. The corridor door had been closed. As the last group merged with the main body, Brody took that moment to climb smoothly onto the stage by throwing a leg over the ledge. Without looking back, he walked stiffly across the stage, past the gold altar, to the rear passage that became more apparent as he approached. He wasn't sure how many people might've been watching him from behind, but he guessed at least Zayed would notice he was doing some quick recon.

Brody entered the limestone passage. As soon as he turned the corner from the sight of the main room, he placed his back to the limestone wall and touched his nose. The epoxy was peeling from too much sweating.

He heard echoing voices ahead so he continued with caution. The passage of limestone became a hallway of cement walls with a low ceiling lit by lightbulbs once again. Closed, nondescript doorways led left and right along the hallway. A figure clothed in a black robe and hood crossed the hallway from doorway to doorway ahead of him. Thankfully, the person didn't look toward him.

Trying the first door on his right, Brody found that it opened to a dark room, so he slipped inside. He felt the wall for a light switch and flipped it on. It was a filing room of some sort, eight-by-twenty feet, with seemingly no computers or digital access. A small vent in the ceiling cycled air. He resisted the urge to pull down a few files off the nearest shelf. No one would probably ever infiltrate this far again, but he couldn't allow himself to be distracted by gathering intel.

Turning out the light, he checked the corridor. Yes, at the far end past a dozen more doors was a stairway leading upward. Another way out! If he could find Nicole now, he could escape without further incident. Zayed could find his own way out, which he would understand when Brody didn't return from his short recon.

Muffled voices reached Brody's ears, but in the cement corridor, the sound was distorted. He had a tranq-pen in one hand, but if he came upon more than one foe, he risked someone alerting others. Even though he suspected the other stairway was an exit, they were still far underground, and to where would it exit? It might emerge at the police station, where many officers were corrupt and probably already owned by GLOW. Such a gathering as this, involving so many powerful people, was certain to be already on the police radar.

At the next door, he put his ear to the metal door. Running water! He opened it a crack.

"It's occupied," said a man's voice with an Australian accent. He stood in a black robe before a toilet. The sink's water ran freely. "Give me a minute."

Brody didn't mind taking advantage of the man's vulnerability. He tranqed him in the shoulder and lowered him to the floor. The man was in his sixties and several inches taller than Brody, but Brody couldn't scout around for another robe. Before anyone else entered the bathroom, he peeled off the man's robe and fit it over his own clothes. The robe ended mid-ankle on Brody, but when he donned the droopy hood, he knew he'd found the answer to his peeling artificial nose.

The hallway was still clear, so Brody dragged the man by his shoulders down to the file room where he left him on the floor. As a final thought, Brody checked the man's pockets. He found a phone and a lighter, both potentially useful.

Now in his latest disguise, with the hood hanging low and his face shadowed, Brody walked slowly up the hallway to the stairs. He looked up three stories to a metal door illuminated by a single orange bulb.

A door opened behind him. He turned to see five robed figures emerge from a room—five in black and one woman in a white gown. *It was Nicole!*

One robed figure looked back. Brody froze.

"Let's go, Dante," a robed woman said with a wave, then continued.

Brody hustled to catch up to the five in robes. He made six. As he trailed behind, he acknowledged that two of the five were women and three were men. One of the men held onto Nicole's right arm and guided her awkwardly before him in the narrow passage. She wasn't a willing participant as he suspected.

They reached the cavern section, then emerged into the large room where torches burned black smoke, illuminating about two hundred observers.

Nicole was led to the gold altar on the stage where she was forced to stand atop it. The robed figures gathered in a semi-circle around her and the altar. Brody was second from the right, his head so low that he struggled to see anything past his hood but the feet of those nearest him. He turned his head only slightly and saw Zayed below the stage in the front of the crowd. It was too dangerous to give him a signal. This was their moment to act, but any action taken now only seemed foolish since it would end in their demise at the hands of dark hearts.

A man on Brody's left stepped up to Nicole and turned her to face him. Brody lifted his head enough to watch. The man produced what looked like a black electrical cord and bound her wrists. Nicole's eyes were red, her cheeks hollow, her frame slumped in the otherwise beautiful white gown. They had defeated her somehow to the point that Brody guessed she would welcome death without needing to be bound at all. She didn't appear abused or beaten, but perhaps starved or sleep deprived. There seemed to be no will to live left in her.

Turning her to face the crowd, the man then took his place again next to Brody.

Then the man to his right stepped to the altar. From beneath his robe he drew a twelve-inch dagger, its hilt gold, its blade polished steel. Brody's head jerked up at the prospect of them killing Nicole without further fanfare. He couldn't stand by for that!

But then he checked his impulse to step in. The man laid the dagger at the foot of the altar. Brody glanced about with concern that he'd revealed himself by flinching at the sight of the knife. In that instant, his head was raised enough to allow torchlight under his hood. He saw recognition on Zayed's face. Before anyone else could notice that he didn't belong, he lowered his head again and stood still as stone.

The man now at the altar pushed back his hood to reveal his face. He was a black man about fifty, his brow stern, his shoulders muscular under the robe. Brody knew the man's face from somewhere—maybe a televised briefing or a magazine or UN assembly footage.

"Brothers and Sisters!" His baritone voice with an African accent shook the cavern air. He raised his arms and fists like an athlete claiming victory, but no one cheered or moved. "We have come so far under our banner, but the planet cries to us for greater change. The people are ripe for rule. Our vision is nearly fulfilled.

Greatness is the victor's reward! I will lead us to that greatness. That is my honor to accept for you. And we will know triumph together in this new age of enlightenment!"

His face turned toward Nicole. Brody was close enough to see her tremble in the cool air, but she didn't raise her eyes to look at her tormentor. He lifted a thick arm and pointed a stubby finger at Nicole's face.

"This woman is the past. Who among us will deliver us into the future? From ruin to riches, from blood . . . to bounty?"

Brody's eyes widened. Something inside him screamed, *Now!* He stepped forward smoothly. There was no way to know the schedule probably carefully choreographed in secret, but the man on his left had done his part, and the man on his right had called for blood. It seemed to Brody that he would be the man to shed that blood. Even if he wasn't the man expected to pick up the knife, he hoped that no one robed or otherwise would interfere in the order of the ceremony.

He stooped between the speaker and the altar and picked up the blade. The gold hilt was ice cold. When he rose upright, he passed a tranq-pen from his left hand to his right, so that he held both tranq-pen and knife in his right.

The speaker backed away and returned to the semicircle. Brody stepped up behind Nicole so close that his breath rustled her auburn hair. His left arm reached around her, across her chest, so that his forearm touched her chin. Pulling her into him, he reversed the knife grip in the folds of his robe.

"Don't fear, Nicole," he whispered. "Jesus Christ hasn't forgotten you."

He thrust his fist into her back along her spine. The tranq-pen easily pierced her gown, all while Brody dragged the tip of the dagger across his own ribs, making a cut through robe and jacket and flesh. The pain was so sudden and almost paralyzing that he nearly dropped the knife. Blood soaked his hand. Nicole went limp, but he held her up.

With a motion as if removing the blade from her, he drew his arm downward. The moment seemed to demand flourish, so Brody raised high the bloody tool, crimson up to his wrist. He held the knife above for a few more seconds, counting on everyone to note the blood and not his reversed grip on the hilt.

Slowly, he lowered his arm and dropped the knife to the altar stone. Sheer adrenaline stopped him from collapsing or gasping aloud. He lowered Nicole to the altar, though careful to continue holding her close and bowing over her as his own blood soaked and trickled onto her white garment.

Finally, he rose, keeping his hood on, and returned to his place in the semi-circle. He felt so many eyes on him that he was tempted to try to read their faces that night to indicate their intentions, but he remained still, his side bleeding under the robe. His wound felt to be six inches long and diagonal along his ribs. Untreated, he would bleed out, but since he hadn't penetrated deeper than his ribs, he believed he had some time.

The speaker beside him raised one arm to still the crowd.

"One man answered, and no man intervened. You are not witnesses but participants. Until tomorrow evening's gathering, we conclude this night's burden and transition of power. From ruin to riches."

"From blood to bounty!" the crowd said as one in a monotone voice.

The crowd below turned to mingle and whisper amongst themselves, but Brody noticed a definite shifting toward the exit. The far door opened. Only Zayed continued to stare up at the stage and altar. Brody wondered if he too thought he'd slain Nicole. The blood shining on his robe might've seemed to have come from her.

People funneled out of the cavern room. Brody squeezed his eyes shut for a few seconds, channeling the pain as of broken ribs, but he knew he'd only slashed as deep as bone across them.

"You idiot!" The black man at his side grabbed Brody by his robe's collar and nearly lifted him off his feet. "That was supposed to be me! We agreed--!"

Brody was nose to nose with the brute, too weakened to fight effectively. In his flash of anger, the man's face revealed his sudden surprise, though he didn't recognize Brody.

Since the tranq-pen was still in Brody's blood-soaked fist, he clicked the top for a fresh water-soluble needle and eased it into the man's own ribs. He let go of Brody and staggered backwards, clutching his left side.

"He's having a heart attack!" Brody warned an instant before the man dropped to the ground.

"Bosco!" A robed woman rushed to his side, shrieking. "Bosco, hang on!"

Backing away, Brody let others kneel over their comrade. Zayed leaped onto the stage as Brody waved him to hurry.

"I'll get help!" Brody announced, then held his side and limped toward the rear cavern passage. When he glanced back, Zayed was collecting Nicole in his arms. Nobody noticed or stopped him.

In the passage, Brody fell against the wall for a few seconds. The sharp pain threatened his consciousness. There was no easing the agony except to hope he hadn't caused an immediate, mortal wound. He continued forward and reached the hallway and the first door. He threw it open. It was the records room. While holding his breath against his misery, he grabbed an armful of files and threw them at the door and hallway. Again, more files, until he'd heaped them inches deep. Zayed staggered over the paper debris, his arms easily carrying Nicole's thin frame.

"Keep going!" Brody waved and drew the lighter from his pocket. He lit one file on fire, then dropped it to spread. Finally, he went to the fallen man whose robe he'd worn and dragged him into the hallway and beyond the growing flames. No one would be coming up that hallway for at least a few minutes.

Brody hustled after Zayed who'd reached the steep stairs ahead of him. At the bottom of the stairs, Brody tugged off the robe and gasped against the movement that enflamed his side. Tearing desperately at the robe, he found a seam that gave way. He wound a strip of fabric around his chest, hoping to stem the flow of blood.

He started up the stairs, pausing every few steps and watching Zayed draw farther ahead. When he reached a landing, he collapsed and rolled onto his back. Smoke from the fire drifted along the ceiling, rising to the promise of outside air. A door slammed above or below. Brody couldn't discern the echo.

Now out of breath, he understood this was his end. It wasn't a bad end, not after the tumultuous life he'd lived. At least he'd see his Lord soon. And he'd see Gail again. Zayed would see Nicole returned to America to face the consequences of her many crimes. But surely not before he gave her the gospel message. She would hear of the One who'd died for her so she might live in the freedom of complete forgiveness.

※

Nicole forced a yawn to clear her ears as the plane reached cruising altitude. But her ears were a minor annoyance compared to the discomfort of the deep bruise along her spine. She still couldn't believe she'd wakened—*alive!*

The man named Zayed had given her fresh clothes from the rear cabin. He'd said the jeans and sweatshirt belonged to a young woman named Marcy who sometimes traveled with them, but Zayed hadn't yet told her who "they" were. Even now, the Middle Eastern man was back in the private cabin tending to the man with the wound. Nicole had found enough blood on her white gown to realize someone had bled quite a bit to protect her, but she wasn't yet sure when or why. All she could remember was standing on the gold altar, waiting for Bosco to cut her throat.

The cabin door opened and Zayed emerged.

"He's awake." He was a solemn man, yet kindness was apparent in his eyes. "And he's asking for you."

"What's his name?" Nicole rose unsteadily and he caught her. "Oh, whatever drug that was isn't out of my system yet."

"It'll wear off." He guided her to the door. "Just sit with him. He's a little weak himself."

Nicole entered the cabin and Zayed closed the door behind her. She eased into a padded chair next to the queen-sized bed where lay a disheveled pale man. The sheet reached only up to his waist where his naked torso revealed fresh bandages across his ribs. But this was a man clearly acquainted with hardship. His arms, shoulders, and torso showed traces of whitish scars, some many years old. He was a soldier of some sort, which didn't surprise her since it would've taken nothing short of a small army to free her from the clutches of that Bangkok cavern.

The man stirred. His hand went to his bandage and his eyes opened. His eyes were brown and his hair was blond, though it appeared to be dyed.

"That man doesn't have a gentle touch." He chuckled then winced. "It's Nicole, right?"

"Yes, though I'm not accustomed to younger men calling me anything but Ms. or Senator Pitney."

"No formalities here." He limply waved his hand. "When I shed blood for someone, I start to think of them as family, if I hadn't already."

259

"Well, I . . . thank you for your sacrifice. I was trapped, you understand. I would've willingly died that way only to avoid a worse death."

"And now you can live to consider a better eternity."

Nicole blinked.

"That's an odd thing to say, but I'm still grateful. Was it Bosco who stabbed or cut you?"

"Bosco." Brody shook his finger in the air. "Ahh, the Prime Minister of Congo. I knew I'd recognized him."

"He's been after my position for years. My recent misfortunes in Washington gave him the justification."

"Sometimes what seems like a misfortune is just an opportunity—an opportunity for yourself."

"I've thought of that, though I'm not sure how to recover what I've lost. I'll be arrested unless you have a safe place to take me. I'm assuming you've thought all this through?"

"Yes, I have. We have."

"I have money—beyond measure."

"It's okay. We're rich in other ways."

"So, it was Bosco who added another scar to your canvas there?"

"No, this was self-inflicted during the ceremony. Once I took the knife, I was expected to wet its blade. In the folds of my robe, I cut myself and tranquilized you. It was an illusion for them meant to save you from any serious injury."

"Oh." Nicole's hand went to her mouth. "I had no idea. Zayed didn't say anything. You could've died for me, young man, and I don't even know your name."

"We all must die, Nicole." His eyes—yes, this was a man who knew hardship, but such gentleness! "It's not when we die or even how we die that matters, but that we die well. Dying for you to live again would've been a good death to undergo."

Nicole was overcome with emotion. His face was weathered, but not unhandsome. She'd paid for lovers and their company her whole life, but here was a man so genuine, so compassionate, and heroic!

"You don't even know me."

"I know you. Give me your hand." He opened his muscled hand next to him on the bed. She leaned forward and placed her small hand in his. "You are a woman who has gone her own way for a lifetime."

"It's a hard world for a woman like me to make it in."

"All these years, I never imagined how we would meet—or that I would one day hold your hand and pity your life."

"Pity me?" With her other hand, she wiped at her tears. "Yes, my future is unknown. I've been ruined to some extent, but I'll find a way to come back."

"No, not this time. Nicole, you may want to run back to what you were, but others have already taken advantage. You've been replaced."

"But the vision still carries on. The planet will see renewal and I could still lead. I'm sure I can reinvent myself and—"

"*No.*" His hand tightened on hers. "Nicole, it's over. It's time to stop. Yes, the vision will continue. Whatever may come of this world, it's now out of your hands. New, young men and women have risen. Now, you must think of your soul."

She studied his firm hand and his face, so pleading yet so forceful.

"My soul?"

"Nicole, it's *me*. You've searched for me and I've searched for you. Finding each other like this—it's no accident. I would've given my life for you, but only because Jesus the Son of God loves you and gave His life for you already."

She froze. The words seemed to numb her. Seconds passed before she jerked her hand away to rub it like she'd been stung by a scorpion.

"Who are you? You're not GLOW!" She was offended enough to try to make her words biting, but they came out more inquisitive than accusatory. "What do you mean, I've searched for you?"

"Admit that you know I care for you, and I'll tell you who I am."

"Enough games!" She stood abruptly, then felt silly standing over this defenseless man and sat down again. "Fine. I admit you care for me. I never had a son, but if I did, I'd wonder if you were him the way you look at me."

"Very well." He took a deep breath. "You have called me your greatest enemy, or so your soldiers have sworn when I have captured and questioned them."

She blinked.

"No. It can't be."

"But it is. I'm Brody Sladrick."

Staring at him, she realized she could see it now. He was older than sketches and blurry photos she'd seen through the years. Instead of fear or anger, she found herself trying unsuccessfully to hate someone who'd proven his compassion. *He'd saved her life!*

"What do you want with me?" She held up her chin. "You have a plan, no doubt."

"You were created to be loved and to share love."

"I don't want to hear your vile lies."

"It doesn't matter what you call me or the Lord God who made you. You've already admitted that I care for you. Any opposition you attempt now is just stubbornness. I've shown you God's love. It breaks through the emptiness of your vision for humanity and this fallen planet."

"You're . . . twisting everything up in my head."

She slowed her breathing. This was worse than Bosco capturing her and gloating over her, humiliating her in front of the GLOW leadership. No, that wasn't true. Brody Sladrick was without doubt showing her something completely different, something greater than what she'd feared from him for so many years. He couldn't destroy what she no longer had. All she was left with now was her life, and he wasn't even mocking her in her poverty and weakness.

"Nicole, give me your hand. It's okay. I mean you no harm."

A tear rolled down her cheek. *Not Brody Sladrick!* She placed her hand in his again, noting the warmth of it this time. He closed his hand tenderly over hers.

"I'm not going to abandon you through what must follow."

"What must follow?"

"You have been acting on behalf of yourself at the expense of others for a long time. I understand you have an emotional vision for this planet, and you feel that GLOW has been a vehicle to bring some ruin to countries you wanted to rebuild."

"But like you said, I'm out of all that now. I've been replaced."

"The consequences of your secret and harmful activities are before you. I'd rather you faced ridicule here for your crimes, and yet call upon God in His mercy to forgive you before you stand before Him in judgement."

"There is no God."

"I think you know there is. Or you used to know it. But it's been more convenient to deny His existence to maintain your own passions. God is merciful. He's the One who taught me to risk my life to rescue you from the hands of selfish, wicked people. You are loved, Nicole. The question is, will you take the side of the One who loves you and forsake your disdain for Him?"

Nicole clamped her mouth shut, but her silence was so uncomfortable that she had to respond.

"You've given me a lot to think about." Then she scoffed. "Look at us. Brody Sladrick, telling me about God and Jesus. I almost wish I could take back what I said about you being like a son to me."

"Yeah, we're quite a pair, huh? Mother and son?"

"If you're not going to abandon me, then this is the kind of dry humor I have to put up with? Great."

"You'll learn that the One who is willing to bleed for you means you no harm."

"I know you're talking about Jesus."

Brody grinned.

"Yeah, I guess I was."

Zayed stood in a black suit at the rear of the gathering so he could monitor the funeral and surrounding grounds. California's sunshine warmed the cool morning and the dew evaporated from the grass around the casket. About thirty adults were in attendance, mostly from Sam Garrity's local church—perhaps those who'd known Ram in his youth.

At the moment, Kim Ward stood at the head of the casket and read a prepared eulogy. Brody had flown her and her father down from Seattle for this important celebration of life. Zayed had been in the room when Ram had died in Kim's arms, but he hadn't offered to speak. What Kim could testify to about God was more powerful since she'd been a victim of Ram's, surviving as a trafficked teen and then leading Ram to Christ in his final moments.

Everyone knew now from Kim's statement that Ram had died saving her life. He'd been a criminal in life, but a child of God in his final breaths before death.

Also in attendance was another survivor of Ram's Texas network, Aaron Ridgewood and his wife. The border patrol agent had embraced Brody like a family member, and instead of sadness, Aaron beamed from where he stood, his wife at his side weeping for joy as Kim shared the details of her experience that began and ended with Ram Garrity.

Zayed guessed that no one had spent more time with Ram than Brody, and no one had known him better since they'd traveled closely during Ram's last few weeks. But no one had asked Brody to speak either, and that was okay, he'd said. He was there for the family and to witness Kim's powerful testimony. This was a moment to celebrate what the Lord had done, not only on the cross but also in a quiet infirmary in a castle in Poland.

Sam Garrity and daughter Carmen stood in awe of Kim's report. No one had previously told them the details of Ram's death. But Zayed had heard they were devout believers, so they weren't too shocked at how God had answered their prayers for their son and brother to come to a crossroads before death.

Across the cemetery, a lone black town car stopped on the narrow driveway, then a van pulled in behind it. Zayed walked away from the funeral to stand and face the vehicles. He had no qualms about making himself a target if enemies were prowling nearby. New GLOW operators had certainly been hired to search out Brody and to kill anyone close to him if they couldn't destroy him personally. Brody was still recovering and would be for several weeks. His ribs were sore, his breath shallow. As a doctor, Zayed had informed his brother that he'd caused more tissue damage across his ribs than first thought.

"It doesn't matter," Brody had responded. "Mission accomplished. The rest is in God's hands."

Zayed understood he meant that saving Nicole Pitney's life had been worth it—with the hopes that she'd open her heart one day to Christ's gift of salvation. She sat in a Washington, D.C., jail cell under protective custody, arranged by Senator Madison. Her crimes against humanity were many, and she was expected to betray her old GLOW companions for leniency from federal prosecutors. But Zayed agreed with Brody—after the media grew weary of her story, the government would cover up Nicole's testimony. She knew too much dirt on too many important people. As an elderly woman already, Zayed guessed she would die in prison, forgotten by the world she'd victimized, despised by those who continued her trafficking enterprise.

But Brody wouldn't forget her. His interest in her could've been one reason why she hadn't already disappeared into a European black-site prison. Brody wanted to visit her often, and Madison had reluctantly agreed to permit him. It was hard to deny Brody a compassionate request after he'd rescued so many women and children over the years from her traps. The government couldn't make her disappear since someone like Brody had made known his care for her.

Two suited men in dark sunglasses emerged from the car across the cemetery. One of the men reached into his suit jacket and drew a sidearm as they walked toward the funeral attendees. They may have been there for Brody, or maybe for Kim, since she'd been outspoken about her trafficking experience and her deliverance by the hand of God.

Zayed drew out two tranq-pens, one for each hand. His disarmed grenade remained in his breast pocket. He walked calmly toward the two strangers. He wasn't afraid. God was with him.

Thanks for reading *Shadow Slave!* I pray you were blessed by this fictional story and will **find the following End Notes & Resources helpful**. Please pray for those caught in this horrible slavery and pray the trafficked might be rescued. —*David Telbat*

D.I. Telbat

END NOTES FOR
SHADOW SLAVE

Now that you have learned about trafficking through this fictional story, we introduce you to a **real ministry based in the United States** called—

RESCUE AMERICA

You can find the following material on their website (https://rescueamerica.ngo/), used here with permission. Visit them to learn more.

Right now in our world, there is a slave trade entrapping an **estimated 40 million victims across the globe**; it's **called human trafficking**. Every day, millions of people are being bought, sold, and exploited for the benefit, profit, or gratification of someone else.

To bring it down to a national scale, there are currently **an estimated 403,000 people being trafficked in the United States**. That is roughly 1 in every 800 people in our nation, and according to our research, there are more trafficking points of sale in America than there are Starbucks. **It is happening in all 50 states, and in every zip code across the U.S.**

Human Trafficking comes in various forms, but according to *Polaris*, the **top ten types of trafficking** include Escort Services; Pornography; Illicit Massage, Health and Beauty; Residential-Based Commercial Sex; Personal Sexual Servitude; Outdoor Solicitation; Domestic Work; Emerging Types; Bars, Strip Clubs, and Cantinas; and Illicit Activities.

Although human trafficking is so widespread, it is **still an issue that many are unaware of in our nation**. However, trafficking can happen to anyone, anywhere, and it's important to understand how. **The majority of victims have some type of prior relationship with their traffickers**.

In 2020, **42% of sex trafficking victims were trafficked by a family member**, and 39% were brought into trafficking by an intimate partner or a marriage proposition. In cases of **labor trafficking, 69% of victims were recruited into trafficking by a potential or current employer**, and 15% of victims were recruited by a family member.

Do you know where sex trafficking is happening in the United States? Because of what's often portrayed in the media, you may think sex trafficking only takes place in developing countries, or on street corners in crowded cities, or through kidnappings by strangers.

The truth? Sex trafficking isn't just happening overseas. It's not just taking place in big cities, and in most cases, it doesn't happen through unlikely kidnappings as it appears in the movies. The reality is, sex trafficking is much more common than you might think, and **it's happening all around us**—in your town, down the street from your house, and in every zip code in America.

There is hope for rescue, no matter where a survivor is located.

Traffickers use several tactics to entrap their victims, but **one of the most common methods is called grooming**. Grooming is the process of a trafficker building a relationship and gaining trust with their potential victims. Traffickers prey on the vulnerabilities of their victims—whether it be unstable family life, mental health concerns, financial needs, job insecurities, relational desires, a low sense of self-worth, or more—and they step in to fill those gaps and meet those needs. Once trust is established, traffickers will begin to exploit their victims for their own gain through forced labor or commercial sex.

Rescue America exists to rescue, revive and empower the sexually exploited through a 24/7 Rescue hotline and emergency care response. We believe there is a redemptive solution for every victim of sexual exploitation who desires to exit the life. **How does all of this work?**

Rescue – Through direct outreach and our 24/7 Rescue hotline, we connect with survivors ready to exit the life and help facilitate their safe exit alongside trained volunteers.

Revive – Upon exit, survivors are transported to a secure location where their most pressing and practical needs are the first priority: food, water, sleep, and safekeeping.

Empower – Based on individual assessments, survivors then find stabilization and professional support to address their mental, emotional, and spiritual needs, preparing them for long-term placement in partner homes across the US.

Survivors can call our hotline (833.599.FREE) from anywhere in the country and immediately receive a rescue response, be provided with food, clothes, and other necessities, and be placed with and transported to a care program that best fits their specific needs. We work closely with each survivor throughout the entire process, empowering them to make decisions for their next steps as we facilitate their exits to safety.

As we care for survivors through our Rescue hotline, we spend time weekly in prayer for those we are currently serving; **our hope for each one of them as they exit the life is that they will learn to hear the Lord's voice, experience His presence, and be transformed by His truth that replaces the lies they've believed for so long.**

It is our honor to be able to serve, pray for, and care for them as they walk that out. Only God's voice can drown out the lies that tell survivors all they are good for is their body, that they will never be loved for who they are, and that there is no other option for them. **God's truth speaks a better word over them—that they are**

loved, valued, and worthy—and that word is transformative.

We believe every survivor who calls our 24/7 Rescue hotline is priceless to the God who created them; a relationship with Him is accessible to all, and **He longs to draw them to Him, no matter what their past looks like or what they've done.** Each one of them individually is so important to God that He would leave the 99 and go after the 1 time and time again, just as He explains in Matthew 18:12-14:

"What do you think? If any man has a hundred sheep, and one of them has gone astray, does he not leave the ninety-nine on the mountains and go and search for the one that is straying? If it turns out that he finds it, truly I say to you, he rejoices over it more than over the ninety-nine which have not gone astray. So it is not the will of your Father who is in heaven that one of these little ones perish."

God's heart is to rescue His flock. Our God is the God of redemption. The God of not only grace and mercy but of new life.

Since 2014, we have seen hundreds of brave survivors walk out of the darkness of sex trafficking and begin their journeys to healing and new life, and every rescue is made possible by our incredible volunteers and supporters. Everyday people took steps to educate themselves about the realities of sex trafficking, and then they took steps to make a change. **We believe the first step is awareness.**

What can YOU do to fight this issue and stand up for the freedom of survivors? **One of the first steps is raising awareness**; you can do that by simply learning the facts and having conversations about what you learn with the people in your life. **The more people learn about it, the more people can join the fight to combat it.** You can then play a part in ending modern-day slavery by getting involved as a volunteer or financial partner with organizations whose missions are to serve survivors and end trafficking.

Join us at the next **National Human Trafficking Awareness Day** (https://nationaltoday.com/national-human-trafficking-awareness-day/) on **JAN 11** to increase your own awareness, receive monthly insights into the realities of sex trafficking in our nation, and hear redemptive survivor stories from the frontlines.

Visit the Rescue America website (rescueamerica.ngo/) to find much more, including rescue stories.

~

Other Resources:

If you or someone you know have been sexually exploited and want out of the life, please call **Rescue America's 24/7 – Rescue hotline number at 833.599.FREE**.

Visit: *Hidden Humanity*, Book One by D.I. Telbat, (https://books2read.com/b/HiddenHumanity), to read more about trafficking in his **Author's Note** at the front of the book.

Visit: Vision Beyond Borders/women (https://www.visionbeyondborders.org/women/)– Also, there is more about VBB in the **End Notes of *Hidden Humanity***, Book 1, about their ministry to trafficked women and children.

Visit: **Polaris* at https://polarisproject.org/; and https://polarisproject.org/telling-the-real-story-of-human-trafficking/

Visit: Phantom Rescue (phantomrescue.org/)

Visit: Restoring Hope Nepal (https://www.restoringhopenepal.org/)

Visit: Truckers Against Trafficking (https://truckersagainsttrafficking.org/)

To report a trafficking tip, please call the **National Human Trafficking Hotline** at **888.373.7888**.

ACKNOWLEDGEMENTS

This series wasn't in my sights until Patrick Klein with Vision Beyond Borders suggested I write a fictional book/series with a fresh voice to expose human trafficking to the Christian church. His initially shared intel and experience set me to task! Thank you, Patrick. Thanks also to Dee for her willingness to tackle yet another series that encourages God's people to live like Christ. I thank our local proofreader, Sharon L., for her time and insight, as well as many helpful Beta-Readers who have offered invaluable time to help edit and advise in the final stages of this project. We are humbled by their assistance to make this the best novel possible! My thanks also to Mark York for sharing with us about *Rescue America* for use in the End Notes. May God be honored by the work of our hands.

OTHER BOOKS BY D.I. TELBAT

The COIL Series: Christian Suspense

The COIL Legacy Series: Christian Suspense

COIL Legacy Collection: 3 Books in 1 Volume

The Resolution Series: America's Last Days

The STEADFAST Series: America's Last Days

STEADFAST Collection: 6 Novellas in 1 Volume

Last Dawn Series: America's Last Days

Leeward Set: Where Christians Dare

Never Lost Series: Trafficking Rescue Novels

~

Arabian Variable

Called To Gobi

God's Colonel

Soldier of Hope

Short Story Collections

~

Coming Soon

The ELM Series

More *Short Story Collections*

ABOUT THE AUTHOR

D.I. (David) Telbat is a Christian author best known for his **clean, Suspenseful Fiction with a Faith Focus**. This includes his bestselling and award-winning *COIL Series, Steadfast Series, Last Dawn Series*, and other Christian Suspense and End Times novels. He wrote his first book at age 14, and he hasn't stopped since!

David studied writing in school and worked for a time in the newspaper field. Getting into serious trouble with the law as a young man became a turning point in his life. The Lord used that experience to draw David into a personal relationship with Him. Re-focusing his life for Christ, he now seeks to honor God with his life and writing by doing what he loves most—writing and Christian ministry.

Subscribe to receive David Telbat's FREE, bi-weekly **D.I. Telbat Newsletter** with one of his Christian short stories, or an Author Reflection, or his Novel News Update. You'll also receive **exclusive subscriber gifts**, such as his *Three For Free*—three-novels-in-one eBook! You can join the adventure by visiting his site at books2read.com/DITelbat/ and click on the "**Follow this Author**" button.

www.ingramcontent.com/pod-product-compliance
Lightning Source LLC
Chambersburg PA
CBHW030808210726
48290CB00002B/477